City of Ghosts

Bali Rai

Doubleday

www.**rbooks**.co.uk

CITY OF GHOSTS
A DOUBLEDAY BOOK 978 0 385 61169 5

Published in Great Britain by Doubleday,
an imprint of Random House Children's Books
A Random House Group Company

This edition published 2009

1 3 5 7 9 10 8 6 4 2

The Random House Group Limited supports the Forest Stewardship Council (FSC),
the leading international forest certification organization. All our titles that
are printed on Greenpeace-approved FSC-certified paper carry the FSC logo.
Our paper procurement policy can be found at www.rbooks.co.uk/environment.
Set in 13/15.6pt Bembo Schoolbook by
Falcon Oast Graphic Art Ltd.

RANDOM HOUSE CHILDREN'S BOOKS
61–63 Uxbridge Road, London W5 5SA

www.**kids**at**randomhouse**.co.uk
www.**rbooks**.co.uk

Addresses for companies within The Random House Group Limited can be
found at: www.randomhouse.co.uk/offices.htm

THE RANDOM HOUSE GROUP Limited Reg. No. 954009

A CIP catalogue record for this book is available from the British Library.

Printed in the UK by CPI Mackays, Chatham, ME58TD.

Mixed Sources
Product group from well-managed
forests and other controlled sources
www.fsc.org Cert no. TT-COC-2139
© 1996 Forest Stewardship Council
FSC

A big thank you to everyone at
Random House Children's Books for all their hard
work; and to Penny my agent for being so great.

To everyone who helped me during the writing of this
novel – most of you know who you are. Some of you
may even be in this book . . .

A big thank you to Asian Dub Foundation for their
song 'Assasin'; the original spark for this novel and a
wicked tune to boot.

Finally, to the memory of Udham Singh (*aka* Ram
Mohammed Singh Azad) and all the ghosts of
Jallianwalla Bagh.

Also by Bali Rai:

(UN)ARRANGED MARRIAGE
THE CREW
RANI AND SUKH
THE WHISPER
THE LAST TABOO
THE ANGEL COLLECTOR

For younger readers:

SOCCER SQUAD: STARTING ELEVEN
SOCCER SQUAD: MISSING!
SOCCER SQUAD: STARS!
SOCCER SQUAD: GLORY!

Prologue

Caxton Hall, Westminster, London,
13 March 1940

Udham Singh (aka Ram Mohammed Singh Azad)

Udham Singh watched the chairman of the meeting, Lord Zetland, gathering up his notes as another member of the panel answered a question. He looked at his watch and saw that it was half past four; the meeting was nearly over. The Tudor Room was packed with guests and other interested parties. Two banks of chairs sat in front of the panel, with channels through the middle and to both sides. The chairs were full, as were the channels, and Udham was standing in the perfect position, to the right of the speakers, by the first seated row. Zetland, who was Secretary of State for India, put his hand to his mouth as he let out a yawn. Two places to his right sat the man Udham had come to see.

Sir Michael O'Dwyer was a distinguished-looking gentleman with silvery-white hair and pale skin. Age had caught up with him and the skin around his jaw line had begun to sag. But his eyes retained the steely determination that had seen him through his time as Governor of the Punjab two decades earlier – or at least that's what he wanted the public to believe. He sat perfectly still, listening with interest to those around him. What a shame, thought Udham, that O'Dwyer hadn't listened to the voices of the people he'd governed all those years ago.

Lord Zetland brought the meeting to a close and the audience gave a small round of polite applause. As he heard the clapping, Udham found himself drifting back to that fateful afternoon in Amritsar in 1919; to the event that had set him on this path and given his life purpose. There he was, stumbling aimlessly through the smoke-filled darkness . . .

For twenty-one years Udham had bided his time, travelling to many countries and planning his revenge. Eventually he'd found himself in England, in the heart of the beast that had taken hold of his motherland. Now here he was, a revolver tucked into his waistband, ready to satisfy the ghosts of Amritsar; to help those restless spirits find their peace.

'So many you kill,' he whispered, directing his remark at O'Dwyer. Not that anyone could hear him. People had begun to stand up, preparing to leave. This was his chance . . .

He pushed his way through the crowd, past chatting white men and women, until he was in front of the panel. His eyes hardened and his heart raced. He pulled out the gun, looking directly at O'Dwyer. The old man seemed unable to understand what was going on at first. The skin around his eyes began to crease, however, when the truth dawned. His mouth opened and formed a perfect O.

Udham said a silent prayer, and fired.

Part One

The Orphan and the Rich Girl

Amritsar, 17 January 1919

Gurdial watched Jeevan as he tried to juggle three onions. They were sitting on a low wall within sight of the Golden Temple, watching people go about their business.

'I *can* do it!' Jeevan insisted.

Gurdial smiled and shook his head. My best friend is a buffoon, he thought to himself. Jeevan had always been the same, ever since they'd been thrown together as children at the orphanage. He was never beaten, never wrong. Once he got an idea in his head, stubbornness and a degree of vanity meant that he had to act it out. However many people told him he was wrong, he would spend the entire day insisting that he was right. Most people considered Jeevan spoiled and irritating, but for Gurdial, who knew him better, it was part of what made him who he was.

Everyone at the orphanage assumed a mask and

Jeevan was no different. It was how they dealt with their past misfortunes. Gurdial knew that beneath the front, Jeevan was warm-hearted, kind and loyal, and whenever his friend played up, Gurdial simply ignored him and talked about something else.

'The postmaster is having an affair' – Gurdial was repeating two-month-old gossip.

As Jeevan picked up his onions once again, he pulled a face. 'Tell me something new, *bhai*,' he said. 'That old goat has been news for weeks.'

Gurdial yawned. They had been up since dawn, beginning their day with a wash, followed by prayers and lessons. Now, in the warmth of the afternoon sun, his eyelids felt heavy and sleep was on his mind. But there was no way he could head back to the orphanage for a nap. The couple who ran it, Sohan Singh and Mata Devi, would have a hundred and one chores waiting for him, and Mata Devi in particular would beat him for being so lazy.

Instead, Gurdial turned his attention to the busy street. The myriad colours and sounds and smells made him smile. Amritsar was a wonderful city, constantly changing yet always familiar too. A city of tall, inward-leaning buildings and narrow alleyways where the sun never shone; of wide open spaces too, bathed in sunshine and filled with numerous brightly coloured trees and plants and flowers. White marble buildings ringed the pool of *amrit* or holy water that in turn surrounded the Golden Temple.

People of all religions lived in the city. Each afternoon, after their chores were done, Gurdial and Jeevan would head down the streets and alleyways, looking for fun. The people they met were Muslim and Sikh, Hindu and Christian. Some were as dark as the night sky; others had yellow skin and hair. There were green eyes and blue eyes and brown eyes. The *goreh* were pink – their women were often tall and wore dresses and sun hats, many of them showing off their arms and legs, constantly smoking cigarettes. The men wore far too much clothing and strutted around like peacocks, forever puffing on pipes or cigars, their faces red and their hair and moustaches always perfectly oiled.

Today, the streets were as busy as ever, and across the road from where they sat Gurdial saw two soldiers talking to an old man in a white turban. He was wondering what they were discussing when a hand clapped him on the back. He turned and saw Bissen Singh standing by his side, smiling at him.

'Here you are again, idling away the hours,' Bissen said to them.

Jeevan put the onions in his pocket, hoping to disguise the fact that one of them had begun to rot and smelled.

'Bissen-ji – where have you been?' Gurdial asked.

'I went to visit my family,' he told him.

Bissen Singh was in his twenties but had already done more than Gurdial and Jeevan could have imagined in a lifetime. He had fought in the Great War – the one that had just ended – alongside the British. He'd been injured in a country that Gurdial had never heard of, called France, and been sent to England to get better. He still walked with a slight limp, and on certain days Gurdial had noticed that his gaze grew distant, as though he was dreaming of faraway places and different people. Gurdial often dreamed of fighting alongside Bissen Singh and wondered if he would ever experience even half as much during his own lifetime. As Bissen ruffled Jeevan's hair, Gurdial asked how his family were keeping.

'Good, good,' he said. 'And what about you two — keeping out of trouble?'

Gurdial nodded as Jeevan spoke up: 'When you were in the war,' he said, just as he always did whenever he saw the soldier, 'did you have to cut your hair?'

Bissen laughed but his thoughts were elsewhere for a moment: back in England, sitting in front of a mirror as a young nurse cut his locks away.

'No, no!' he replied, snapping back into the present. 'They let us wear our turbans, although in the trenches it was very difficult to keep them clean.'

'Did the rats try to eat it?'

Bissen had told them a story about the English soldiers. How some of them would be woken during the night by rats licking their hair, attracted by the taste and smell of the creams they used to keep it in place.

'Not my hair,' he said patiently. 'I kept mine under my turban.'

'Did you have to eat the rats?'

'No,' replied Bissen. 'We just shot at them.'

As a farmer trundled past on a wooden cart pulled by two huge bullocks, Gurdial wondered whether to tell Bissen Singh what was really on his mind. The problem was that Bissen would react exactly as Jeevan had. Gurdial was in love with a merchant's daughter – a rich girl from a well-to-do family. He spent each night dreaming of her, hoping to find the courage to ask for her hand in marriage. But deep down, he knew that his dreams were hopeless. There was no way her father would consent to the marriage – Gurdial was too poor and from a lower caste. People like him did not marry girls like Sohni. Ever.

'You look as though the troubles of the world are upon your shoulders,' Bissen told him.

Jeevan smirked. 'He is in love, *bhai-ji*.'

'Shut up!' demanded Gurdial, turning red with embarrassment.

'What's this?' asked Bissen. 'Have you found yourself a nice young girl?'

Gurdial groaned.

'Tell him, *bhai*,' urged Jeevan mischievously.

'It's nothing!' insisted Gurdial. 'It's just a girl I've seen—'

Jeevan snorted. 'The daughter of a rich man, *bhai*,' he told Bissen.

'Oh. Which man is this?'

Gurdial shrugged. 'It is Gulbaru Singh's daughter.'

Bissen raised an eyebrow. 'The cloth merchant?'

Gurdial nodded. 'It doesn't matter anyway. It is nothing – a dream – and it won't ever come true.' His heart broke as the words left his lips.

'But what's the point of dreaming?' Bissen asked him. 'What's the point of hope?'

'I don't understand . . .' said Gurdial.

'If everyone thought like you, then no one would ever achieve their dreams,' explained Bissen. 'Dreams do come true – not all of them, I agree, but they do sometimes.'

Jeevan shook his head. 'But Gulbaru Singh is an evil, nasty man,' he told Bissen. 'He hates poor people. There is no way he'll allow Sohni to marry a penniless orphan.'

'Then perhaps Gurdial needs to go and find his fortune,' said Bissen. 'No one knows what Fate holds in store for them. No one.'

'I *know*,' Gurdial replied. 'But Jeevan is right. Sohni is just a dream . . .'

Bissen put his hand on Gurdial's shoulder. 'Have you spoken to her?'

Gurdial nodded. 'We meet in secret sometimes, when she can get away. Her mother died when she was young and her father remarried. His new wife does not allow Sohni to do anything. We have to be careful.'

'And is your love mutual?'

'Perhaps,' Gurdial replied with a shrug. 'She tells me it is, but how can she want someone like me? I have nothing and I will never have anything.'

'We are orphans,' added Jeevan. 'We are of a lower standing than her.'

Bissen frowned. 'When I was in Europe fighting for the English I learned a great lesson,' he told them. 'At the end of the day, when it really matters, there are no higher or lower people. When Death comes to call, he doesn't ask if you have money. He does not care if you wear rags or are dressed in the finest cloth known to man. No one has the right to regard themselves as better just because they have money. The Gurus teach us that we are all equal.'

Gurdial saw a bead of sweat breaking on Bissen's forehead. 'Are you feeling hot, *bhai-ji*,' he asked him.

Bissen wiped his brow and nodded. 'Just a little under the weather,' he lied. 'I need to go and take some medicine.'

'Oh.' Gurdial was a little disappointed. He loved to listen to the soldier, to learn of new things. Bissen was like an older brother – a wise head to ask for advice.

'Perhaps you can come and see me tomorrow,' Bissen suggested. 'We can talk some more.'

Gurdial smiled. 'I'd like that,' he said.

As Bissen walked away, Jeevan shook his head. He removed the onions from his pocket and noted that the rotten stench was gone.

'What's the matter, *bhai*?' asked Gurdial. 'Why are you shaking your head?'

Jeevan grinned. 'He is lying to us.'

Gurdial looked shocked. 'About what?'

'He's not ill, Gurdial,' teased Jeevan. 'I can't believe you could be so stupid—'

'What are you talking about?'

'*Pheme*,' replied Jeevan. 'He is a drug addict.'

Gurdial frowned. 'I know we are brothers,' he told his younger friend, 'but if you ever tell lies about Bissen-ji again, I'll slap the skin from your face!'

'But—' began Jeevan.

Gurdial didn't wait for him to finish. He slid off the wall and walked away, heading for the crowds in Hall Bazaar.

18 January 1919

Gulbaru Singh's house sat in the centre of a walled compound, three storeys high and painted a light, minty green. The pale yellow wall was five feet high, and inside it were thick hedges that grew up half a foot higher than the wall. The front of the house had two verandas that flanked a heavy wooden door. The gardens were mature, with tall plants and well-established evergreen bushes. To the left of the house were eight mango trees and a single peepal with a thick trunk and a high canopy; to the right stood a majestic old banyan tree, its gnarled trunk looking as though it had been twisted by the hand of a giant.

Around the back, the garden had two plots, divided by a well-worn dirt path. On one side was a vegetable patch and on the other, more bushes and plants. A single narrow gate in the back wall led to the dark alleyway beyond. It was at this gate that Gurdial stood patiently, waiting for Sohni. A single pale blue butterfly fluttered around his head, a rare sight during a Punjabi winter. Gurdial was wondering where it had come from when he saw Sohni coming down the garden path. He smiled and waved, his heart jumping madly inside his chest.

Sohni reached the wooden gate and threw back the bolt. The ancient rusty hinges squeaked, the gate opened and she stepped out into the tree-shrouded alleyway. The sun was high in the sky but the trees did their best to stop the light from penetrating. What little there was created a dappled effect on the dusty ground, as though the earth had caught yellow measles. Caper bushes grew along the edges of the path, their inward-curving spines like claws. The path led off into almost total darkness in one direction and out into the narrow street in the other. The young lovers chose the darkness.

'I didn't think you'd be able to come,' Gurdial said to Sohni, taking her hand.

'I was waiting for my stepmother to leave,' she replied.

Gurdial grinned.

'What's so funny?'

'You didn't call her a witch for a change,' he replied.

'She was throwing plates around earlier,' Sohni told him. 'Screaming at the walls as though they'd eventually answer her.'

'Where is your father?'

Sohni shrugged. 'At the shop. He is hardly ever at home, and when he is, all they do is fight.'

Gurdial pulled her to him; the heat from her body sent his senses wild. Her skin was as smooth as a pebble that had been washed in holy water and her light blue eyes were full of life. He leaned forward and kissed her, hoping that she wouldn't pull away. She didn't.

'I can't believe you are mine,' Gurdial said after their kiss.

'And why is that?' asked Sohni as they made their way down the path, heading for the privacy of the trees and the fields of tall grasses beyond.

'Because you are so beautiful, and I am so ordinary.'

Sohni let go of his hand and stroked his cheek. 'You have such a warm smile,' she told him. 'And your eyes make me feel safe. No *ordinary* person could make me feel that way.'

They entered a clearing and found a place to sit on the grass. Sohni sat between Gurdial's legs, facing away, his arms wrapped around her. Gurdial took in the smell of her hair, like vanilla and peaches, and closed his eyes, hoping to forget that he was a penniless orphan and Sohni the daughter of a rich man. Their love was secret because it needed to be. Sohni's father would kill both of them if he found out, and Gurdial worried that it was only a matter of time before he did. Someone would see them together or Gulbaru Singh would get suspicious and follow her. And such thoughts stopped him from relaxing fully.

'Are you still worried?' Sohni asked, knowing that he was.

Gurdial nodded before resting his head on her shoulder.

'Perhaps we should meet further away,' she suggested.

The clearing, although private, was barely half a mile from her father's house. But no one ever wandered down the dark alleyway and into the trees because the path didn't lead anywhere. That was what made her feel safe.

'There is a stream,' replied Gurdial, lifting his head. 'It's in a copse about twenty minutes' walk from the city, to the south past Nawan Kot.'

Sohni giggled. 'Is it your usual hiding place for all the other girls,' she teased.

'No, no! There are no other girls.'

'But you must have seen other beautiful girls in the city,' continued Sohni.

Gurdial held her tighter. 'I've never looked,' he replied truthfully. 'Until I saw your face I did not think of girls at all.'

'So how do you know of this copse?'

'I used to go and hide there,' Gurdial said. 'When I feel lonely or upset I go there to talk to my parents.'

Sohni shivered. 'I'm sorry.' She turned round so that she faced Gurdial. 'It must be so hard for you.'

He shook his head. 'It's the same for you.'

'How can it be? I still have my father, no matter how

badly he treats me. But that's because he wants a son, not a daughter.'

'But you lost your mother,' said Gurdial.

'I never really knew her,' Sohni told him. 'All I have are the memories of other people and they aren't the same. They don't belong to me. Do you remember your parents?'

He nodded. 'Not very much; just their smiles and some smells. And I can see flowers in a courtyard too. They are blue and pink; beautiful.'

Sohni took his face in her hands; tears were streaming down her cheeks.

'Why are you crying?' asked Gurdial.

'Because of you,' she said.

Gurdial felt a wave of love wash over him. His skin prickled with electricity.

'What do you say when you speak to your parents?' Sohni asked.

'Just everyday things. I tell them how I'm feeling and what is going through my mind; things I don't tell anyone else.'

'Can you tell *me* those things?' Sohni wiped away her tears.

Gurdial nodded. 'I would like to.'

'Then I want you to. You can tell me anything.'

Gurdial grinned, hoping to make Sohni smile. It worked. 'Anything?' he asked.

Sohni nodded.

'What if I commit a crime or do something wicked?'

'Then I will tell you off.'

'What if some other girl attempts to lure me away from you?'

'Then I will lock you in a room.'

'But what if I starve?'

Sohni shook her head. 'Don't worry. I'll bring you bread and water.'

'Like a pet?' Gurdial asked.

'Yes,' she said. 'A dog . . .'

Gurdial pulled a face.

'A very handsome dog,' added Sohni. '*Very* handsome.'

'Do you think about the future?' Gurdial asked, changing the subject.

Yes,' she replied. 'And it's always with you. I don't care about my father. I would give up anything to be with you.'

Gurdial swallowed hard. He wanted nothing more than to spend his life with Sohni too, but her father was no small barrier. Deep in his heart, he knew that their chances of being together were slim. But he decided to bury that thought.

'So you'd have me even if we ended up living in the sewers?' he joked.

Sohni looked him in the eye. 'Even the sewers,' she whispered, pulling him to her and kissing him.

Hidden in the tress that skirted the clearing, the woman smiled as she watched the young lovers before turning away to allow them privacy.

'Let the young ones have their day,' she said to herself. 'You can no more deny the young their feelings than you can stop the sun from shining. It is nature's way, and who are we to challenge nature?'

And then, as if to mock her own question, she vanished into the darkness.

19 January 1919

Gulbaru Singh woke suddenly, thick, salty beads of perspiration dripping from his brow. For three nights his dreams had been invaded by evil spirits and he had no idea how to get rid of them. The most recent, the one that had left him sitting up in the darkness, drenched in sweat, had been the worst yet.

In the dream he was sitting in his office at the rear of his shop, counting the day's takings, when a sudden gust of wind threw the door wide open. Startled, he jumped out of his seat, the stout club he kept for security gripped tightly in his right hand. He was expecting bandits and ready to break heads, but to his amazement a small male child, no more than two years old, crawled through the door. The child stopped in front of him and sat down, then looked up, holding out his arms. Gulbaru put down his club and knelt, asking him where he'd come from. The boy began to cry.

Unsure of what to do, Gulbaru felt his right hand start to burn. He looked at it and found himself holding a bloody knife. The handle burned into his skin but he could not let it go. He shook his hand, flailing as the searing pain made him feel faint, but still the knife remained stuck to it.

And then he was lying spread-eagled, his hands and feet tied to wooden pegs pushed into the ground. He looked around and saw that the shop had vanished and he was in some sort of clearing, out in the woods. The baby sat by his head, shaking what appeared to be a rattle. The noise brought stray dogs out from the shadows; mangy, sharp-toothed mongrels with blood and flesh dripping from their jaws. Gulbaru tried to scream but there was no one to help him. The baby boy, oblivious to the danger, continued to shake his rattle. Something else crawled out of the darkness to his left, edging towards Gulbaru: a baby girl with eyes of burning fire and daggers for teeth.

From the right came an identical baby girl, this one followed by hundreds – no, *thousands* of rats. The baby boy continued to shake his rattle until the other babies, the dogs and the rats surrounded Gulbaru. And then he heard it – a voice he'd almost forgotten – as it gave the order. The first baby girl opened her mouth, drew back her head, snarled and then ripped a chunk of flesh from Gulbaru's chest with one bite. The mongrels howled with bloodlust as the rats began to clamber over his body, picking at his skin with their teeth. The largest of

23

the dogs jumped onto him. Its hot, bloody mouth was wide open, little pieces of flesh falling from the teeth. It arched its back and struck . . .

Now, as he sat up in bed, he wondered what the significance of his dreams was. No doubt his wife, Darshana Kaur, would interpret them for him. But she was soundly asleep, her back to him, snoring loudly. Gulbaru got out of bed and walked over to the water gourd on the table. He poured himself a drink, downing it in one, and then made his way back to bed.

As he got under the covers, his wife stirred and turned round. 'What is it?' she asked him.

'Nothing,' he lied. 'Go back to sleep.'

Darshana ignored him. 'This is the third night you've woken me,' she said.

'Bad dreams,' he admitted.

Darshana sat up and let the covers fall from her. Even in the darkness Gulbaru could make out her crooked nose and mono-brow. The heat that rose from her body carried the stench of onions and dirt. He turned away and tried to close his eyes.

'I know you want a son,' she told him, hoping that he was still listening, but knowing in her heart that he was not. 'And I know that I am not the beauty I was when we met. But I love you, Gulbaru Singh, and I always will. We have been through too much, done too much, to be apart . . .'

Darshana looked at Gulbaru's back, stroked it, and for a moment prayed silently that she might provide him

24

with a male heir. God knows, she had tried everything she could; listened to every old wives' tale, but to no avail. Now, no matter how much she tried to deny it, she knew that his love had died. It would not be long, she realized, before he cast her aside and found a younger woman to be with. And that thought ate away at her day and night.

'Do you remember those nights after we first met?' she said to him. 'The way you never wanted to leave me when dawn broke?'

Gulbaru said nothing but his memory took him back to a time when Darshana had been truly beautiful; to the little room where they had spent so many nights. He recalled taking her away from the brothel owner just as he was preparing to put her to work. Threatening to cut out the man's heart with a dagger to have the woman he dreamed of. Theirs had been a savage, animal passion but the fire was long dead, the embers faded to grey.

'I am still the same girl,' she insisted. 'I may not look the same but I *am* her and I still love you.' She lay back down, facing his back, her left hand caressing his shoulders and neck. 'I promise that I will provide you with a son,' she added.

Gulbaru remained silent and listened to his wife crying herself to sleep.

On the other side of the city, lying on a thin mattress on the floor, Gurdial dreamed of happier days, of finding a better place. His thoughts were flooded with images of a golden future with Sohni. The two of them holding hands in the sunshine, laughing in a garden filled with flowers. A house, not dissimilar to Sohni's, stood behind them, freshly painted, its doors and windows thrown open. Jeevan and Bissen Singh were there, sitting on one of the verandas, drinking spicy tea and chatting idly about the state of the world.

Inside the house, around a large table fashioned from rosewood, a meal was waiting. Large clay bowls filled with dhal sat on the table next to plates of *roti* and fresh fruit – slices of juicy mango and plump lychees. From the kitchen came the sound of a couple laughing. Gurdial watched himself walk through the door to find Mata Devi and Sohan Singh cheerfully preparing the rest of the meal, their faces turned away from him.

A bright green lizard crawled across one of the walls, throwing out its tongue, searching. Flies buzzed in and out of the windows as a huge wasp hovered above a wooden pail of water-buffalo milk. In the corners, spiders wove their webs and small mice scuttled about. From the back door came the croak of a toad, the cry of an eagle and the gentle rustle of a cooling breeze. And in the distance, a car horn *pap-papped*.

Gurdial approached Mata Devi and touched her plump shoulder. She turned and smiled at him, and suddenly he found himself looking up at an open sky, blue with gentle wisps of white cloud floating in it. The smell of citrus oil invaded his senses, and then the

26

smiling face of a woman looked down at him. He smiled back at her, trying to speak, but the sounds were simply the little gurgles of a baby. The woman kissed his forehead and cooed gently.

He felt the presence of a man but could not make him out. He saw a smile and sensed a voice but no more than that. And then he found himself sitting opposite the Golden Temple, its reflection shimmering in the water. Jeevan was at his side, holding rotting onions, telling him a story. A hand took hold of his shoulder, forcing him to turn. Gulbaru Singh's face confronted him, his eyes blazing with hatred, his breath sour.

'Did you think I would let you live?' he spat.

'But I . . .' Gurdial heard himself stutter.

Gulbaru Singh raised the machete in his right hand and brought it down in an arc towards Gurdial's head—

Gurdial sat up, his breathing shallow, his heart pumping. Across from him, Jeevan stirred and woke up too.

'What's the matter, *bhai-ji*?' Jeevan asked.

'Nothing,' whispered Gurdial.

'You sound unwell.'

'Just a bad dream.'

'All right,' said Jeevan, settling back down.

Gurdial lay down too but kept his eyes open, wondering why his dream had turned into a nightmare so quickly. Was it some kind of message to leave well alone? However hard he tried to banish them, the insecurities he felt over Sohni stayed with him, day and night. Was he a fool for believing that they had a future together? Was he really so naïve? Outside the open window he heard a pack of stray dogs howling. In the corner of the room something scurried across the floor. Gurdial closed his eyes, hoping to fall asleep, but he was soon in his dream again, back at the beginning. Holding hands with Sohni in the sunshine.

21 January 1919

Darshana Kaur led her guest into the kitchen and poured some tea for him. He thanked her in heavily accented Punjabi and took the chair she offered. She remained standing, watching him as he sipped at the cup.

'Do you know why you are here?' she asked him.

'Yes,' he replied, his cat-like green eyes searching the room around her.

'Where are you from?'

The man smiled. 'From across the mountains to the north,' he replied.

'From China?'

He nodded. 'From the empire of dragons,' he said, smirking.

Darshana wondered how old he was. His hair was long and straggly and completely white. A long white beard hung from his face and his teeth looked canine.

His skin was dry and his ears seemed too large for his head.

'How do you come to speak our language?' Darshana asked.

'I have lived in your country for many years. I was brought here by a rajah who employed me for a decade.'

'What did you do for this rajah?'

The Chinaman smiled. 'Whatever I could,' he replied. 'Spells and potions and curses . . . But you know all about me. That is why you asked me to come.'

Darshana nodded. 'I am told that you are the best there is,' she told him. 'Expensive, but very good.'

'That I am. Once I am in your employ, there is nothing I cannot do, if you ask me.'

Darshana was about to ask him another question when the Chinaman shushed her.

'You long for a male child,' he said to her. 'You have already had two . . . shall we say, *unsuccessful* attempts at childbirth.'

'But how do you—?'

'*Silence!*' he ordered. 'It is what I do. Now, I can help you but it won't be easy. You must do as I say, whenever I say.'

Darshana nodded slowly.

'Take all images and artefacts of God or religion from the house,' he said.

'But . . .'

The Chinaman frowned. 'Do as I say or find another.'

'When do I—?' began Darshana.

'Now,' he whispered. 'I shall finish my tea as you collect them and then we shall go into the garden.'

'The garden?'

'In order to burn the offending items. The magic does not work if it is tainted by religion.'

Darshana sat where she was and thought for a moment about her husband. Would he be angry if she did as the man asked? The answer was probably no. Gulbaru Singh was not a religious man, unless you counted the worship of money.

'I'll do it,' she replied. 'But be warned – I am not a woman to cross.'

The Chinaman nodded. 'I know this. Now get on with your task. And make up a bed for me. I will be staying in your house until my work is done.'

Darshana left the kitchen, muttering as she went. She had taken an instant dislike to the Chinaman. But as long as he served his purpose she would put up with him.

Twenty minutes later they were in the garden – a pile of religious artefacts burning on a small fire in front of them.

'Do you have any broken or cracked dishes?' the Chinaman asked Darshana.

'One or two,' she replied. 'Why?'

'Bring them out too. And anything else that is broken. Such things will stop you falling pregnant.'

'Is there anything else I need to burn while I'm at it?' she asked sarcastically.

The Chinaman smiled. 'In many parts of this country, a bitch such as you would know her place. But here, you are queen.' He chuckled to himself. 'I mean nothing by those words,' he told her. 'That is just my way. Do not take it to heart.'

Darshana looked him in the eye. 'You dare to call me a bitch again,' she said quietly, 'and I will pull your eyeballs from their sockets and feed them to the rats. You say you know all about me: tell me, am I serious?'

He nodded. 'You and I will make formidable allies, madam. I apologize for any offence.' He began to chuckle once more.

'Let me go and find those broken dishes,' she said.

When she returned, the Chinaman inspected the dishes closely before smashing them on the ground. Once they were in small pieces he took a broom and swept them into the fire.

'Kneel down, madam,' he told Darshana. 'I am going to see what it tells us.'

'How?'

'Many things are made clear in this way,' he said.

They knelt before the fire and looked into it. The flames were small but hot enough to make the skin on Darshana's face prickle. The Chinaman looked unperturbed. He sat completely still for five minutes, not even looking away when Darshana stood up, her face red with the heat. Finally he turned and looked up at his mistress.

'You may not like what I saw,' he said, 'but we are allies and I must tell you.'

Darshana helped him to his feet. 'What did you see?' she asked, desperate to know.

The Chinaman fixed her with his feline eyes. 'The magic of love has gone from your marriage,' he said softly.

Darshana nodded sadly.

'Your husband looks for a new love. And, as he has done before, he thinks about ridding himself of his burdens.'

Darshana's eyes grew wide with shock as she digested the Chinaman's words. 'I am his burden,' she said in a whisper.

He nodded. 'He sleeps badly and he dreams of ghosts. And each day, as he sits making money, he wonders what a new woman could give him. And thinks of what *you* cannot give him.'

Darshana shuddered. 'A son,' she said.

'Yes, madam.'

She wiped away her tears and steadied herself. 'This remains between us,' she told him.

'As you wish,' he replied. 'If the time comes, I will be ready to help.'

An image of Gulbaru lying on her bed in the morning light, his eyes shiny with love, came to her. He called out to her, telling her that he wished to lose himself inside her. That he would never, *could* never, touch another woman. Was God so cruel that he could kill such a beautiful love? she asked herself. Despite all they had done, they *had* loved each other. And now it was gone. She had known, deep inside, that it was over, but it had taken the Chinaman to make it sink in.

'But if I . . . If he . . .' she stuttered. 'I will end my life alone. What man will want this broken thing that I have become?'

The Chinaman took her hand. 'Broken things can be mended,' he told her. 'Perhaps your husband is the evil that has infected your body. Perhaps when he is gone, you will become again the flower that you once were.'

Darshana wiped her eyes again. 'Do you think so?' she asked hopefully.

'Yes, madam,' replied the Chinaman. 'Now let us go and drink some more tea.'

26 January 1919

Sohni wiped her eyes and followed her stepmother's instructions.

'It had better be finished by the time I get back or I will take my cane to you!' Darshana Kaur warned her young stepdaughter.

'It will be finished,' Sohni replied, eyeing the pile of washing that sat in front of her. Her scalp stung from having her hair pulled, a punishment that her step-mother often used. She picked up the washing stick, a thick piece of darkened hardwood that was used to beat the clothes clean, and ran her fingers over its smooth edges. Resigned to her fate, she picked up one of her father's shirts, dipped it in the bucket of soap and water at her feet, and then laid it down on a stone slab to her right. She took the stick and began to beat the shirt.

An hour later, when the last piece of clothing had been washed, she looked down at her chapped hands.

'What man is ever going to want me?' she asked herself. 'I have the hands of a forty-year-old widow.'

A sudden gust of wind made the shutters rattle and Sohni felt herself grow cold. She shivered and picked up the wet clothes, preparing to hang them out to dry. The wind dropped as suddenly as it had arisen and she made her way out into the large courtyard. She hung out the clothes before sitting down on a wooden seat – a seat that her mother had used when she was still alive. Sohni rubbed her hands together, ashamed of the calluses that had formed, and thought of Gurdial.

She wondered what he was doing – whether he was smiling or frowning, what thoughts were going through his head. She smiled as she pictured his curly black hair and big brown eyes with lashes that were thick like a woman's. His strong yet gentle hands and the way he cocked his head towards her whenever she spoke to him. She looked back down at her hands. Gurdial would have her even if she was an old hag, toothless and smelling of dung. Gurdial was her hero, her dream.

'I wish I could tell my father,' she said to herself.

'Tell him what, child?' said a friendly voice behind her.

Sohni turned to see Mohni standing there, his old hands covered in dust. He had worked for her family for as long as she could remember – he was like a grandfather, and a mother too. She confided in him and he listened to her. He was from a so-called lower caste, a *choorah*, but he was a thousand times more loving than her father had ever been. He smiled gently and then held out his arms. Sohni sprang from her seat and went to him, comforted immediately by his touch and by the dusty scent, like mouldering mushrooms, that clung to him – the same scent she remembered from her childhood.

'What is it, my daughter?' asked Mohni.

'It's nothing, *chacha-ji*,' she replied, wishing that she was truly his child.

Mohni ruffled her hair and grinned. 'Ever since you were a little girl I have been able to tell when you are lying,' he reminded her. 'Have you ever pulled the wool over these eyes? I may be an old goat now but my mind is still young.'

Sohni took a step back and looked at him. 'I'm sorry. But what can I tell you, *chacha-ji*? It is the same problem as always.'

'Your stepmother?'

'Yes . . .'

'Perhaps we should throw her down a well?' suggested Mohni with a glint in his eye.

Sohni smiled. It was his stock reply. 'I just wish I could get away from here,' she said. 'Somewhere far away . . .'

'With Gurdial?'

As with everything else in her life, Sohni had told the man she called uncle all about her love. 'Yes,' she replied.

Mohni sighed. 'I watched your mother fall madly in love with a boy when she was your age. But the Gods had a different plan for her . . .'

'She married my father instead – I know.'

Something passed across Mohni's face – a shadow from the past.

'What is it, *chacha-ji*?' Sohni asked.

Mohni smiled sweetly. 'It is nothing, child. Just an old memory of your mother. Each time I look at you I see her . . .'

Unaware of the lie, Sohni smiled back and gave her uncle a hug. The old man hated lying to the girl but he had promised her mother many things. And in a lifetime that stretched across eighty-two years, he had never once broken a promise.

'I promised your mother that I would look after you until you became someone's wife,' Mohni added. 'And I shall do just that. It is the only thing that keeps this wreck of a body going.'

Sohni shook her head. 'Who are you trying to fool?' she said. 'You are as strong as an ox.'

Mohni smiled weakly. 'Only my heart,' he told her. 'If it wasn't for my heart, the rest of me would have returned to the earth long ago.'

'Your heart?' asked Sohni, confused.

'Why, yes, my child. It beats only as long as you need me. Once you are settled, this old goat can move on to the next journey.'

Sohni tightened her hold on the old man. 'But I will need you for ever,' she teased.

'Well, in that case I will become a very old goat indeed,' he replied.

A door slammed shut inside the house. Sohni's step-mother had returned.

'Quick!' warned Mohni. 'Don't let the witch see us together.'

Sohni let her uncle go and walked slowly back into the house, hoping against hope that her stepmother would take an afternoon nap. Perhaps then she'd be able to sneak out and meet Gurdial.

But it was not to be. Once inside she saw that her stepmother was agitated. The lines on her forehead were pronounced, and the single brow that sat above her eyes like a caterpillar was lowered. Even her crooked and hooked nose twitched with anxiety. She was not a happy woman. Standing next to her was an old Chinaman, with hair as white as blossom, stooped over with age. His skin looked fragile, as if it was made from dried rice paper. However, his eyes blazed out like emerald torches.

'Get me a hammer!' Sohni's stepmother ordered.

'A hammer?' she queried.

'Don't question me, you bitch!'

A fire raged inside Sohni but outwardly she remained calm. The last time she had shown her true feelings, she had borne the resulting bruises for two weeks. She was in no mood for another savage beating. 'Very well,' she replied.

She walked round to her father's workshop, found an old hammer and returned to the house. The Chinaman was pulling five-inch nails from a cloth bag. He raised one up to the light and studied it carefully. Satisfied, he took the hammer from Sohni, went calmly over to the front door and proceeded to bang the nail into the wood. Once he had finished he repeated the process with a new nail. On his fourth such act, Sohni quizzed her stepmother.

'To your room!' spat Darshana Kaur. 'Before I put out your eyes!'

Sohni decided not to argue and left the room gladly. But instead of going to her own room, she stood behind the kitchen door and listened as her stepmother began to chant incantations and the Chinaman continued to damage the door. Sohni smiled to herself. It had to be another fertility ritual. The one thing that was driving both her stepmother and her father mad was the lack of a male heir to their fortune. Darshana had borne two daughters, both of whom had died as infants, but had yet to produce a son. And Sohni was well aware that her father would rather burn everything he owned to ashes than hand it over to her – a girl.

'Stupid old witch,' Sohni said under her breath, before going off to find something else to occupy her time.

Out in the garden, Mohni stood by the moss-covered wall, talking to a woman he usually met in the market-place. She wore a white *salwaar kameez* and her face was wrapped in a black scarf which would, on closer inspection, have proved to be made of the finest silk that money could buy. As they spoke, the woman gestured towards the house. Mohni grinned and whispered something to her, moving his head towards hers. They shared a moment of laughter before the woman spoke again. Mohni nodded his agreement and then waved the woman away. She turned and made her way back down the lane. Mohni watched her leave before stooping to pick up the basket of vegetables at his feet — vegetables the woman had brought him. When he looked back down the lane, the woman was gone. A single butterfly, the colour of a cloudless summer sky, fluttered past Mohni's face.

'Butterflies in winter?' he said to himself with a sly grin. 'How very odd.'

28 January 1919

The walk took Gurdial twenty minutes, along a dusty, rutted and potholed road. He had left the city at midday, heading south, along one of the routes taken by the farmers who brought their goods to market each day. The nearest village was another ten minutes' walk but Gurdial left the road where he always did, just past two giant trees. The field he entered was L-shaped and dropped away from the road, its steep banks overgrown with hemp plants. He worked his way through them until he had reached the stream, then followed the slow-running water towards the copse where Sohni was waiting for him.

As Gurdial approached he could not stop staring at her. She was more beautiful than anything or anyone he had ever seen. Her sunlight-coloured hair was tied up in a bun and her smooth alabaster skin had a rosy hue. When she saw him, her eyes, as blue as the *amrit* that surrounded the Golden Temple, sparkled. She looked like a princess. Gurdial felt himself gulp down air as his heart began to race in his chest.

'You're late!' she teased. 'I thought I would have to find myself another boy.'

Gurdial smiled warmly. He knew that she was teasing, but even so, hearing her talk of another boy stabbed at his insides.

'What's wrong?' she asked, seeing beyond his smile.

'It's nothing,' he told her. 'Just me being foolish. I cannot even joke about you being with another . . .'

Sohni grinned. 'You are so silly sometimes,' she scolded playfully. 'How could I ever meet anyone as kind and considerate as you?'

Gurdial shrugged. 'I am just a simple man,' he replied. 'And you are the most beautiful girl in the whole of the Punjab. Every man who looks at you wants you. You could have anyone you wish.'

Sohni closed her eyes. 'And I wish,' she told him, 'I wish for a slightly silly yet remarkably loyal and utterly handsome boy from the Khalsa Orphanage.'

She opened her eyes again. 'Do you know anyone who fits that description?'

Gurdial took her hand and squeezed it tight. 'You are so kind to me. But what if you can't have me?'

Sohni frowned. 'Then I will live my life as a spinster!' she insisted. 'It's you or no one.'

Gurdial felt a warm shiver work its way down his spine. He took her other hand and pulled her towards him. Her scent, a dreamy collision of lavender and vanilla, sent powerful urges through his body. He held her tightly.

'One of these days,' she said to him, 'we will be together properly. And there will be no more secret meetings.'

Gurdial smiled. 'But I love this place,' he said. 'Even after we are married I would like to meet you here – it is our place.'

Something splashed in the stream, and above them a white dove circled. A gentle breeze whispered through the leaves. They sat down on the grass and looked out across their hiding place.

'It's so beautiful here,' said Sohni. 'I can see why you like to come here. It's like a dream . . .'

Gurdial nodded. 'I worry,' he said.

'About . . . ?'

'Dreams,' he replied. 'What if that is all we ever have?'

Sohni lay back on the grass and looked up at a perfect, cloudless sky. 'I won't allow it,' she said.

Gurdial lay down at her side and turned towards her. 'But there is so much that stands in our way. Your father will never consent to our wishes.'

Sohni sighed. 'I know,' she said quietly.

'I have spent each night since we met playing it over and over in my head,' he told her. 'And each time I ask your father for your hand he laughs at me. It will be no different when I do it for real.'

Sohni turned to look at him, her eyes wide with surprise. 'You are going to ask him?'

'Yes,' he replied.

'When did you decide on this?'

'Just now. Right here, this very minute. It is the only way . . .'

Sohni felt her heart jump before her stomach clenched with nerves. 'When?'

Gurdial shrugged. 'I do not know. Everyone I've spoken to thinks I am crazy . . .'

Sohni smiled. 'By everyone, I take it you mean Jeevan?'

Gurdial nodded.

'How is your pig-headed friend today?'

'As stubborn as always,' he told her. 'He is trying to learn how to juggle and carries three onions wherever he goes. One of them is beginning to rot . . .'

'And is he any good?' asked Sohni.

'Useless,' replied Gurdial. 'But you can smell him coming a mile away.'

Sohni ran her hand down his chest. 'So who else have you spoken to about us?'

Gurdial wondered whether to tell her about Bissen Singh. After all, she didn't know him and perhaps she would worry that they might be caught out. But Gurdial trusted the soldier and he trusted in his love for Sohni – there should be nothing that cannot be said between us, he told himself.

'A soldier,' he admitted.

'A British soldier?'

Gurdial shook his head. 'He fought for the British in

their war, but he is a Punjabi: Bissen Singh. He is a wonderful man – full of good advice.'

Sohni asked whether he could be trusted.

'You could trust him with your life,' Gurdial replied. 'He is the one who told me that I have to do the right thing and ask your father. He also told me that a dream is not worth having if you don't believe that it can come true.'

Sohni moved closer to him and put her head on his shoulder. 'He seems to be a good man, from what you say,' she said. 'And he speaks sense. Mohni told me the same thing. What good is a dream if you don't try to realize it?'

Gurdial pulled her closer still until her breasts pushed against his side and he could feel her breath on his cheek. He ran his hand along the curve of her hip and let it rest on her thigh. Even through her clothes, he could feel the heat that emanated from her skin. He longed to touch her bare flesh, to ease into her and listen to her as she whispered her love into his ear.

'So when will you ask my father?'

'I don't know,' replied Gurdial.

'And what if he says no?'

'Then we will have to think of something else.'

'We could run away,' Sohni suggested.

'Perhaps,' said Gurdial. 'But where would we go?'

Sohni turned and lay on top of him. She looked into his eyes and smiled. 'I don't care where we go,' she told him. 'As long as we go together.'

46

Later, as Sohni sat in the kitchen with Mohni, her stepmother asked her where she had been all afternoon.

'I went to run the errands you gave me,' she replied.

'And it took *three* hours?' snapped her stepmother,
looking at her with disgust. Who did the little bitch think
she was? 'If you are lying to me I will slap you,' she
warned.

'I'm not lying,' said Sohni. 'Ask anyone. I was at the
market and then I went to see my friend, Yasmeen—'

Darshana spat in horror. 'The Muslim girl?'

'Yes!' said Sohni.

'How dare you spend time with that whore when
you should be here,' fumed Darshana.

'But I was only doing what you—' began Sohni.

Before she could finish Darshana pounced on her
and began to beat her about the face. Sohni cowered
from the blows but did not cry. She knew that her stepmother was a weak woman; that her rages subsided
quickly. By the tenth blow Darshana was red in the face
and breathless. The sour, dank smell from her armpits,
like rotten vegetables and putrid milk, made Sohni want
to heave.

'We shall see what your father has to say,' her stepmother told her, before storming out of the kitchen.

Once she was gone, Sohni washed her face and
straightened her hair. As Mohni apologized for not
being able to help her, she took his hand.

'I don't want you to help,' she told him. 'She'll

only take it out on you and I'd rather she hit me first.'

'But—' began Mohni.

'No,' replied Sohni.

'I should have cut out her heart on the very first night she arrived here,' whispered Mohni. 'Your mother always knew that she was an evil woman—'

Sohni started in shock. 'My *mother*? How did she know who Darshana was?'

Realizing his mistake, Mohni backtracked. 'She used to work in the market,' he lied. 'Your mother never liked her, always making rude comments and swearing at people. There were rumours that she practised witch craft too.'

'Oh,' replied Sohni. 'I didn't realize that she was around when my mother was still alive.'

Mohni cursed himself silently. There were many things the young girl didn't know and it was best that it remained that way.

'How would you?' he asked Sohni. 'You were only a child.'

'One day you will have to tell me everything,' she said to him.

Mohni smiled. 'You know it all, my child,' he lied again. 'Perhaps I can fill in the *minor* details.' He looked away in shame.

2 February 1919

Gurdial stopped at a stall and feigned interest in the brightly coloured fruits.

'What are you doing now?' asked Bissen.

The young man shrugged.

'Come on,' urged Bissen. 'Don't lose your will now.'

They were on their way to confront Sohni's father. After days of trying to get Gurdial to change his mind, to think more carefully about what he was doing, Bissen had given up. If Gurdial wanted to do what he thought was the right thing, then so be it.

Bissen had tried to reason with the boy. He'd told him that he and Sohni were still young and had plenty of time to consider their actions. That Sohni's father, Gulbaru Singh, would not be open to his request if it came out of the blue.

'But he won't say yes, anyway,' Gurdial had replied.

'Perhaps. But he might be more willing if there was a

more . . . er . . . adult approach made on your behalf.'

'And what adult can I send?' the boy had asked. 'I have no mother, no father and no older brothers.'

It was good to see the determination on the boy's face but Bissen also knew that once Gulbaru Singh found out about them, the young lovers would have trouble meeting. Hope was hope and dreams were dreams but the reality of life in Amritsar was harsh. The poor never married the rich – never – and that was just the way things were.

The problem for Bissen was trying to justify his arguments to himself: it was something he just couldn't do. Here he was, a lovesick fool, waiting for an invitation to return to England – to the woman of his dreams – hoping and praying that she would ignore the social taboos inherent in English society and step away from her own race and religion and culture. And yet he was telling Gurdial that taboos could never be broken, and at the same time urging him to follow his dreams. The opium-induced fog in his head had grown so thick that he jumped from contradiction to contradiction like some kind of agitated toad.

'What if he laughs at me?' asked Gurdial as the stallholder shooed him away.

Bissen sighed. Laughter would be the least of Gurdial's worries. 'We've already spoken about this, Gurdial. You can't control how he will react.'

'And that means . . . ?'

'It means what it means,' said Bissen. 'Don't worry about his reply before you've even asked the question. Once he makes that reply, then you can try to do something about it.'

'I don't want to make things difficult for Sohni.'

Bissen shook his head and placed a hand on Gurdial's bony shoulder. 'But what you're about to do *will* make things harder,' he told him. 'That's something both of you already know. It's the risk you've both chosen to take.'

Gurdial put his hands to his head in confusion. 'Oh, why can't this be easy?' he cried.

'Because nothing ever is. Because if things were easy, life would be much less interesting.'

'Now you're just teasing me,' complained Gurdial.

'No I'm not. I'm just trying to explain how things are.'

Gurdial stepped aside as a short, squat market trader barged past them, his eyes blazing with anger. The man swore at them before beginning an argument with a younger, taller trader.

Bissen ignored the disagreement and pulled Gurdial after him. 'Come,' he said. 'It's now or never.'

Gulbaru Singh was a happy man because he was making money – lots and lots of money. The Rowlatt Act, introduced by the British to try and keep a lid on the growing tensions in the Punjab, had also pushed prices up, and that suited Gulbaru down to the ground.

After all, people were never going to stop buying cloth, were they? No matter how expensive it was, they were still going to need it – no one was going to start walking around the streets of Amritsar naked.

His shop, situated in the middle of the main shopping street, was packed with buyers. There were overbearing mothers buying expensive material for their daughters' weddings, and grim-faced fathers hoping not to have to spend too much; men looking for turbans, and women who wanted the latest fabrics for their *salwaar kameez* and saris. And all of them were going to have to pay much more than they would have even three months earlier.

'God bless the British,' Gulbaru said to himself as yet another mother dragged her daughter into the shop.

He turned to his assistant. 'Moti-Lal – run and fetch some tea!' he ordered.

'Yes, boss,' replied Moti-Lal.

The very least he could do was offer them some tea, Gulbaru thought to himself. After all, they were about to make him even richer.

'*Bhai* – how much is that new fabric over there?' asked a woman with a pronounced widow's peak and three large moles on the left side of her face.

Gulbaru looked at the fabric she was indicating and smiled to himself. 'What can I tell you, sister?' he said with a fake sigh. 'This Rowlatt business is killing me.'

The woman scowled as he told her the price. Her husband, a man half her size, went red.

'But,' added Gulbaru, 'it is the freshest design we have. Perfect for any daughter.'

'Brand new, you say?' asked the woman.

'Arrived yesterday,' Gulbaru said, lying through his rotting teeth. 'As yet no one in Amritsar has bought even a scrap of this fine cloth . . .'

He pulled a length from the roll and laid it out on the counter in front of the customer. 'Feel how opulent it is,' he told her. 'And ask yourself if your daughter is worth the extra premium that you'll pay – I know mine is—'

'And no other person has this?'

'No,' replied Gulbaru. 'I swear on the life of my own beautiful daughter.'

'I'll take it,' decided the woman.

Gulbaru tried not to grin as the husband went even redder and started to cough. As he asked the woman how much fabric she wanted, a gunshot rang out in the street. Everyone in the shop ran to see what was happening. Across the road, a group of policemen had detained two young men at gunpoint. No one seemed to have been hurt. A crowd had gathered and three British soldiers tried to keep them at bay. It was yet another incident in a growing catalogue. Amritsar was heading for trouble.

'These rebels are making things very difficult,' said a red-turbanned man.

Gulbaru shrugged. 'How is an honest man supposed

to make a living?' he asked as a gaunt-looking youth walked past him.

The man in the red turban scoffed at Gulbaru's words. 'Some of us,' he said to no one in particular, 'are making plenty of money.'

Although his remarks were aimed squarely at Gulbaru, the cloth trader ignored him. Instead he watched his assistant returning with the tea. 'Quickly,' he ordered. 'Get them back inside before they change their minds . . .'

Moti-Lal took the tea inside and then returned to round up the customers. '*Chai – chai!*' he shouted. 'Come inside and drink.'

Gulbaru watched as his customers returned to the store. 'Now let's see if we can't lighten your pockets for you,' he whispered to himself.

Bissen Singh stood at the entrance to Gulbaru's shop. It was much like every other store in Amritsar: open to the street. At the end of the day, all the merchandise was shut away in a storeroom to the rear and wooden shutters locked across the opening. It sat between a jeweller's and a food store, with a narrow gulley running between each shop. The gulleys were overgrown with weeds and stank of human and animal waste. Stray dogs and homeless beggars used them as resting places, away from the bright glare of the sun.

Gurdial stood behind Bissen, his eyes wide with fear and anticipation. His mouth felt as dry as kindling and his stomach made strange gurgling noises. He looked into the shop and saw Sohni's father talking to a customer.

'I'm not sure I can do this,' he said to Bissen.

'It's too late to turn back now.'

'But I am an orphan,' Gurdial moaned. 'An orphan who wants to marry a rich girl.'

Bissen sighed. 'Very well. It's decision time. Either you go in and speak to him or we leave right now and never come back.'

Gurdial looked at his mentor. His eyes filled with tears and his heart sank. A creeping realization dawned on him. Whether he asked Sohni's father or not, it did not matter. There was no way Gulbaru Singh was ever going to agree, so it mattered little whether he went inside or skulked away like a thief.

'Well?' asked Bissen. 'Are you going to live on your knees or be a man?'

Gurdial wiped away the tears and stood up straight, shoulders back and chest out. 'I'm going to ask him,' he said defiantly.

Bissen put his hand on the boy's shoulder. 'Come on then,' he said sympathetically. 'I'll be at your side, brother. But for God's sake do not tell him that you are already lovers.'

Gurdial waited a moment longer before striding into the store with as much confidence as he could fake. Bissen paused for a few seconds, shook his head and followed.

* * *

Inside Gulbaru Singh's shop the temperature was stifling. A layer of greasy sweat clung to Gurdial's forehead as the sour smell of body odour and musk and incense made him swallow air. Despite the heat, he felt as though someone was stabbing him in the guts with an icicle. He found himself unable to look Sohni's father in the eye as the words he had so carefully rehearsed disappeared from memory. He turned to leave but felt Bissen's hand in the small of his back, preventing any escape.

Gulbaru Singh, for his part, had barely noticed the arrival of the two men. His eyes were firmly fixed on the bosom of a short Hindu woman in a tight gold and yellow sari, who was looking at various fabrics. Gulbaru studied her rounded hips and strong buttocks and wondered whether such a woman would have provided him with the male heir he so desperately craved. With his first wife dead, her replacement had promised much but delivered nothing. Each evening she ate away at Gulbaru's patience and showed herself for the useless whore she had always been.

Now she resorted to pills, potions and black magic to try and conceive a son. Nothing worked, as if he had been cursed for some reason. But Gulbaru Singh had always had plans – his whole life had been run according to them – and he was not about to let his second wife deny him his due. Perhaps there were more permanent solutions to his problems, he thought to himself. And the fresh scent and, perhaps, virginal touch of a new bride was certainly something he would welcome. He sighed to himself.

Gurdial stepped forward and tried to get Gulbaru's attention, his heart pounding in his chest. Blood thumped behind his eyeballs.

Sohni's father looked up and sneered. 'What do you want?' he asked Gurdial, looking at him with contempt.

'I . . .' began Gurdial, but the words failed him.

'Are you begging for something?' spat Gulbaru. 'You poor people are always asking for something.'

'No, sir,' replied Gurdial. 'I wanted to speak to you.'

Gulbaru sneered again. 'And what would a snivelling wretch like *you* have to talk about?'

Gurdial cleared his throat. 'It is delicate,' he told him. 'Can we speak outside?'

Gulbaru looked beyond Gurdial to Bissen. 'Are you with *him*?' he asked the soldier, dismissing the young man with a nod movement of his head.

Bissen nodded but said nothing.

'So what does this boy have to tell me? Is it some sort of scam?'

Bissen shook his head. 'It is a delicate matter, *bhai-ji*,' he replied respectfully. 'It would be much better if we spoke in private.' He nodded at the customers in the shop, all of whom were now listening in to their conversation.

Gulbaru thought about it for a second and then

shrugged. He picked up a thick wooden club from the counter as he made his way towards the back of the shop.

'Let's talk then,' he said to Bissen and Gurdial without looking at them. 'But be warned: I have broken the heads of better men than you.'

Bissen looked at Gurdial and gestured for him to follow Sohni's father. 'You can be sure, *bhai-ji*,' he told Gulbaru, 'that it is not a trick.'

The customers watched the two men and the boy go into the back room of the shop with interest. When the door was closed they turned to Moti-Lal.

'Is there something wrong?' asked the woman in the gold and yellow sari.

The shop assistant shrugged. 'I do not know. But I cannot imagine that Gulbaru Singh has business with either of those two.'

As they returned their attention to the back room they heard Gulbaru Singh break out in howls of laughter. Not the warm laughter of a man who had been told a good joke but the cold, heartless, arrogant laughter of one who could not believe what he was being told by men he knew to be his inferiors.

'Surely this is some sort of joke,' said Gulbaru.

Bissen shook his head.

'But it must be. You come to me with this orphan boy, this penniless wretch who reeks of sweat and mouldy onions, and you ask me if I will allow my daughter to be his wife? Do you think I am mad?'

'No, *bhai-ji*,' answered Bissen.

'Then do not waste my time,' spat Gulbaru. 'Can you not see that I am a busy man with money to make?'

Gurdial cleared his throat. 'I will do anything you ask of me, sir,' he insisted.

Gulbaru waved his hand in the boy's face. 'And what can *you* do for me?' he asked, his eyes cold. 'You are a beggar and a fool. What could you *possibly* bring me or provide for me that would matter?'

'I will do whatever you ask of me,' repeated Gurdial, his hopes fading.

Gulbaru thought for a moment. Then something in his eyes changed. The coldness remained but a spark of mischief also appeared. He smiled at the orphan boy. 'Very well,' he said.

Gurdial's eyes widened in shock. Was he dreaming or had Sohni's father just agreed to their union? He shot a glance at Bissen, who remained calm. 'So you are happy for me to marry Sohni?' he asked hurriedly.

Once again Gulbaru began to howl like a demented hyena and tears flowed down his cheeks. His laughter echoed around the room. Gurdial realized that he had misheard.

'I would be happier if she married a dog!' Gulbaru told him.

'But you said very well . . .'

Gulbaru shook his head. 'Listen to me, boy, and listen well. I will allow you to marry my daughter on one simple condition and one alone. You have until Vaisakhi to bring me the most precious thing in the whole of India.'

Gurdial looked at Bissen, unsure of what to say or do.

'Are you simple?' asked Gulbaru. 'Do not look at him, boy! I want the most precious thing in the whole of India by Vaisakhi or I will personally remove your head from your shoulders for daring to ask for my daughter.'

Gurdial realized he had no choice. He nodded.

Bissen stood up straight and looked into Gulbaru's eyes. 'I have witnessed this agreement,' he warned him, 'and I will hold you to it. If the boy does as you ask then you will allow the marriage—'

Gulbaru snorted.

'Remember,' Bissen went on, 'I will keep you to your word or I will die trying.'

Gulbaru cackled like an old hag. 'Die trying then,' he told him. 'It will be far easier than taking me on.'

Bissen turned to Gurdial. 'Come! Let's go.'

He opened the door for Gurdial.

'Remember!' Gulbaru shouted after them. 'Until Vaisakhi!'

The laugh that erupted from him was almost demonic.

Gurdial sat on the steps of the orphanage with his head in his hands and wondered why God had made his life so difficult. How on earth was he to know what the most precious thing in India was – and even if he did work it out, how was he supposed to get it? It could be anywhere, from the beaches of Kerala to the plains of Rajasthan and everywhere in between. And all before the festival of Vaisakhi, which fell in the second week of April.

'We'll find a way,' said Bissen, who was sitting next to him.

Gurdial looked up and shook his head, his eyes watering. 'We will *never* find a way, *bhai-ji*,' he replied, resigned to his sorrow. 'Sohni and I will *never* be together.'

'But you can still run away,' Bissen reminded him.

'We can,' Gurdial agreed, 'but that isn't what honourable people do. And it will be difficult with no money—'

'But it *can* be done. Nothing is finished and nothing is certain. And for now you must hold onto that. You knew that the chances of Gulbaru Singh agreeing to your request were slim. Now you must find another way, that's all.'

The door to the orphanage opened with a loud creak and Mata Devi looked out onto the steps. 'Gurdial – where have you been?' she asked. 'I had some errands for you this afternoon.'

Gurdial turned to make some sort of excuse but Bissen beat him to it. 'Good afternoon, Mata Devi-ji.'

'*Sat-sri-akaal*,' she replied. 'And why are you sitting on my steps?'

Bissen smiled at her. 'I needed some help today. My wounds have been playing up and I asked Gurdial to give me a hand.'

Mata Devi smiled and asked him if he wanted to come inside and have some tea.

'No, no,' replied Bissen, 'I must hurry home and attend to something but I want to thank you for raising these young men so well. Gurdial has been a great help to me.'

'I'm glad to hear it, my son,' replied Mata Devi. 'He is a good boy with a kind heart. Now, are you sure you won't come in and eat with us?'

Bissen shook his head. 'Perhaps tomorrow.'

'Come along then, Gurdial,' said Mata Devi. 'There are still chores left to do.'

Gurdial stood up and dusted himself off.

'Come and find me tomorrow,' Bissen told him. 'If you have the time.'

Gurdial nodded before turning to his guardian. 'Is Jeevan back yet?' he asked her.

Mata Devi shook her head and led Gurdial inside as Bissen took his leave. 'I'm not sure what is going on with Jeevan,' she told him. 'He just isn't his usual self at the moment. Do you know where he's been going?'

Gurdial shrugged. 'No, Mata-ji,' he lied.

Gulbaru Singh waited until his daughter had left the room before speaking to his wife.

'A strange thing happened to me today,' he told her.

Darshana Kaur looked up at her husband and arched her single brow. Her beady eyes searched his face for clues. What was he talking about? Behind him, an old mirror threw her reflection back at her. She winced. Before marrying Gulbaru, when they were lovers, she had been a strikingly beautiful creature. Her hair had been long and lustrous and her eyes had sparkled. Her skin was once smooth and her teeth perfect rows of white enamel. Her young body had been strong and hard, with full breasts and enticing curves. But from the day they'd married everything had changed.

Now she was a hag – her teeth brown and rotten, her hair greasy and thin; her once admired figure had gone, and hair had begun to sprout on her chest and back and no amount of sugaring or shaving stopped it. And worse still, even more perplexing and maddening, was the smell that she carried with her – of rotten vegetables and rancid milk, a scent that she could not remove, no matter how many times she washed herself. And all of it had begun after they'd wed – barely six months after his first wife had died, butchered by their hands. How long would it be, she asked herself, before Gulbaru plotted her demise too? A second glance at her reflection told her that it would not be very long at all.

'A strange thing?' she asked quietly.

'*Very* strange,' replied Gulbaru. 'Apparently my daughter has a suitor.'

This time the black caterpillar that sat above

Darshana's eyes arched of its own accord. 'A *suitor*?'

Gulbaru nodded.

'And this man is willing to take her off our hands?' At last, Darshana thought to herself, a husband for the little bitch. For many years she had wanted to get rid of Sohni, in much the same way as she and Gulbaru had rid themselves of the two daughters she'd borne. Now the opportunity to remove Sohni *without* killing her presented itself. She smiled.

'Oh, I've no doubt that he will take her off our hands,' Gulbaru told her, 'but he is only a boy. And a poor one at that.'

'A poor boy?' asked Darshana, her smile fading. In her husband's eyes she saw rage. 'Shall I fetch her from the kitchen?'

Gulbaru thought for a moment and then shook his head. 'For now this remains between us. Besides, there is no hope of the boy ever fulfilling the quest I have set him.'

'What *quest*?' enquired Darshana.

'The beggar told me that he would do anything to gain my daughter. So I told him to bring me the most valuable thing in all of India, by Vaisakhi.'

Darshana frowned in confusion.

'Are you *demented*?' spat Gulbaru. 'There is no way on earth that I will allow my daughter to marry such a dog! I have set him a task that he has no hope of fulfilling, and while he wastes his time I will work out how to kill him.'

'Ah,' said Darshana. 'Do you want me to take care of that part?'

Gulbaru shook his head. 'This is something I want to do alone. This wretch wishes to make me a laughing stock but I will not allow it. No, what I want *you* to do is watch my daughter like a hawk. The boy insists that they have never met but I don't believe him. I want you to follow her, to find out if they are already lovers.'

Darshana nodded. 'And if they are?'

'Then Sohni can join her mother. No one will destroy my reputation – no one!'

Darshana's smile reappeared. 'I understand . . .'

She stood up, walked over to him and began to knead his shoulders with her warty hands. 'Does this feel as good as it always did?' she asked.

Gulbaru grunted.

'The Chinaman thinks that we have a very good chance of conceiving a boy,' she added.

'Does he really?' replied Gulbaru sarcastically. 'For the amount of money he takes from me, he had better be right.'

Darshana let her hands wander down her husband's chest. 'Perhaps we should try now?' she suggested.

Back in the shadows by the front door, Mohni stood silently and averted his gaze. He'd heard everything the couple had plotted and knew he had to act. Quickly, he let himself out and made his way to the narrow lane that ran down the side of the house, looking around to make sure he wasn't being followed. The lane was dark but Mohni knew it well.

She was quick to arrive, her appearance heralded by the sweet aroma of mangoes and cream.

'*Sat-sri-akaal*,' said Mohni.

'You have news?' asked the woman, adjusting her black shawl.

Mohni nodded and told her everything he'd overheard.

When he was finished the woman sighed. 'There is much evil at work. What about the boy?'

'I'm not sure what to do about him,' replied Mohni. 'This quest – I don't even know if he will begin it. I think it would be best if they left.'

'No,' insisted the woman. 'Sohni cannot leave her home. You leave the boy to me.'

Mohni nodded in agreement. 'So you will help them soon?'

'No,' she said. 'I will help them when the time is right – until then I will watch over them.'

'And what about Gulbaru and the witch?'

The woman smiled. 'I'll take care of that too – perhaps keep them occupied until I can think of something.'

Mohni asked her how she would do that.

The woman chuckled. 'There is much that we can do. Perhaps one day you will find out.'

It was Mohni's turn to laugh. 'It is something I should

have discovered long ago – this power. But I made someone a promise and I intend to keep it.'

The woman nodded. 'Be careful. You are also in great danger,' she told him. 'The witch will come after you. Be prepared.'

'Let her come,' answered Mohni.

Part Two

The
Brothers

Amritsar, 13 February 1919

Mohni could feel his legs as he walked into the market-place. There was a dull ache that stretched from his knees down to his ankles. He stopped for a moment and shook them but it made no difference.

'A consequence of age, you old goat,' a woman's voice said.

Mohni looked at a fruit stall piled high with mauve lychees, bright red pomegranates, pale lemons darted with green, and oranges so deep and rich in colour that they seemed to glow. Each pile threw out a powerful, sweet scent, as if the various fruits were competing for the attention of the people walking past. Their colours seemed otherworldly, too bright and too vivid for Mohni's milky, cloudy old eyes. Standing to the right of the stall was the woman who had spoken.

'There you are, daughter,' Mohni said with a grin.

'I am always here.' Her honey-coloured eyes sparkled. 'And there too . . .'

'Here, there and everywhere,' said Mohni. 'Like a ghost.'

The woman gave Mohni a smile so warm, so comforting, that he could have melted.

'And who are you watching today?' he asked her.

'Everyone and no one,' the woman replied, smiling at the warm, musky smell that emanated from Mohni and his clothes; a scent that unleashed happy memories from her own childhood.

To most people her reply would have seemed unduly cryptic but Mohni knew her well and simply nodded his almost hairless head.

'Who are you watching in *particular*?' he asked.

The woman nodded towards a stocky teenage boy with jet-black hair and a thin moustache. 'This one,' she said. 'He has a great duty to fulfil and I need him to stay safe until it is done.'

Mohni squinted at the boy. There was something about him that seemed familiar. 'I have seen him before, but where I do not know.'

'He is another who grew up in the orphanage,' she told him, just as two boys who were also orphans walked past. One of them carried three rotting onions.

'Ah,' said Mohni. 'Gurdial – the love of Sohni's life.'

The woman smiled. 'And the possible cause of great sorrow and danger,' she added.

'You do not approve of their love?'

'Fate does not care for approval,' she replied.

'There is also the small matter of your own interest in Sohni,' Mohni reminded her.

'Yes, there is that too. Her father and stepmother must never see them together. You must protect her.'

'Until my dying day,' he said. 'I made a promise to her mother before she died.'

The woman nodded. 'Has anything happened since you told me of her parents' plans?' she asked.

Mohni shook his head.

'Good. But stay vigilant: Gulbaru and Darshana are infected with evil.'

Mohni waved his hand at a fly that was trying to settle on his long thin nose. 'So apart from the orphans and Sohni, is there anyone else you watch over?'

'There is also a soldier who will very shortly buy some oranges from me,' the woman said.

Before Mohni had a chance to reply, a proud-looking young man wearing a blue turban and walking with a pronounced limp asked the woman for five oranges.

The woman smiled at him. 'Just five oranges, Bissen?' she asked him.

Surprise flooded the young soldier's face. 'How do you know my name?'

She adjusted the black shawl she wore and shrugged. 'You are well known. The soldier who fought for the British in their war.'

'But—' Bissen began.

She shook her head. 'You must not think that I'm judging you, Bissen,' she told him. 'There are many here who dislike what you did for the *goreh* but I am not one of them. I merely wish you to eat more oranges.'

The soldier eyed her with suspicion. 'More oranges?'

She nodded. 'Your skin is dry and your face is drawn. I know that the pain of your injury keeps you this way but fruit is very good for you.'

'My mother keeps telling me the same thing,' he replied.

'Here – take ten oranges.' She put the fruit in the cloth bag the soldier had given her.

'But I only wanted—'

The woman looked into the soldier's pale grey eyes and he stopped abruptly. Mohni, who had seen many people react to her in this way, grinned.

'There is no charge,' she said.

A thought passed across the soldier's face. 'I have a strange feeling . . .' he told her.

'A sense of *déjà vu*,' she replied. 'I know. Memory can sometimes play tricks on all of us. Here . . .'

The soldier took the bag, thanked the woman and walked away, his face full of confusion.

'A special case, that one,' the woman told Mohni.

'Aren't they all?' he replied.

Gurdial and Jeevan walked through the marketplace and into the Hall Bazaar, looking for something to do. As wards of the Khalsa Orphanage, they spent their mornings praying, going to school and running errands for the couple who took care of them. By mid-afternoon they were usually to be seen wandering the streets of Amritsar. Jeevan, who was the shorter of the two, nodded towards a unit of Gurkhas moving slowly down the street, their uniforms dusty and their faces determined. Every now and then they would stop and stare into the open shop fronts.

'What do you think they are looking for?' Jeevan asked his friend.

Gurdial grinned. 'Perhaps if you put down those onions you're carrying, you wouldn't have to point with your head,' he suggested.

'They *are* a bit smelly.' Jeevan was still using the onions to practise juggling and they were beginning to rot, especially where his clumsy fingers had caused indentations.

'*Bhai* – they smell worse than the opium addicts.'

Jeevan screwed up his face.

'Nothing smells *that* bad.'

Gurdial looked across the street at an alleyway that ran between two store fronts. It was so narrow that only one man could pass at a time – if they could get through the overgrown weeds, which stood as high as a horse. Along the middle of the alley ran an open sewer.

'What about that *nali*?' he asked Jeevan, pointing at the sewer.

'No,' said Jeevan. 'The addicts are worse than that too.'

'But not as bad as your onions.'

Jeevan sighed. 'Very well. I'll get rid of them, but I have no money left to buy any more.'

'You didn't *pay* for them last time, you fool,' Gurdial said with a laugh.

'Will you help me to get some more?' Jeevan asked.

'Yes, *bhai*. I know stealing is against the teachings of the Gurus but you *are* my brother.'

Jeevan smiled.

'And besides,' said Gurdial, 'these merchants are making a fortune from the Rowlatt Act.'

Gurdial had heard people talking about the Rowlatt Act but didn't really understand what it meant. As far as he could tell, the act was making rich people richer and everyone else poor. As for its details, Gurdial wasn't sure he'd understand even if they *were* explained to him. Not that it mattered. In the great scheme of things he was a penniless orphan and his station in life had been decided. That was the way of Kismet and it was beyond his control. It was better to live a simple existence and to know your place. Too many dreams didn't help anyone, and besides, Gurdial had already gambled on his biggest dream: Sohni.

'Are you thinking about that girl again?' teased Jeevan.

Gurdial nodded. 'I'm going to meet her later.'

'Be careful, *bhai*,' Jeevan warned. 'If her father finds out, I will be arranging your cremation.'

'I'll be fine. Gulbaru Singh is too busy making money.'

Jeevan was unaware that Gulbaru Singh also knew exactly how Gurdial felt about his daughter. Even though he felt bad for hiding something from his brother, Gurdial knew that telling him would do no good. For now, he told himself, the problems he had were best kept hidden.

Jeevan nudged Gurdial and nodded towards the Gurkhas once more. The patrol was outside a food shop that served thick, crispy *paratha*, deliciously fiery lentil *dhal* and hot, spicy tea. It was a place where young men gathered and had sparked the Gurkhas' interest. The two boys watched as the patrol leader questioned a tall, thin man wearing a black fedora hat. The soldier seemed to be pointing at the man's waistband and asking a question. Very quickly a crowd began to gather. Gurdial took Jeevan's arm and pushed through to the front, eager to get a ringside view.

The tall man was protesting to the soldier. 'It's nothing!' he shouted at the Nepali.

'There!' replied the soldier. 'Take it out slowly!'

He was pointing at a bulge at the man's waistband, a bulge that was covered by his shirt. To Gurdial it seemed obvious that the man was concealing a pistol.

'*Leave him be!*' a voice from the crowd shouted.

'*British dogs out!*' another cried.

The soldiers began to look nervous. The crowd was swelling and they were hopelessly outnumbered. The patrol leader put a whistle to his lips, ready to call for reinforcements. As he did so, someone threw a stone at the Gurkhas. The man with the pistol saw his chance and ran. But the patrol leader was too quick for him. He blew on his whistle and then took aim with his rifle. A single bullet tore through the man's hat, shattering his skull, and he was dead before his body hit the ground.

The crowd began to scatter, shouting and screaming. More soldiers ran down the street towards them.

Gurdial grabbed Jeevan. 'Come on!' he shouted. 'Down the alley!'

Behind them, the soldiers arrested and handcuffed three of the dead man's friends and bundled them into a patrol van. As the last of the men was forced in, he turned and shouted for India to be set free:

'*INDIA ZINDABAAD!*'

14 February 1919

Bissen Singh sat on the steps outside his lodging house, watching the world go by. The entire right side of his body felt numb and his scalp itched beneath his royal blue turban. The morning sun was weak, its rays watery, and there was a chill in the air. The narrow lane was crowded in on both sides by two- and three-storey buildings painted in burnt sienna and ochre and vibrant pink. Bir Singh was sitting on a wooden stool outside his shop across from Bissen, adjusting his orange turban. As far as Bissen could tell there was very little that Bir Singh didn't sell, and as a result his business was popular. Bissen raised his hand in greeting and Bir Singh replied in kind. In the middle of the lane a gang of children were playing catch with a small blue ball, shouting and screaming at each other.

Further along, a two-man army patrol stood at the corner where the lane joined a main street, watching for trouble. There had been an increase in incidents since the turn of the year; incidents that had been branded as terrorist by the British. The clamour for an end to British rule over India grew with each day, and Bissen, for one, did not understand it. The *Engrezi* had brought much that was good, and India had prospered as a result. Having spent time in England during the war, Bissen longed to see his own country modernize in the same way. Not once in all his time in England had he seen an open sewer or packs of stray dogs. The poor were apparent but they did not sleep by the sides of the roads and there was no caste system – although social class was another matter. But at least the poor of England could eat. In India, to be the lowest of the low meant starvation and disease, and infant mortality was like a cancer, eating away at the very core of the country.

But then again, thought Bissen, perhaps he could also understand the revolutionaries who were rising against their masters. The British did not help themselves with their taxation and their reliance on the gun. The Rowlatt Act in particular had led many people to the door of the militants. Prices were rising as the cost of raw materials soared. All around the city, Bissen had seen the effects of the new law, and the army patrols had doubled in number. Amritsar was like a cooking pot, full to the brim with water and simmering dangerously.

A small butterfly, as blue as the most beautiful

summer sky, fluttered about Bissen's face. He watched it closely, wondering why it had come to life so early in the year, when his senses were suddenly filled with the scent of mangoes and fresh cream. Someone sat down at his side.

'Good morning, Bissen.'

He turned to see the woman from the marketplace at his side. A black shawl with silver threaded through it was draped over her head.

'How did you—?' he began.

She turned to him. Her skin looked as though it was sculpted from marble, smooth and flawless. Her lips were bright red and full and her face perfectly symmetrical. Bissen felt himself getting lost in her butterscotch eyes. His thoughts took him back to England, back to the woman who had nursed him through his injuries. He shivered.

'Your eyes tell me many things,' the woman said to him.

The lane seemed to brighten and the chill in the air disappeared. Bissen felt himself warming, relaxing.

'This is not the place for you, is it?' she asked.

Bissen shook his head.

'Where is it you wish to be?'

'With her,' Bissen replied, unable to control what came out of his mouth.

'She is beautiful,' the woman continued.

'How can you know this?' he asked.

She put her delicate hand on his shoulder. 'You have

looked at her so many times that her reflection has become imprinted on your eyes.'

'I don't understand.'

'When I look into your eyes, I can see her face,' she explained.

Bissen's head told him that this could not be. But his heart told him to trust the woman. Even though he had only met her once before, he felt as if he'd known her his entire life.

'The pain is deep,' she continued. 'And there is nothing that you can take to stop it.'

He nodded.

'But you do take something . . .'

Bissen's eyes fell. '*Pheme*,' he admitted. 'To take away the pain of the injuries.'

The woman nodded. 'I understand your need,' she told him. 'But be careful that your love for opium does not outgrow your love for Lillian.'

It took a few seconds for her words to sink in. 'How can you possibly know her name?' he asked.

But when he looked up, the woman had disappeared.

Just past midday Bissen made his way to the post office, just as he did every day. On his return he stopped to buy food from one of the many street vendors in Hall Bazaar. He was served up a small earthenware pot of thick *dhal* which he ate at a counter top made of ancient blackened hardwood. Beside the pot sat a cup of steaming hot tea, made from the dense, treacly milk of a water buffalo. Along from Bissen sat a group of young men, all of them eyeing the soldier with distaste. He had grown used to such reactions. He was just one of a number of men who had fought for the British and had now returned to the city. Resentment towards the *Engrezi* was often taken out on those whom the militants saw as traitors: the police, civil servants, ex-soldiers and even some teachers bore their wrath. Instead of reacting, Bissen simply ignored the young men and quietly ate his lunch.

Once he'd finished, he made his way to the Golden Temple and sat on a low wall, watching the light as it reflected to and fro between the golden walls and the deep blue water that surrounded them. Bissen often sat in the same place watching the worshippers enter the temple. There were people on the stone steps by the water, watching as others bathed in it. The water was blessed – a pool of holy nectar called *amrit* – and most of the worshippers cleansed themselves there before entering the *gurdwara*. Bissen found himself gazing long-ingly at a stout, curvaceous woman washing herself some fifteen yards away. She held up a towel to cover her modesty but the curve of her mocha-coloured breast was more than apparent. Bissen, feeling ashamed, looked away.

'She'll come and clip you round the ears!' he heard a young voice say from behind him.

He turned and saw Gurdial and Jeevan standing together, grinning at him.

'Her husband will be after your blood!' added Gurdial.

Bissen shook his head. 'I wasn't looking at her,' he replied.

'Why *not*?' asked Jeevan. 'Is there something wrong with you? She is beautiful.'

Bissen smiled. 'Are you still playing with onions?' he said, changing the subject.

Jeevan held out the fresh onions in his hands. 'I'm getting better,' he boasted. 'Look!'

As Bissen and Gurdial watched, Jeevan proceeded to throw the onions into the air. One by one they fell to the dusty ground.

'A monkey could juggle better than you,' teased Bissen.

'I'll try again, *bhai*,' replied Jeevan, picking up the onions.

Gurdial made a face. 'We saw a man being killed yesterday,' he told Bissen, hoping that he'd be impressed.

'*Killed?*'

Gurdial nodded.

'He was running from a patrol,' added Jeevan. 'They shot him—'

'Where was this?'

Gurdial gestured with his head as he replied. 'Hall Bazaar.'

'I was there earlier,' Bissen told the boys. 'No one spoke of it.'

Jeevan came and sat next to Bissen on the wall. To the

boys, Bissen Singh was more than just someone they saw every day in the street; he was a hero. He had done so much in his twenty-four years, much more than either of the orphans could even imagine, despite being only eight years older.

'Did you kill many people when you fought for the *Engrezi*?' Jeevan asked.

Bissen nodded. 'I was only a boy when I went to fight,' he told them. 'I did many things . . .'

Each time he met the boys they asked the same questions, and each time Bissen answered patiently.

'In that country you told us of?' asked Gurdial.

'France, yes.'

The idea of the outside world was difficult for many Indians to grasp. Boys such as Gurdial and Jeevan would probably become old men and never travel further than the next large city. Most of the people Bissen knew were insular without even knowing it.

'What did it feel like to kill people?' asked Jeevan.

Bissen shrugged. 'It was my duty. I didn't think of it properly until afterwards. When we were fighting, we just thought about staying alive.'

The boys were staring at him now, engrossed.

'I can't even remember the first one,' added Bissen. 'They say that you always remember, but not me. I find it easier to forget.'

Jeevan began to ask another question but Gurdial, realizing that Bissen's last reply had held a message for them, nudged his friend in the ribs.

'*Ow!*' moaned Jeevan.

'Tell me more about what happened in the bazaar,' Bissen said.

This time Gurdial shrugged, unconsciously apeing the soldier, whom he regarded as an older brother. Bissen's talk of things being easier to forget had turned on a switch inside his own head. Gurdial had lost his family at a very young age, and the memory of them grew less clear as each year passed. The image of a small house encircled by plants and bushes that were bright with flowers seemed to have lost its vibrancy. What had once been the faces of two people was now just separate pairs of loving eyes, looking down on him. And there was the smell of citrus, neither orange nor lemon but a sharp infusion of both. The recollection made him happy and sad at the same time: there was a vast, empty hole that he carried in his soul; a void that could only be filled when he found himself a new family. Tears welled in his eyes, and with a sense of shame he turned his head away from Jeevan and Bissen.

'The soldiers shot him,' he told Bissen, hoping that he wouldn't see the tears. How stupid he felt, crying in front of his friends. But thinking of the emptiness he held inside always brought tears to his eyes. It wasn't something he could control.

'Why?' asked Bissen.

Jeevan sighed. 'He was hiding a gun, *bhai-ji*.'

Gurdial wiped his eyes, then turned back to his friends. 'The dust is always getting in,' he lied.

Bissen and Jeevan said nothing. All three were lost and longing to find some sense of belonging. That was the nature of their friendship. It was why they were brothers. Not that they had ever discussed it. It was just something that was there between them, as silent as a ghost, and as loud as thunder too.

15 February 1919

Jeevan watched as the couple who ran the orphanage hugged Udham Singh with unconcealed delight.

'You have returned!' cried Mata Devi, her eyes streaming with tears.

Mata-ji was a large woman, and as she sat on a stool by the open fire, the overspill from her buttocks obscured its legs. Her dark hair was scraped back and tied into a ponytail. Her face was warm and generous and her eyes still held the mischievousness of the young girl she had once been.

'It has been so long,' added her husband, Sohan Singh.

Sohan was as thin as a cane of sugar and his clothes were tatty and torn. His greying turban was loosely tied and seemed too big for his head. Grey whiskers spread across the lower part of his face and his brown eyes danced with intelligence. His skin was the colour of sheesham wood and seemed parched.

Udham Singh, who was a few years older than Jeevan, seemed a shy, quiet man. He stood only a few inches taller but his frame was stocky with it, whereas Jeevan was reedy and waif-like. Udham's arms were thick with muscle, his hands like clubs, covered in dark hair. He wore a thin moustache and had jet-black hair and his eyes were as black as coals. Compared to Udham, Jeevan felt like a little boy.

'It has been too long, *chacha-ji*,' Udham replied to Sohan. 'Are you both well?'

The couple nodded.

'And who is this?' he asked, nodding towards Jeevan.

'Another one like you,' sighed Mata Devi. 'There are so many boys whose lives are empty.'

Udham smiled at Jeevan. 'You look like you could use some more of Mata-ji's food,' he joked.

Jeevan, unsure of himself, shrugged. Udham was well known to the boys at the orphanage. He had been sent there as a boy, along with his brother, who had died soon afterwards. But despite the hardships he'd faced, Udham became a hard-working member of the group, and to some of the boys he was a role model. At the age of sixteen he'd left for Basra in Iraq to work as a carpenter for the British. But he was soon sent back to India, although he'd never fully explained why. Now he found work in and around the city and had yet to turn twenty years of age.

'Do you have a name?' asked Udham.

'Jeevan. You used to call me and my friend Gurdial monkeys when we were younger. We annoyed you all the time.'

'Ah! I remember you two! Well, in that case, my brother, would you kindly pour me some tea?'

A smile burst onto Jeevan's face. 'Yes!' he replied, pleased that Udham remembered him.

'And perhaps you'd like some food?' Mata Devi added. 'I've just made *aloo gobi*.'

Udham nodded as Jeevan brought him some tea. 'Thank you, *bhai*.'

Jeevan stood for a moment before remembering that he had arranged to meet some friends. 'May I go out now, Mata-ji?' he asked.

The old woman asked him if his chores were complete.

'Oh, let the boy alone!' Sohan told her. 'He has done enough chores for five young men.'

Mata Devi sighed. 'Be careful, *beteh*,' she warned. 'There is danger in the air nowadays.'

'I won't be long, Mata-ji,' replied Jeevan.

'See you around,' Udham said to him.

'You too, *bhai-ji*.'

Gurdial was busy chasing after Gulbaru Singh's daughter so Jeevan made his way to the railway bridge to meet some other friends. He arrived well before time, and wary of the army patrols stationed at each end of the bridge, he found a patch of grass and sat down, careful not to stare at the soldiers. The grass was slightly damp and smelled of the rain. Jeevan turned to face the tracks and wondered whether he would see a train pass by on its way to the station. To his left were tall poles carrying the telegraph wires that allowed the British to make contact with each other. And across the tracks, outside the old city, was the British quarter; and beyond this, the heavily defended fort.

The houses in the British quarter were much larger than those in the old city and the roads and lanes around them much wider. Each house had its own walled compound, the walls painted in pastel shades of yellow, blue and pink. A large variety of trees and bushes filled the gardens. From where he was sitting, Jeevan could make out the trailing bougainvillea hanging from some of the compound walls, the flowers cream, purple, pink and crimson. Wild caper bushes with thick, sharp spines grew from cracks in the ground, and teak trees stood tall, their whitish-grey bark shimmering like silver in the sunshine.

The caper bushes took him back to his own child-hood, to the days before his mother had been killed. Her scent, a mixture of lychees and ripened sugar cane, seemed to reach out to him across the years, and he could picture her smile. He thought back to all the stories she used to tell him at bedtime, to the *mooliwale paratha* she'd make each Sunday morning before they visited the village *gurdwara*. As a widow with no other family, she had lived a hard life but she had

91

never let her troubles discolour his day, not even once.

And then he saw himself cowering in the corner of the room they had called home as the blood began to thud in his veins, making them bulge. The bandits had come during the cold of a winter's night, seven of them, carrying rifles and machetes. They had thick facial hair and none had any semblance of light or life in their eyes. They were soulless and evil and they carried with them the stench of carrion. While he'd looked on help-lessly, those animals had used his mother, one after the other.

'Don't look,' his mother had begged him. 'Please turn away!'

But Jeevan had frozen, his eyes wide with shock. The last of the bandits, once satisfied, had turned to him.

'Now you are all alone,' he'd sneered before cutting Jeevan's mother's throat from ear to ear.

The bandits raped and killed four women in the village and murdered several men before night gave way to dawn, but only one of them had mattered to Jeevan. And she had been taken away from him. Had he been blessed with a father, with a gang of strong elder brothers, his life would have turned out so differently. But there had been no one to help him save his mother; no one to defend her from men who had the hearts of jackals.

Now, as he sat alone watching the railway tracks, Jeevan wondered how it might feel to have a family. Mata Devi and Sohan were wonderful, kind souls, but they had many orphans to fend for. Jeevan was just one of the many. What he longed for more than anything in the world was to feel special. That was what had drawn him to Gurdial: they were the same age and each of them had an emptiness that they held inside. Gurdial had been at the orphanage for a few years when Jeevan arrived and had taken him under his wing. Before long they became like brothers, looking out for one another and telling each other what they held back from everyone else. When Gurdial shed tears, Jeevan thought no less of him because he knew what the tears represented.

But now Gurdial had found Sohni, the merchant's daughter, and Jeevan felt his place being taken. Not that it was unnatural, for what else was a young man to do but find a woman to take care of him? Jeevan felt no anger towards Gurdial and his secret love; he longed for his brother to be happy. But he no longer felt special, and that was hard to take. And then there was the small matter of Sohni's father, Gulbaru Singh. He would never allow his daughter to marry a penniless orphan. But Gurdial was blinded by love and could not see reason, and each time Jeevan tried to open his brother's eyes, Gurdial grew cold and sulked.

'People are like the seasons,' Bissen had told him. 'It is natural that things change, and that is equally true of human beings. Perhaps Gurdial is moving into summer whereas you are not yet ready to let go of spring?'

'Perhaps, *bhai-ji*,' Jeevan had replied.

A meaty hand took hold of his shoulder and broke into his thoughts. 'Good afternoon, *bhai*!'

Jeevan turned to see the giant frame of Ram Singh standing over him. '*Bhai-ji*,' he replied.

'Cheer up!' Ram bellowed.

'I'm fine,' said Jeevan. 'I was just lost in my thoughts.'

Ram smiled and helped Jeevan to his feet, holding out a shovel-like hand. Two years older than Jeevan, Ram Singh was pale-skinned, a shade over six feet tall and still growing, his chest the size of a barrel and his neck as thick as the trunk of a peepal tree. Next to him stood Rana Lal, a short, skinny boy with oily black hair and acne-pitted cheeks, who was six months younger than Jeevan.

'*Sat-sri-akaal, bhai-ji*,' said Rana.

'*Sat-sri-akaal*,' replied Jeevan.

Ram looked across at the bridge and the army patrols. '*Saleh bhenchoord goreh!*' he said. 'Look at them eyeing us, here in our own land . . .'

Jeevan turned and saw that the white men on the bridge were watching them.

'Perhaps they think we are rebels?' said Rana. 'Ghadar Party men.'

The Ghadar Party had been created by Indian workers in a far-off land called California, or so Jeevan had heard. They were revolutionaries, and one of them, not much older than Jeevan, had been hanged by the British four years earlier for conspiring to commit terrorist acts. The name of Kartar Singh Sarabha was known to all the young men of the Punjab; a martyr who had been no more than a boy when he died.

'Let's go,' said Jeevan, remembering the rebel he had seen killed by troops a few days earlier.

'When we are ready,' replied Ram Singh defiantly. 'I could crush them with the fingers of one hand.'

Jeevan shook his head. 'But they have rifles, *bhai-ji*. Just the other day I saw them kill someone.'

The defiance in Ram seemed to wither. He looked at Jeevan and then nodded. 'Come,' he said, 'let's go to the bazaar.'

As they set off for the central thoroughfare of the old city, Rana asked Jeevan what he had seen.

'It was someone with a gun,' he explained. 'The soldiers asked him to stop and he ran. One of them shot him in the head.'

Rana nodded, his eyes wide with a mixture of horror and fascination.

'Their time is coming, *bhai*,' said Ram Singh.

Jeevan wondered what his friend meant but said nothing.

21 February 1919

The assistant postmaster shook his head, just as he did each day, and Bissen turned away, hoping not to show the sadness he felt.

'Perhaps tomorrow, *bhai*,' the postmaster said to him, hoping to make him feel a little better.

'Perhaps,' Bissen replied without looking back.

He hurried out into the street. The air seemed as thick as treacle and Bissen fought to breathe. He found an upturned crate and sat down, wondering where the air in his lungs had gone. A merchant emerged from the post office, his copper beard neatly trimmed and freshly coloured, and stopped in front of Bissen.

'Can I help you, my brother?' he asked.

Bissen shook his head. 'I'm fine, *bhai*,' he replied. 'Just a little tired.'

The merchant shrugged. 'We are *all* tired, *bhai*,' he said. 'May Allah bless you.'

'And you too,' said Bissen as the merchant walked away.

A shout went up on the other side of the busy road. Bissen looked over and saw a man being led into the police station. A crowd had gathered before he could blink and insults were being thrown.

'*LET HIM GO!*' demanded the crowd.

'*Death before dishonour!*' shouted one of them.

It was obvious that the police had picked up a rebel and the crowd were unhappy about it.

'*Traitors!*' a young man shouted.

This man stood taller than the rest of the crowd, his shoulders square and his face proud. A black turban made of the finest silk sat on his head and he wore a silver *kurta pyjama*. He was very obviously the son of a wealthy family and Bissen wondered what he was doing there.

'Who knows?'

Bissen turned to see the woman from the market once again. She smiled and told him not to worry about the motives of people he didn't know.

'That young man will earn his own fate,' she added. 'And his path does not intersect with yours.'

Bissen shook his head, wondering whether the opium was beginning to mess with his mind.

The woman shook her head. 'You can blame it on the *pheme* if you like, *beteh*,' she told him. 'But I am as real as the ache in your heart.'

'I don't understand how you can know so much

about me,' said Bissen. 'I don't even know your name.'

She laughed. 'You do not need to know my name to understand that I am a friend.'

Bissen stood up. 'A friend?'

'Yes,' the woman said, nodding.

He felt confused. There were so many things about her that made no sense and yet he felt completely at ease in her company.

'No joy for you today?' she asked, nodding towards the post office.

'Is there anything you don't know?' Bissen wondered.

'Very little,' she replied. 'Everyone can see you walking to the post office each day. You walk with a sense of purpose and your stride is long, despite your injuries.'

Bissen thought about her words and found that he was nodding in agreement.

'But when you leave the post office your face has fallen. Your shoulders sag and your sense of purpose disappears. It is obvious that you are waiting for something.'

'I see,' replied Bissen as a gang of youths ran past, heading for the police station.

'There is a storm coming,' the woman said, changing the subject. 'I can smell the anger of the people in the air—'

'Have they caught another rebel?' asked Bissen, gesturing towards the police station.

She smiled. 'They have a *boy* in custody; a boy whose father they shot dead,' she told him. 'The father threw a bomb at the patrols. He killed two Indians and a

Nepali. But two years ago the boy's mother was killed during a shoot-out between soldiers, policemen and rebels – the father was taking his revenge.'

'So it has nothing to do with revolution then?' asked Bissen.

The woman shook her head. 'It has everything to do with it. Everything and nothing . . .'

Bissen raised an eyebrow. 'You speak in riddles.'

She nodded but said nothing.

'What do you mean when you say that?' asked Bissen. 'I'm not as clever as you.'

'There is always some excuse for such deaths,' she explained. 'The boy will want to avenge his father; a father who wished to avenge his wife. But the soldiers will want to protect themselves and their comrades. They also have a duty to their superiors and to the British Empire. Each killer will find some justification for his actions.'

A memory shot through Bissen. A young German soldier, no more than a boy, his eyes filled with tears, his voice pleading.

'You killed men in that war,' the woman said to him. It was neither a question nor a statement. It was as if she was reading Bissen's own thoughts out loud.

He nodded. Behind them two larger patrols arrived and twenty or so soldiers began to disperse the crowd. The policemen stayed inside the police station – the *kotwali*. The new troops were led by the superintendent of police, a man called Rehill.

'I killed *many* men,' admitted Bissen as he watched Rehill take charge of the situation.

'And how did you learn to accept that?'

Bissen shrugged. 'I thought you knew everything,' he replied, making the woman smile.

'I could tell you, but then you would think me some kind of witch,' she joked.

'So you are not a witch?'

She shook her head. 'I am just a woman who sees the world around her for what it is,' she told him. 'So how *did* you come to terms with killing so many fellow humans?'

Bissen looked down at his toes. 'I didn't,' he replied. 'At first it was my duty to king and emperor. But that soon wore thin and I realized that I was fighting to survive. I knew that I had to shoot to stay alive. If I hadn't, then the enemy would have gunned me down. Either that or my superiors would have executed me for desertion.'

The woman nodded and put her hand on Bissen's shoulder. He gazed at her fingers, so long and slender, as yet another memory crashed through him like the giant waves he'd seen on his passage back to India. Lillian's face, her eyes, her smile. He looked away, wishing he had never left England; had never left her.

'You wait for a letter,' the woman told him. 'A letter from Lillian.'

Bissen found himself nodding. He wanted to ask her how she knew Lillian's name but found that he couldn't. Something was stopping him.

'Your letter *will* arrive, Bissen,' she said, her voice as soothing as honey.

'How can you know that?' he asked.

'I just know.'

She held out her hand and Bissen felt himself drawn to her. He reached out and took her hand.

'Her letter will come before the storm,' she added. 'Leave as soon as you get it. Do not wait. Do not walk in anyone else's path; not even for a moment. Do you understand?'

Bissen shrugged.

'When it comes, take the letter, gather your things and go,' repeated the woman. 'I can only warn you once.'

'I don't understand . . .'

'Others will embroil you in their lives. When the time comes, leave them to their own fates and walk away.'

The woman smiled at him. 'Come and see me at the market tomorrow. I will have some more fruit for you.'

Bissen smiled back. 'I would like that.'

And then, realizing that she wanted to take her leave, he looked away, towards the scene of the disturbance. He knew that when he turned back she would be gone.

22 February 1919

Jeevan made a face at his friend. Gurdial, feeling a little guilty, tried to cheer him up.

'Why don't we go out when I get back?' he suggested. 'We could go and spy on the drunks.'

Jeevan shook his head. 'We'd have to sneak out, and if Mata-ji catches us, she'll beat us for sure.'

Gurdial shrugged. 'I'm sorry,' he said, 'but I promised Sohni I would see her.'

'No, no, *bhai-ji*, you go,' replied Jeevan. 'Besides, I have other friends I said I would meet.'

Gurdial nodded. Jeevan had mentioned Ram and Rana many times. The thought of Jeevan's new friends left him feeling torn. Part of him felt envious of the time Jeevan was now spending with them, but another part of him was pleased too. Gurdial had Sohni, and the thought of Jeevan kicking his heels when they weren't together made him feel guiltier still.

'It is good that you have Ram and Rana,' he said. 'Perhaps I can meet them too.'

'Ram is very clever,' Jeevan told him. 'He knows so much about the British and the rebels. His father was a Ghadar Party member.'

'Really? Is he still active?'

Jeevan shook his head. 'The *Engrezi* killed Ram's father in Lahore,' he said.

'Be careful, *bhai*,' warned Gurdial. 'Don't get involved with the revolutionaries – the British want them all dead.'

'I won't,' he replied. 'But I want to learn what I can. The British treat us as slaves in our own land. Someone has to make them go away.'

Gurdial sighed. He needed to go, yet part of him wanted to stay and make Jeevan listen. The revolutionaries were every bit as dangerous as the British. In the end it was ordinary people who would suffer, just as Bissen had told them. There were too many so-called rebels in Amritsar and Gurdial didn't want Jeevan caught up with them. It would only lead to trouble.

'I have to go,' he told Jeevan. 'Meet me later and we'll talk some more.'

Jeevan nodded. 'Be careful you don't get caught,' he teased. 'You would not suit the life of a eunuch.'

Gurdial swore at his friend and then grinned like a madman before going to meet Sohni.

★　★　★

103

An hour later Jeevan was sitting on the grass inside Jallianwalla Bagh with Ram Singh and Rana Lal. The Bagh, a disused piece of land to the east of the Golden Temple complex, was enclosed on each side by the two- and three-storey buildings that were common in the old city. Although the land had a private owner it was commonly used as a park. The ground was dry in summer and bog-like during the rainy season, with large bare patches amidst the sparse brown grass. Sewer *nalis* cut through the Bagh, and behind Jeevan and his friends was an old well; the air was often thick with the stench of sewage and rotting food, the barely covered channels a fecund breeding ground for disease.

'It stinks here,' complained Rana. 'And I'm sure there are rats in the *nali*.'

Jeevan looked over to the sewer channel and saw movement. It could well have been a rat.

'It's not going to eat you,' replied Ram.

'Why are we here?' asked Jeevan.

Ram shrugged. 'What else is there to do?' he said.

'We could take a walk into the city,' suggested Rana.

'We'll do that later.'

'Why, what are we doing later?' asked Jeevan.

'There is someone I want you to meet, *bhai*,' replied Ram.

Jeevan flicked away a fly before scratching his nose. 'Who?'

Rana Lal smiled. 'A girl!' he said, moving his head from side to side.

104

Ram Singh began to laugh.

'A beautiful young thing with big eyes and even bigger—' continued Rana, only to stop suddenly when he saw that a middle-aged woman passing by. She gave him an evil look: just another wastrel talking dis-respectfully rather than doing something constructive. She shook her head and muttered under her breath.

Once the woman was out of earshot, Jeevan teased his friend. 'Are you such a coward? What was that old bag to you, your aunt?'

'Why didn't you finish your sentence?' added Ram. 'Were you ashamed?'

Rana Lal went red and shook his head. '*Theery Maadhi . . .*' he swore.

Ram looked at Jeevan. 'I think we've upset our brother,' he said.

'I think you are right,' agreed Jeevan.

'If we were brothers,' said Rana, his voice rising in pitch with each word, 'then you wouldn't be laughing at me.'

Jeevan thought that Ram would continue to tease Rana but his eyes suddenly grew cold and he stood up so that he towered above them. His face was flushed with pink.

'Any Indian who doesn't lie with the British dogs is my brother!' he said in a determined voice.

Jeevan looked away as Rana listened in silence.

'Don't ever question my love for my fellow Indian,'

Ram continued. 'My father gave his life for his brothers and I would happily do the same.'

Rana gulped down air. 'I sorry, *bhai-ji*,' he replied weakly. 'I did not mean to question you.'

Ram knelt down and put his hand on Rana's shoulder. 'Don't be sorry,' he told him. 'I am your brother and I always will be – just like the others.'

Jeevan wondered who the others were. He asked Ram what he meant.

'The people we are meeting later,' Ram explained. 'They are just like us – together we are one big family—'

'But I don't understand,' said Jeevan.

'Don't worry,' Ram told him. 'You'll find out later.'

Suddenly Rana cried out and sprang to his feet. 'It's there by the *nali*!' he shouted, pointing towards the sewer channel.

Jeevan looked over and saw a giant rat. It stared at them for a few seconds before sliding slowly and gracefully into the foul, stinking water and swimming away.

'We should go and catch it,' Ram joked. 'There's enough meat there to feed half the city.'

Rana shivered. 'I hate rats,' he said quietly.

Jeevan took hold of Rana's arm. 'Then I'll kill every rat I see, *just* for you.'

Rana broke into a broad smile.

'Come!' bellowed Ram Singh. 'Let's go before the rat comes back with its friends.'

★   ★   ★

That evening Ram led Jeevan and Rana down a dark alley in the notorious Kucha Kurrichan, the red-light district, and stopped outside a three-storey house with dark wood shutters and bars on every window. A group of raucous men, high on some intoxicant or other, stood at the entrance; across the alley, a busty woman in a tattered green *sari* was in heated conversation with a thin, weasel-faced man with a shaven head. Gold rings hung from his ears and a peacock tattoo rose from the base of his neck up onto his crown.

'Is she a prostitute?' Jeevan whispered to Ram.

'Yes,' replied Ram, 'and that man owns this place.'

Jeevan looked up at the building and then down each side of the alley. Although it was narrow, it seemed very busy. At the far end, where it led into a wider street, raised voices told of yet another argument. And in the other direction the shadows also told a tale – of secret lanes and dark corners and locked doors that kept the outside world at bay. A maze of passageways devoid of the morality that Jeevan had been taught since the day he'd entered the orphanage.

'Why are we here?' he asked.

Ram told him to be patient, then pushed the men in the doorway aside. None of them complained once they saw Ram's size, and Jeevan and Rana quickly followed. They found themselves in an internal courtyard with a stone staircase in the middle, leading to the upper floors. Around the edge of the courtyard were several rooms, all with stout locked doors. Ram led them to one of these doors, tucked away in the far corner, and rapped out a code with his knuckles. Very slowly the hinges groaned and the heavy wooden door swung open.

'Quickly,' someone hissed from inside the dimly lit room. 'Get inside!'

The only light in the room came from an oil burner and there was a heavy odour of perspiration and mould. In the middle stood eight wooden chairs and a table. Ram told Jeevan to take a chair. The other two men in the room studied him closely. The first was older than the rest of them. He wore a black *kurta pyjama*; he had a closely shaven head, a thin moustache sitting under a beak-shaped nose, and a gold ring in his left ear. His tall, athletic frame strained against his clothing. The thick, sinewy muscles in his neck seemed ready to pop and his hands looked as hard as rocks. His eyes were dark and imposing and his jaw looked as though it had been carved from granite.

'This is Jeevan,' said Ram.

The older man nodded but remained silent. The second man smiled at Jeevan. 'Welcome, brother,' he said.

'*Sat-sri-akaal*,' replied Jeevan politely.

Ram and Rana took their seats as the second man continued talking to Jeevan.

'Ram tells me that you are a fine young man,' he said.

Jeevan, unsure of what to say, shrugged.

'My name is Pritam,' the second man added. 'And this family needs fine young men.'

The oil burner flickered, throwing a little extra light across Pritam's face. His skin was as pale as Ram Singh's and his features proud. He wore a black turban of the finest material and a grey *kurta* that looked silvery in the dim light. The muscles of his upper arms seemed ready to tear through the fabric that covered them.

'So what has Ram told you about us?' Pritam asked.

Jeevan cleared his throat, hoping to sound manlier. 'Nothing really,' he replied. 'He told me about his father and the Ghadar Party.'

Pritam nodded. 'Ram Singh's father was a hero, Jeevan. A man of the people who died for his mother.'

Jeevan was confused. 'His mother?'

'Mother India,' explained Pritam. He was about to continue when the older man stood up and looked directly at Jeevan.

'You are an orphan, aren't you?' he said.

Jeevan nodded.

'Don't worry,' said the older man with a grin. 'Ram Singh told me all about you.'

Jeevan looked across at Ram, who nodded too and then winked.

'My name is Hans Raj,' the older man said, 'and we are part of a brotherhood here—'

'A brotherhood?' asked Jeevan.

'Yes. Now tell me what you think is wrong with our beautiful Mother India.'

Jeevan felt his palms grow clammy and he gulped down air. 'I . . . er . . .' he began to stutter.

'Think about what you saw the other day,' Ram reminded him. 'The man who was shot down.'

Jeevan nodded. 'There was a rebel who was killed by the British,' he said.

'And why do you think there are rebels in Amritsar?' asked Hans Raj.

Jeevan shrugged. 'Because—' he began.

Hans Raj held up his hand, palm open, and Jeevan stopped. 'Why are Indians being killed in their own country by people who don't belong here?'

'I don't know,' admitted Jeevan, realizing that it was something that he'd never given any thought to.

Hans Raj came around the table and put his hand on Jeevan's shoulder. 'Don't worry,' he said in a soft voice. 'We are not here to make you feel stupid, Jeevan. There are many of our brothers and sisters who don't realize how serious things are.'

Jeevan looked up at Hans Raj, unable to hide his confusion.

'The British have enslaved our people,' continued the older man. 'They have taken what is ours and made it their own. We cower in front of their guns, and the traitors among us make fat profits in return for selling their souls. Our mother, our beautiful, rich, plentiful mother, is being raped in front of our own eyes and we do nothing!'

Jeevan's thoughts raced back to the night of his mother's death. His stomach churned and his eyes welled with tears. He looked away as the memories tore into his heart.

'I can see that you understand,' Hans Raj said in a soothing voice.

Jeevan nodded slowly.

'They call people like you orphans. They tell you that you have no family. But India is your family, *beteh*. As long as you understand that, you need never feel alone in this world.'

Pritam smashed his hand against the table top, making Rana Lal jump. 'Join us!' he demanded of Jeevan. 'Let us become your family. Help us to free our mother!'

Hans Raj threw Pritam a look that seemed to extinguish the young man's anger instantly. He looked away, his eyes burning with intensity. Jeevan looked across to Ram Singh, his eyes questioning.

'Let me walk you back to the orphanage,' suggested Hans Raj. 'I have things I wish to tell you.'

'What do you want to tell me about?' Jeevan asked in a voice that was no more than whisper.

Hans Raj smiled. 'Patience, my son,' he replied.

The walk took twenty minutes, and along the way Hans Raj explained many things to Jeevan. He told him about the history of British rule in India and of the countless rebellions and martyrs. He spoke of men who had defied the military power of the British and fought with what little they had to try and save their own country.

'There is a country called Russia,' he said, 'where the

JJJ

people have taken over. Each man in that country will be given his own plot of land and everyone will work for the benefit of the whole country. There will be no hunger and no poverty, not like we have here. The people will rule.'

Jeevan thought about Bissen Singh and the war he'd fought for the *goreh*. Was that what he had been fighting for too?

'We only want what is right,' Hans Raj continued. 'We don't hate the British because they are white. We hate them for what they do to us. India should be ruled by Indians. Not the traitors who work with the British but the people themselves, just as they do in Russia.'

'Is everyone who works with the *goreh* a traitor?' Jeevan asked.

'Yes,' replied Hans Raj. 'Even if they don't know it themselves. If you help them in any way, you are hurting India.'

Jeevan wondered whether to mention Bissen Singh, worried that Hans Raj might think badly of him for having such a friend. But Hans Raj seemed so intelligent, so wise; far more so than the soldier, it seemed. Bissen was like an older brother but Hans Raj was old enough to be Jeevan's father and had far more experience of the world.

'There is a soldier . . .' he said tentatively.

'A soldier?'

Jeevan nodded. 'I know him. He fought in the war

for the British but now he is just like you and me, living in Amritsar.'

Hans Raj shook his head. 'No, my son,' he explained. 'This soldier will never be like you or me. He may not be fighting for the *goreh* now, but he did.'

'And that makes him a traitor?' asked Jeevan.

'I'm afraid it does. There will be many who fail to help us. Some of them will be our own brothers and sisters, but we cannot falter; the path is set. India can only be free if we fight.'

They had reached the road that led down to the orphanage and Jeevan thanked Hans Raj for walking back with him.

'Do not ever thank me again,' Hans Raj said sternly. 'We are family, *beteh*, and this is what we do: help each other. Understand?'

'Yes, I think so,' replied Jeevan.

Hans Raj ruffled his hair with a meaty hand. 'Good boy,' he said. 'Come and meet us tomorrow. We'll be in the bazaar during the afternoon.'

Jeevan nodded.

'And perhaps tomorrow you can tell me about the pain that sits in your eyes,' added Hans Raj.

'But—'

Hans Raj shushed him. '*Family*,' he said. 'You can talk to me about anything, my son. Now, go before you get into trouble.'

24 February 1919

Bissen sat, his legs crossed, on the north side of the Golden Temple complex. Behind him was the Clock Tower Gate, a white marble building with domes at each of its four corners. In the centre sat the tower, the clock set into it. The tower itself was topped with a fifth dome, much larger than the others.

Bissen sat at the edge of the man-made lake that surrounded the Golden Temple, watching the world go by. He remembered sitting in the exact same place as a young child, with his father explaining the history of the city to him. The lake had already existed, sitting among trees. For many hundreds of years it had been a place of contemplation and worship, frequented by the Buddha and Guru Nanak too. It had been excavated by the fourth Guru, Ram Das, who increased its size. The *sarovar* was now full of *amrit*, holy water provided by an underground spring. It was this spring that gave the city its name, he'd been told.

Bissen often came to sit by the lake to ease his mind. There was a sense of calm about the area; a tranquil energy that reinvigorated and soothed. He looked across the water to the single causeway that linked the temple to the rest of the city. The temple itself, Harmandirsahib, was a three-storey building. The ground floor had walls of shining white marble, while the first floor was gilded with gold leaf. A third floor, smaller in area, sat at the top, surrounded by a low parapet. On top of this was the large dome. Both the dome and the walls of this floor were also gilded. When the sun was shining, the gold leaf reflected the light, and the image that was cast across the water shimmered. It was a truly magical place and Bissen had need of its calming effect.

His dreams had been dark and disturbing of late, filled with the horrors of the war and the screams of the dying. Each night the ghosts of his fallen comrades invaded his dreams, urging him to join them in the twilight world of the spirits. Bissen understood that their souls were not at rest. They were lost, much like him; and like him, they searched for peace and could not find it anywhere. The dreams had encouraged Bissen to increase his dependence on opium, a situation which he found depressing. He longed to stop taking the drug but knew that if he did, the spiders that crawled inside his head would only multiply.

So instead he sat within sight of the temple, taking in the sense of peace and trying to clear his thoughts. He closed his eyes to shut out the world and concentrated on the face of the woman he had left behind. He felt someone touch him on the shoulder. He opened his eyes to see Gurdial standing beside him, a concerned expression on his face.

'Are you well, *bhai-ji*?' asked the boy.

'I was just meditating,' he replied. 'Or trying to at least.'

'I'm sorry,' said Gurdial. 'I've disturbed you.'

Bissen stood up and smiled at him. 'No matter. It's always a pleasure to see you.'

Gurdial was reassured. 'I was hoping to see you,' he admitted. 'There is something I wish to talk to you about.'

Bissen raised an eyebrow, wondering what it was.

'It's Jeevan,' said Gurdial, pre-empting the question. 'I'm worried about him.'

'Jeevan? Is he in trouble?'

Gurdial shook his head. 'No,' he said. 'But he may be about to get into trouble.'

Bissen was confused. 'Come,' he said, 'let me buy you some tea.'

They walked through the Clock Tower Gate and into the busy streets of the city. After five minutes they reached a tea shop. Bissen ordered two cups of spiced tea and came to sit by Gurdial. The boy seemed fidgety, his eyes darting everywhere.

'Does something concern you?' asked Bissen.

Gurdial nodded and leaned closer to whisper, 'There are some men over there, behind us. When we came in they called you names.'

Bissen looked up and saw three young men with stern expressions staring at him. He glanced at Gurdial, then back again. The young men were still eyeing him. 'What did they say?' he asked.

'They called you names because you fought for the *goreh*,' said Gurdial. 'I think they want to fight with us, *bhai-ji*.'

Bissen nodded. 'Don't worry,' he said, aware that the boy was scared. 'They are cowards. Let them say these things to my face.'

'But—' began Gurdial.

'Just relax,' replied Bissen. 'I'll deal with it.'

He stood up and walked over to the young mens' table. As he approached, they looked away. Bissen cleared his throat. 'Is there something I can do for you, my brothers?' he asked.

None of the men spoke up.

'Or perhaps you'd like to say something to me?'

Again there was no reply.

'I'm just over there,' said Bissen, pointing to his table. 'Please come and see me if there is anything you need.'

He turned and walked slowly back to his seat. 'You see?' he said to Gurdial. 'It was nothing.'

'But what if they try to do something?'

'They won't, *bhai*,' replied Bissen. 'Trust me.'

Ten minutes later the young men were gone and Bissen ordered another two cups of tea.

'So tell me about Jeevan,' he said.

'He is spending a lot of time with new friends,' explained Gurdial. 'It's my fault because I keep leaving him alone.'

'And what is wrong with these friends?' Bissen asked.

'I think they are revolutionaries.'

'What makes you think that?'

Gurdial shrugged. 'Jeevan keeps on talking about the Ghadar Party.'

Bissen nodded. The Ghadar Party only existed to force a revolution and its members were responsible for many acts of violence. If Jeevan was getting involved with them, then he was heading for trouble.

'One of his new friends is called Ram Singh,' continued Gurdial. 'His father was a Ghadar member until the *Engrezi* killed him.'

'I see,' replied Bissen. 'Do you want me to talk to him?'

Gurdial nodded. 'I would like that,' he said.

Bissen smiled. 'So what else is new?' he asked. 'What of your quest?'

Gurdial looked down. 'I have been thinking about it,' he admitted, 'but I have no idea what I can do. Where can a poor man like me get such a precious thing? I don't even know what it is.'

Bissen put his hand on the boy's shoulder. 'Is there anything I can do to help?'

'Unless you can find me the most precious thing in India, the answer is no.' Gurdial sounded forlorn.

'Maybe we were too quick to approach Sohni's father,' said Bissen.

Gurdial shrugged. 'What difference does it make? Whether yesterday or tomorrow, my fate is what it is . . .'

Bissen shook his head. 'I know that such fatalism runs in Punjabi blood, but I didn't think you would give up so soon.'

'I have no choice,' replied Gurdial. 'What real chance have I got? I need a guardian angel—'

'Or a different plan,' suggested Bissen. 'Perhaps to take Sohni far away.'

Gurdial looked at him.

'Whatever the solution, Gurdial,' said Bissen, 'it will come to you. Don't give up so easily.'

'What do you think I should do, *bhai-ji*?' asked Gurdial.

Bissen sighed and ordered some more tea.

On the other side of the old city Jeevan sat under a giant banyan tree talking to Hans Raj. It was a mild day and the sun was just breaking through the light grey clouds. The other boys had gone on an errand, leaving Hans Raj free to talk to Jeevan; a situation which he had engineered. He saw the seeds of a convert in Jeevan; in his eyes and in the questions he asked. There was deep anger inside the boy, and if Hans Raj could find its source and tap it, the boy would become a very fine foot soldier.

'Tell me about your parents,' he said.

Jeevan shrugged. 'There is nothing to tell,' he replied, trying to fend off the question.

Hans Raj saw the change in Jeevan's eyes and realized that he had found his way in. A door had opened in the façade and Hans Raj stepped through.

'I can see that it hurts,' he said. 'My parents died too.' The last part was a lie but Hans Raj played his role well. He looked away, gulping down air and letting the corners of his mouth turn down.

'I didn't realize . . .' replied Jeevan, his eyes wide. Was Hans Raj just like him; a lost soul looking for a place to belong?

Hans Raj wiped away the few false tears that he had mustered. What he would have given for an onion . . . 'They were killed when the British attacked our village,' he continued, adding each new layer to his story as it came into his head.

'Why did they attack, *bhai-ji*?'

Hans Raj lowered his head and voice at once. 'They are murderers,' he whispered. 'They pretend they are peaceful but I know better. I watched them kill my entire family.'

Jeevan shook his head slowly. 'Everyone?'

Hans Raj nodded. 'I had to hide in a chest; I was only a boy. The leader of the troop, a tall, white-haired man in a red uniform, he took my mother to one side . . .'

Jeevan's breath came quicker.

'He held her down,' continued Hans Raj, before taking his head in his hands and pretending to weep.

Jeevan leaned over and placed a hand on the man's shoulder. 'Don't worry, *bhai*,' he said to him. 'You are not alone.'

Hans Raj looked up and saw that the door in Jeevan's eyes was now wide open. He wanted to smile but stopped himself. The boy was nearly his.

'My mother was raped in front of me too,' revealed Jeevan, his face set, voice determined.

'No . . .' replied Hans Raj. 'My poor boy . . .'

'Bandits came to our village. They took turns with my mother and then they cut her throat . . .'

Tears flowed freely down Jeevan's face but he no longer cared. He had never told anyone apart from Gurdial about what happened that night; no one else had ever asked or cared about it. Now here was someone who wanted to help him, to look after him; someone he could trust.

'Do you know your history, my son?' asked Hans Raj.

'I don't understand what you are asking me . . .'

'The British use a tactic called divide and rule to conquer us. One of the things they do is to pay bandits to attack villages—'

Jeevan wiped his eyes and glared at him. 'The British?'

Hans Raj nodded, convincing Jeevan that his lie was

the truth. He decided to add more layers: 'When the villages are left devastated, the villagers have no choice but to turn to the white men for defence. That is how they worm their way into the fabric of our country. They are no better than those animals that put themselves inside your mother!'

Jeevan's eyes began to blaze. The bandits had been sent by the *goreh*! No wonder there were men such as Hans Raj and Pritam all over the city. They knew the truth and they were willing to act on it.

'You must have been very scared,' Hans Raj said, 'when they did what they did to her.'

Jeevan nodded. 'I *was* scared. But the feeling of helplessness was worse. I dream about it all the time. I couldn't stop them; I couldn't save my mother.'

Hans Raj stood up and held out a hand for Jeevan. He pulled him to his feet and gave him a bear hug, whispering in his ear, 'You are with us now. There is nothing left to fear. Anything you want you shall have – and don't worry: the chance to save your mother will come again.'

Jeevan pulled away and glared at Hans Raj. 'My mother is dead!' he spat. 'How can I save her?'

Hans Raj bent over and picked up a handful of red-brown soil. 'This is where your mother returned to when she died,' he told the boy. 'This soil is rich with the blood and tears of our people. It is this soil we will defend. The mother you will get the chance to save is *our* mother.'

Jeevan wiped away more tears. 'Mother India . . .' he whispered.

Hans Raj pressed the soil into Jeevan's hand. 'Yes, Mother India,' he said, his eyes burning with hatred.

Part Three

The
Revolutionaries

HMP Pentonville, London,
13 July 1940

Udham Singh (aka Ram Mohammed Singh Azad)

5 a.m.

There is not much more left to say now that I wait to
kiss the hangman's noose. I go to my Maker with no
fear. Rather it is with hope in my heart and longing
in my soul that I face my end. Nothing that these
dirty British dogs can do will strike fear inside me.
They have done all they can. Let them shackle my
motherland. Let them cut my people down with
bullets. They can make us slaves to their imperialist
intentions but they will never take away our hope.

I did it – that's what I told that policeman. I did it
and I'm proud and I'd do it again. And again. And
again. I only killed one – it should have been more

but it was only one. I am sorry. You see, it was never my intention to take another human life. It was never my intention to become what I am. Just like my friend, *Bhai* Bhagat Singh, I sought only to free my country. I hold no hatred for the people of England. As I told the judge, I have more English friends than Indian. It is against this vile government that I have a grudge. It was never my intention. Never . . .

They tell me that my executioner is number one on the government list. The best at what he does. Uncle Tom, they call him. I only hope he is as good as they say. I do not wish to wait any more. I do not wish to delay. Let me go to meet my *bhai*, Bhagat Singh-ji, who went ten years since and waits for me. As I have said, Death holds no fear for me. None at all. How can it when I die for a purpose?

When I am gone, I told Justice Atkinson, I hope that thousands more will come in my place and drive the imperialist dogs from my country. It brings a smile to my face to think of the judge, his face growing redder as he struggled to control my speech. But he did ask me if I had anything more to say. Let my words ring in his ears until the day he takes his last breath. Let them cause him to suffer from indigestion each time he takes his breakfast, just as my people suffer at his government's hand. As they starve for food and for freedom while the British steal all their wealth. Let him be constipated each time he takes a shit as my accusations whirl about his head like the Lal Toofan.

There is nothing more left to say and yet there is so much left to say. When will my country be free? When will my people be given back their dignity? When will the imperialist dogs stop raising their so-called flag of democracy and Christianity with the aid of cannons and guns? It is not their people who commit these acts or order them to be committed. It is the dirty dog rulers who do that. Let them be smashed to pieces again and again until they learn to change their ways. Let them . . .

I hope this Uncle Tom is quick. Let them bring me from this dank hole to a place of light. Let me kiss that noose and take Death as my bride and go to wait for the freedom of my mother.

Amritsar, 7 April 1919

Jeevan considered his friend's words, but not for long.
Gurdial was always moaning about something. *Always.*

'There are two types of people on this earth,' Jeevan
told his friend, recalling something he had been told by
Hans Raj. 'There are those who live on their knees and
those who will die standing up.'

Gurdial shook his head. 'Those are not your words,
bhai. They are the words of that madman, Pritam. I have
seen how you have changed since you took up with his
gang. It's not you, *bhai-ji.*'

'It *is* me – can't you see that?' replied Jeevan, exasperated. 'They are *my* words and *my* feelings and *my*
wishes.'

Gurdial shook his head again. 'I don't believe you.
Talk to Bissen Singh if you want to know of these
things.'

'*Bissen Singh?*' Jeevan spat out the name in disgust.

'That *maachord* who fought for the British in their dirty war? What does he know of freedom? He fought for the very people who keep us down. He is a traitorous dog—'

'No, *bhai* – he is a decent and honourable man. Let us go and see him and maybe he can talk some sense into that fat head of yours,' suggested Gurdial.

Jeevan laughed sardonically. 'Fat head? You spend your days chasing after a dream – pretending that someone as rich and beautiful as Sohni will actually have you for a husband – and I'm the one with a fat head? Look in the *mirror*, Gurdial. Your life is meaningless.'

Jeevan was aware that his words were hurtful but something or someone had to shake Gurdial out of his ridiculous fantasy world. To imagine that the daughter of a rich merchant would lower herself to take the name of an orphan . . .

Gurdial's face fell and his eyes began to water. 'I'm going now, *bhai*,' he said. 'I do not know what causes you to injure me so, but may the Gurus bless you anyway. My door is always open for you.'

And with that he walked slowly off down the road, leaving Jeevan standing outside the orphanage. A small pang of guilt pricked Jeevan's conscience. They had been friends ever since Jeevan had arrived at the orphanage. They were the same age, barely sixteen now, and shared the same story. Poor, rural parents, tragedy and death. But friends were like shoes, just as Pritam had said. And losing your shoes did not stop you from walking, did it? There were always going to be more friends. All that mattered was that India should be free. That was the goal. Ordinary, everyday issues paled in comparison.

Jeevan crossed the road and headed down towards the corner where he was to meet Pritam. The air was heavy with heat and dust, and the smell of *paratha* and *dhal* made his stomach grumble with hunger. The streets were full again after the previous day's *hartal*, when most of the city had come to a complete standstill. Civil disobedience, it had been called. But what difference had it made? They had woken up to find the British still in charge; it had no effect on their power. It seemed pointless to fight bullets with slogans and strikes. That would never work. What Mother India needed was strong, resilient men, just as Hans Raj had told him; men who were willing to lay down their lives to secure freedom. It was the only way to make the British leave.

Beyond a small bookstore Jeevan spotted Pritam. Jeevan often looked at him and wished that he had the same proud bearing. The confidence, the sense of purpose. Jeevan was short and squat, with a pronounced bow in his legs, something he'd been teased about over the years. His features were nothing special either, whereas Pritam had a strong jaw line, pale skin and an aquiline nose. People noticed Pritam in a way they *didn't* notice Jeevan. And that was something Jeevan hoped to change.

'You're late,' Pritam said as Jeevan approached.

'I'm sorry, *bhai-ji*,' replied Jeevan, showing deference to his older friend. Pritam knew so much more of the world. He was like the older brother Jeevan had always dreamed of.

'Don't say sorry, Jeevan,' scolded Pritam. 'Just don't be late.'

'I was waylaid by a friend,' he explained.

'And never make excuses. It makes you look weak-willed.'

Jeevan lowered his dark brown eyes and silently chastised himself for his stupidity. What would Pritam think of him if he continued to make mistakes like that?

Pritam, sensing that perhaps he had pushed his latest protégé too far, put a brotherly hand on Jeevan's shoulder. 'Come,' he said with a smile. 'There is much work to do.'

It took fifteen minutes to walk to the room below the brothel where the gang met. The brothel keeper was a good friend of Pritam's father, a rich merchant, and the room was loaned to them as a favour.

'He thinks we play chess and improve our English,' Pritam had said. 'And besides, he's a whoremonger – what is he going to say? We could build bombs here and he wouldn't say a word.'

The shuttered room was sparsely furnished, as always, with chairs and a table strewn with papers. The walls were painted a dark shade of ochre. It smelled of dampness and dust, and darkness clung to the edges of the room – the only light was cast by the oil burner on the floor. Ram Singh and Rana Lal were waiting for them, looking furtive.

'Today we're going to strike fear into the hearts of these dirty dogs,' Pritam told them. He nodded towards the table. 'That is the poster which we are going to put up on the Clock Tower,' he said. 'An open challenge to the British in broad daylight.'

'What does it say?' asked Rana Lal, his jet-black hair oiled and combed back.

Pritam picked up the poster. He read the words to himself, then turned to his comrades. 'I'll show you in a moment,' he replied. 'For now I have another surprise.'

'What is it, *bhai*?' asked Ram Singh as Jeevan looked on impatiently.

'There is trouble heading this way,' Pritam told them. 'There are things being planned. Hans Raj has been in touch with our brothers in Ludhiana by telegram: the day is coming . . .'

Jeevan's heart jumped. Pritam had spoken of 'the day' before. A day when the *goreh* would sit up and pay attention. A day when the Indian would stand on his own feet. A day that would begin with an act *so* daring, *so* effective, that the British would run home with their tails between their legs. But what would that act be, and would he, Jeevan, get to play a role in it? That was the question that swam through his thoughts as Pritam talked of renewed hope.

'We do not live in fear,' Pritam went on. 'It is not fear

that drives us. It isn't greed or power that motivates us. We are spurred on by hope. By the wish to see our mother free of these chains.' As he found his rage, his voice rose to a shout. 'How dare these filthy bastards come and set foot in our land and tell us that it belongs to them! What nonsense our politicians talk of peace. I don't want peace! I want equal rights! Justice! *Freedom!*'

Jeevan tried not to stare at his mentor but he couldn't help himself. The power in Pritam was immense. His eyes bulged from their sockets and his mouth foamed with rage.

'And if that means that we must die, then we will die. If it means that we must kill, then we *will* kill. Any *gorah* or Indian who dares to stand in our way will *die!*'

As his gang digested the words he had spoken, Pritam opened the poster and showed it to them. PREPARE TO DIE AND KILL OTHERS! it read.

'Let us strike fear in their colourless hearts,' he whispered.

'Is that *all*?' asked Ram Singh, looking disappointed. 'A few words scrawled on a piece of paper? How will this help to free our land?'

Pritam fixed Ram with a cold stare. 'For now, this is all,' he replied. 'But don't worry, *bhai*. There is rebellion in the air. Their taxes are starting to bite. Food is becoming too expensive to buy. When a man is hungry, he will fight. Soon—'

'I say we go out this evening and find a *gorah* to kill!' demanded Ram.

'Patience!' snapped Pritam.

'But—'

'*Be quiet!*' Pritam's voice boomed around the small room.

Ram let his blazing eyes fall to the floor. When he looked up again, the anger was gone. 'Forgive me, *bhai-ji*,' he said. 'I'm eager to avenge my father, that's all.'

Pritam walked over to his comrade and placed a firm hand on his arm. 'Be ready,' he told him. 'There will be time enough for what you desire . . .' He held aloft the poster. 'Come – let us nail this warning to the Clock Tower. Let the English dogs understand that we are ready to fight.'

He turned and threw open the door. Light flooded into the room. Jeevan's stomach somersaulted with anxiety and anticipation. What they were about to do could lead to imprisonment or even death. The Rowlatt Act allowed the British to hold anyone they wanted to – without charge. Jeevan was frightened by this but that wasn't going to stop him. There was a revolution to fight. Fear could wait. For some reason that he failed to grasp, Gurdial's face flashed across his mind's eye. And then he was in the narrow alleyway, heading out into the street, following his gang.

9 April 1919, 7 a.m.

Dr Satyapal urged the young men to remain calm. It was far too early for such nonsense. He hadn't even taken tea yet, and here were these men – honest, good men, but confused and desperate too. He hoped to calm them quickly and send them on their way so that he could go back inside and begin his breakfast. But their anger was great and their patience worn thin. There were seven of them, Hindus, Muslims and Sikhs, standing in the courtyard of the doctor's home, demanding action.

'It is not enough that the Mahatma calls for strikes,' shouted one of them, a young Muslim with an unusually long and thin nose.

'We can't feed our families!' cried a Sikh. 'What will my children eat – dust?'

Dr Satyapal raised a hand and quietened the men. Birds sang in the early morning sunshine and insects

137

buzzed incessantly. It felt as though the day would be hot and long.

'There will be action,' the doctor reassured them. 'There are delegations being sent to the British. Gandhi is this very day arriving in the Punjab. We shall overcome, my brothers.'

'But we cannot speak,' said the Muslim man. 'We cannot gather or debate and no one listens to us anyway.'

'Calm down, gentlemen,' replied Dr Satyapal. 'Am I not entrusted by you to lead?'

Some of the men nodded.

'Then let me lead. I will speak with Doctor Kitchlew later this morning, and we will perhaps pay a visit to the deputy commissioner, Miles Irving—'

'Irving is a dog!' shouted one of the men. 'He will not listen to you, Doctor-ji. He has even banned you from protesting—'

The unexpected sound of breaking glass turned their heads. Someone had thrown a bottle over the wall. It had landed barely five feet behind the doctor.

'What the—!'

Two of the men ran to the wall and looked over. There, in the lane, stood four young men.

'It is a gang of youths, Doctor-ji. Come quickly!'

Dr Satyapal hurried to the gate and threw it open. Angrily he confronted the men in the lane. 'What is this? How dare you throw bottles over my wall? I demand an explanation!'

He searched their eyes. In three of them he saw signs of shame. But in the fourth pair of eyes he identified only darkness and hatred. The youth in question stood proudly, his glare never once leaving the doctor's face. Realizing that he couldn't outstare the boy, Dr Satyapal lowered his own gaze.

'That's right, old man,' said the youth, his tone mocking.

The doctor looked up again, anger rising like a tidal wave in his chest. His heart began to thump. 'Who are you?' he demanded as sweat began to tickle his scalp.

'Nothing to you!' spat the youth.

'What do you want?'

A crowd of neighbours and passers-by had begun to gather. They stood and gawped at the commotion; ordinary, everyday arguements often drew crowds in the city, but *this* was Dr Satyapal – a widely respected leader of men.

'I'm here to tell you that your time is over,' said the young man. 'People like you have silenced the masses for too long. You suckle at the breast of the *goreh*. Well, no more.'

'I cannot say that I agree – Gandhi-ji tells us to—' began the doctor.

'*Silence!*' The young man's voice boomed through the lane. All observers stopped and paid attention.

'*Gandhi?*' continued the youth. 'A dreamer and a coward; a man just like you, with plenty of talk but precious little else. We listen each time you tell us to disobey in a civilized fashion. And what happens? We rise to greet the new day and find a meaty fist wrapped around our throats, squeezing the life from us. We walk into our yards to find our beautiful Mother India raped!'

'He's right!' shouted someone from the back of the crowd.

One of Dr Satyapal's supporters glared at the mob. 'Who said that?' he asked.

When no one spoke, the doctor turned to the youth. 'And what are *you* doing to save our country?'

'More than you,' replied the youth calmly.

'What is it that you want?' repeated Dr Satyapal.

'To end this charade. This pretence that a few delegations and strikes and mass sit-downs will set us free. Never!'

A few cheers went up from the crowd. The doctor glanced nervously about. Was he being set up? he wondered. Was this some kind of trick?

'I know this boy!' someone shouted. 'He is nothing more than a criminal.'

This time the youth turned to see who had spoken. But once again no one came forward. He turned to Dr Satyapal.

'The day is upon us, old man. And in the midst of battle you can carry your pencils and your books and your petitions. I'll be carrying my gun. Let us see who survives.'

The doctor let his gaze drop once again. The young

man before him had an emptiness in his eyes – an emptiness that made the doctor's soul shiver. There was an evil so fierce in the boy that Satyapal began to fear for his life.

The young man turned to the crowd. 'There is a revolution to fight right now!' he cried out. 'And you are either with us, comrades, or against us. Decide which side you'll follow – and soon, because we will not wait. And when we are victorious, men such as the doctor here will be sent packing with the British – collaborators one and all!'

Some of the crowd shouted their support for him. Yet more shouted in support of Dr Satyapal. The boy smiled – a grim, cold smile. Then he turned to the doctor for the last time.

'Enjoy Vaisakhi, Doctor-ji,' he said. 'And watch out for the tide. It is turning faster than you think and you might just drown . . .'

And with that he walked off through the crowd, followed by his gang. As they passed through, one or two members of the crowd joined them. Dr Satyapal stood and shook his head. He had always known that there was anger – *real* anger – that might one day erupt into bloodshed, but he had never envisaged India following the path of Russia. Now he was not so sure. Menlike the one he had just encountered were dangerous; highly dangerous. God only knew how many others he had poisoned with his misplaced rage. He turned to one of his supporters.

'Watch out for that youth,' he said.

'Yes, Doctor-ji.'

Ten minutes later Pritam, Jeevan, Rana and Ram were standing outside a store front. There were two other young men with them, Sucha Singh and Bahadhur Khan, both of whom had joined after the altercation with Dr Satyapal.

'That treacherous snake,' Pritam said. 'One day I will take my blade and cut out his heart.'

'I thought he was on our side,' Jeevan said.

Pritam shook his head. 'Never. That bastard talks and then compromises, *bhai*. There is no room for such things. If our country is to be truly free, then we must fight and fight and fight again. We must kill and kill and kill again. There is no time for these fat, lazy peacemakers.'

'How true that is!' said a voice from behind Jeevan.

He turned to see Hans Raj standing smiling at him – their mysterious leader who always seemed to appear as if from nowhere and then disappear again into thin air. His eyes burned with an intensity that made Jeevan fearful; an intensity that failed to match his smile, as though the two halves of his face had stopped communicating with each other.

'Come!' said Hans Raj. 'Let us get inside and drink some tea.'

The store owner brought them cups of tea made from water-buffalo milk – thick and sugary and steaming hot. Hans Raj silenced his charges. Since he had arrived in Amritsar six months earlier, he had steadily coached these young men. He had lectured them and cajoled them too, telling them of the plight of their fellow Indians, from Lahore to Calcutta. He'd spoken of the thousands who had died at the hands of the British, and of the starvation and poverty that their misrule had created. In Pritam he'd found an ideal captain. A young man with rage burning in his heart and ice freezing his soul, shielding it from any weak moments. From emotions.

The others were raw, but it mattered little to Hans Raj. He had been sent to do a job and he had almost succeeded. Now was the time to put his gang into action.

'Gandhi is due in the Punjab today but the British will bar him,' he told them.

Rana Lal put up his hand like a schoolboy.

'What is it?' asked Hans Raj, showing his impatience.

'How do you know this?'

Hans Raj shrugged. 'From the Brotherhood in Delhi – a telegram reached me this very morning.'

'Oh . . .' Rana Lal looked thoughtful.

The Brotherhood was a group of like-minded men, Hans Raj had told Jeevan. A collection of patriots whose task it was to save India. There were cells springing up all over the country, from the tribal lands of the North-Western Frontier down to the beaches of Kerala. Honest, decent men who would not bow to the British and who saw no profit in a negotiated peace. As the great Sikh armies had done before them, they were prepared to fight to the end.

'I still don't understand what the Brotherhood is,' said Jeevan.

Hans Raj eyed him and then smiled. 'We are just men,' he replied. 'As I told you when you joined our family, we seek to remove the chains that bind us through *real* action – the bullet and the bomb – and replace the *goreh* with a fairer system. A government of the people, led by a small elite, to ensure that *all* the people of India are looked after.'

'Just as in Russia,' added Pritam, turning to his mentor. 'Is that not so, *ji*?'

Hans Raj stroked his chin and then nodded. 'Like Russia,' he agreed. 'But based on what *our* people need.'

'My father needs some land,' said Rana Lal. 'He cannot feed our family. That's why I came to work in the city.'

Hans Raj clapped his hand across Rana Lal's back. 'And land he shall have! Every man shall have at least one plot of his own. That will be our way!'

Rana Lal smiled in satisfaction. Hans Raj turned to Pritam. 'We must talk in private,' he told his protégé. 'You cannot be too careful with these British. Their spies are everywhere.'

'Shall we go to the meeting room?' suggested Pritam.

Hans Raj nodded. 'You men stay here until Pritam returns. He will have tasks for you to perform, and when India is free, I will personally make sure that your deeds are rewarded. For now, however, your reward is tea and *paratha*.'

He gestured to the owner, who came over hurriedly. Hans Raj pulled a wodge of rupee notes from his pocket. 'Feed these boys, *bhai*,' he told him. 'And feed them well. They are foot soldiers in the battle for our mother.'

The shopkeeper took the money and nodded. '*Bhai*,' he said, looking at the rupees in his hand, 'for this money you can send me three more to feed!'

'Perhaps I will!' laughed Hans Raj, before turning to give Jeevan a wink.

8 p.m.

The gang had spent most of the day prowling the lanes and back alleys of old Amritsar. After nailing the poster to the Clock Tower, Pritam had told them that they were going hunting.

'Hunting for what?' Sucha had asked.

'The enemy,' Pritam had replied.

Now, many hours later, they were walking back to their meeting room, exhausted and hungry, without having seen any of their intended prey.

'Not a single *gorah* anywhere,' moaned Rana Lal.

'Perhaps they know what is coming,' suggested Ram. 'Perhaps they have taken to the fort in fear.'

Pritam snorted as they passed a shack that sold tea and food. The owner greeted them as they passed by, but Jeevan was the only one to reply.

'May God bless you,' the shop owner called out.

At the end of the street they took a left, heading for

their meeting room in Kucha Kurrichan. A hundred yards down the lane, and then left again into the dark alley that led to the brothel. A drunkard appeared from the gloom, his face contorted into a grim smile. As Jeevan sidestepped to avoid a collision, the drunkard shoved him aside.

'*Maachord!*' he swore.

Before Jeevan could blink, Pritam was upon the drunken man. He wrestled him to the ground and began to punch his head. The man cried out as Pritam's fists connected with flesh and bone, trying in vain to shield himself. As the rest of the gang looked on in shock, Pritam seemed to gain momentum, his hands a blur. Eventually the man gave up any attempt at resistance and let out a low moan. Rana and Jeevan grabbed Pritam and dragged him away.

'He is finished!' shouted Jeevan. 'Enough!'

Pritam steadied himself and then wiped his hands on his clothes. He turned away from the man. 'Drunken dog!' he spat.

The man sat up against the rust-coloured wall and let out a sigh. His left eye was completely closed over, his right a bloody mess. Still he looked at his assailant and taunted him.

'When you fell from your mother's hole, you were the second man to pass through it,' he whispered softly. 'I was the first and I went in the other way.' Then he began to chuckle to himself.

Pritam stopped and turned back.

'*Nay, bhai,*' begged Jeevan. 'He is drunk and beaten to a pulp. Let him be—'

Suddenly Pritam was in his face, his soulless eyes boring into Jeevan's. 'You dare tell me what I should do?' he whispered.

Jeevan felt perspiration in his armpits. His tongue seemed to convulse and the breath drained from his body. He croaked in reply, his legs twitching with fear. Real fear. '*Nay,*' he managed to get out.

Pritam looked beyond Jeevan to the man sitting by the wall.

'Your mother worked here,' the drunkard added. 'Everyone knows her . . .'

Pritam pretended to smile. As he did so, he drew a small blade from his pocket and went over. The man whimpered only slightly as Pritam slid the blade into his bloody eye.

'*Bhai!*' Jeevan cried out.

'*What the hell is this?*' an older voice demanded from the darkness.

Jeevan turned to see Hans Raj appear from the shadows. He searched his eyes, trying to keep the tears from spilling down his face.

'Pritam . . .' Jeevan whispered.

The other young men stood aside as Hans Raj pushed past Jeevan and knelt beside Pritam and the dead man. 'The rest of you, get inside!' he spat without looking up.

Sucha and Bahadhur Khan led the way. Jeevan

allowed Rana and Ram to follow but didn't move himself.

'All of you!' added Hans Raj.

Jeevan took another look at the dead man, shivered and then followed the others. Behind him he heard Hans Raj tell Pritam to help him drag the body inside. The alleyway remained empty of witnesses, and once the body was inside the meeting room, Hans Raj shut and bolted the door. Then he turned to Pritam.

'What is this?' he asked.

Pritam shrugged. Not even a flicker of emotion passed over his face. 'He insulted my honour,' he explained. 'And that of my mother.'

Hans Raj shook his head. 'What have I told you?'

'He asked for this fate,' replied Pritam.

'And if someone had seen you . . . ? If the *goreh* had been walking past . . . ?'

'We haven't seen a white man all day,' Pritam said. 'Otherwise there would be more than one body to dispose of.'

Hans Raj turned to the others. 'This is nothing,' he said quietly. 'A simple mistake. You did not see this, any of you. Is that understood?'

None of the young men responded. Instead they shot each other glances. Jeevan shook his head.

'You don't understand?' asked Hans Raj.

'I do,' replied Jeevan. 'But this man was not our enemy. He was just drunk.'

Hans Raj came over and placed a hand on his

shoulder. 'They are *all* enemies, my son,' he said quietly. 'What was this man doing to free our country? Walking the back alleys soaked in alcohol, stumbling from door to door, with no purpose and no honour.'

'But—' began Jeevan, only for Hans Raj to stop him with a look.

'No buts, *beteh*. There is no time to waste on these fools. Those who are not with us are against us. Yes – it was wrong, but Pritam is one of *us*. We *must* stick by each other – one family.'

Jeevan shook his head again. 'No, *bhai-ji* . . . He was just a drunk. It's not right,' he said.

Hans Raj turned to look at Pritam. Then he changed tack. 'If we don't defend each other, then the British have *won*,' he told Jeevan. 'This poor man should not have died, but it is the *British* and *their* laws that drive our people to drink and to fight. It is their vile and wicked rule that divides and, yes, sometimes makes us act like animals. Do you think there were drunks and prostitutes and murder *before* they arrived in our country? No! It is *they* who brought their wicked ways with them. And as they grow ever more powerful and stand with an even heavier boot on the neck of a free India, it us *our* people who divide and suffer and *die*!'

Jeevan looked into his face and saw his sincerity. He bowed his head.

'Remember what I told you when we spoke of your mother?' added Hans Raj. 'Of how the British divide us and make us act like animals? This is yet another example, my son.'

'You are right, *bhai-ji*,' Jeevan said. 'I'm sorry.'

Hans Raj sighed and told Jeevan not to apologize. 'There is no need. We are all brothers here. Brothers with a common enemy. There will be many times when we laugh and many *more* when we cry. But we must come through it all as brothers — otherwise what will happen to our beautiful mother?'

Jeevan nodded. 'I understand, *bhai-ji*.'

'Your mother may have been lost to you,' Hans Raj went on, pushing all the right buttons. 'But *we* are your family now. *India* is your mother . . . I will not let you be orphaned again, Jeevan — that was my special promise to you and you alone when we met. Understand?'

Jeevan nodded as a single tear worked its way down his left cheek. He wiped it away in embarrassment. All he had ever wanted was to feel as though he belonged. Not at the orphanage, with countless other poor souls, but out in the wider world, with a real family — people for whom he was special, just like he had been to his mother so many years before.

Hans Raj looked at Pritam, relieved to have defused the situation. The last thing he needed was a weak link in the gang. It would jeopardize everything he had tried to build. He whispered in his ear, 'Keep an eye on him.'

Pritam nodded. The older man turned to the others. 'We will wait until later to dispose of the body,' he told them. 'In the meantime I'll go and find something to put

151

it in. Stay here and let Pritam get you food and drink. And be ready for the fight, my brothers. Tomorrow the British will know they are in for a struggle.'

He drew back the bolt on the heavy wooden door, opened it and stepped out into the internal courtyard of the brothel, with Pritam right behind him. Jeevan watched them go and then went to sit in a corner, his back cooled by the stone wall.

'Are you all right?' asked Bahadhur Khan, coming to join him.

Jeevan nodded.

'You are from the orphanage, aren't you?'

'How do you know that?'

'I know your friend, Gurdial,' replied Bahadhur.

The mention of Jeevan's friend brought back memories of an easier time. Of teasing the girls of the City Mission School; of arriving late for *roti* and receiving a playful scolding from Mata Devi, the only mother he or Gurdial or countless other young men had ever really known. Memories of following Gurdial as he spied on Sohni, and sitting with him in the shadow of the Golden Temple as he composed love poetry, and people bathed in the cool, clear waters that surrounded the holy site, cleansing the bodies and their consciences.

And now here he was, having witnessed and become party to an act that went against everything he had been taught. And much more importantly, everything he believed in. Had his simple, lovesick friend been right about Pritam? Was he really the villain that some alleged? Or was the voice in his heart the most truthful one; the one that told him to respect Hans Raj, to follow him wherever he chose to go? No one else had ever wanted to replace his mother or told him that he was special. Hans Raj and Pritam had taken him in, nurtured him and made him part of their family; could he really turn against that commitment, that love now, and risk losing his family all over again?

'Are you daydreaming, *bhai*?' asked Bahadhur, breaking into his thoughts.

'No, no,' Jeevan replied quickly. 'I'm just tired after today – that's all.'

Bahadhur nodded. 'Do you think that Hans Raj is right? That there will be much fighting tomorrow?'

Jeevan shrugged. 'I think he may be,' he replied. 'He is always right.'

'Always?' asked Bahadhur.

'Always, *bhai*.'

10 April 1919, 9 a.m.

'But that, Doctor Satyapal, is the law of this land. And the law shall be obeyed,' insisted Miles Irving, the deputy commissioner of the Punjab.

Dr Satyapal glanced at his compatriot, Dr Kitchlew. They were in Miles Irving's bungalow, on a compound separated from the old city by railroad tracks and a bridge; they had just found out that the government had decided to deport them.

'I will not add a single word to those I have spoken already this morning,' continued the deputy commissioner.

Miles Irving had only started his posting in February, but already he felt jaded. The interminable politics of the Raj, and of the Punjab region in particular, had worn him out. How he longed for the reassuring smells and sounds of England once more. He'd had his fill of dust and heat; of busy streets and open gulleys and strange languages and customs. India had left him cold. He turned to the superintendent of police, Mr Rehill.

'Are the arrangements in hand?' he asked.

Rehill nodded but didn't speak. Aware of Irving's lack of authority, he turned instead to Lieutenant-Colonel Smith, the civil surgeon. The man who had the ear of the Punjab's governor general, Michael O'Dwyer.

'Sir?'

'Yes, Rehill?' asked Smith.

'Are my orders complete?'

Smith told him that they were. Rehill's face darkened. He asked Lieutenant-Colonel Smith if he might speak with him in private. Smith nodded and they stepped to one side. Commissioner Irving struggled to hide his annoyance at Rehill's open disregard for his rank.

'I'm worried, sir,' Rehill told Smith. 'Removing these two gentlemen might lead to friction in the city.' He nodded towards Satyapal and Kitchlew.

Smith put a firm hand on Rehill's shoulder. 'No need to fret, old chap,' he told him. 'Everything is under control and O'Dwyer is fully aware of our intentions. I don't think we'll have a problem as long as we act swiftly and with the correct degree of . . . secrecy.'

'Yes, sir,' replied Rehill, although he didn't agree.

The two men turned back and Rehill saw anger and frustration on the faces of the two Indians.

'This is an outrage!' declared Dr Kitchlew. 'An absolute crime against decency. Does Mr O'Dwyer know of this?'

Irving sighed. 'The Governor is well aware of our decision, and besides the Rowlatt Act is quite explicit in its terms,' he pointed out. 'If you and your compatriots openly breach the law, you shall suffer the consequences—'

'But we haven't done a thing!' protested Dr Satyapal. 'You ordered us not to commit certain acts and we've followed your instructions to the letter.'

This time Miles Irving snorted. 'You have done no such thing, sir.'

Dr Satyapal shook his head. 'Where is the decency?' he asked forlornly.

Rehill's deputy, Plomer, a rotund man with an unfortunate habit of breaking wind uncontrollably, entered the room. He approached Irving and the others. 'Sirs, there is unrest in the courtyard,' he told them.

'Unrest?' asked Irving. 'Whatever do you mean, man?'

Plomer cleared his throat of the dust that seemed to lodge itself there each day. 'Their fellow . . . er . . . *persons*,' he replied. 'Out in the courtyard. They're causing a rumpus and asking to see these two.'

'Well, go and quieten them down, Plomer,' said Lieutenant-Colonel Smith. 'There's a good chap.'

'I . . . er . . . can't, sir,' admitted Plomer. 'They won't listen to me.'

Smith rolled his eyes and told Rehill to go and help his deputy deal with things in the courtyard. After they had gone, he turned to Irving.

'I don't know about you, Miles,' he said, 'but this

damn country drives me insane. I'm taking my first drink earlier and earlier each day.'

Irving smiled and went over to a drinks cabinet made of sandalwood and carved with elephants and peacocks. He took out a decanter of whisky and two cut-glass tumblers. As he set them down on the table, a small lizard ran across the surface, its bright green tail disappearing down the table leg.

'Damn creatures!' he cried. 'They get everywhere.' He poured two large measures and handed one glass to Smith. 'There you go, dear fellow.'

The two Englishmen sipped their drinks. The two Indians might as well have become invisible.

Out in the courtyard Rehill was trying to calm the attendants who had arrived with Satyapal and Kitchlew. There were six of them in total and they were unmoved by Rehill and Plomer and their so-called authority. While Plomer was clueless and dense, Rehill had vast experience of the region and knew he needed to be discreet. If word of the deportations became public too soon, it would lead to chaos on the streets of Amritsar – of that he had no doubt. And Amritsar was a city on the brink. A city that was harder to control than a herd of elephants. Rehill estimated that, on a good day, the British had effective control of about a third of the city, and that was at full strength. But General Dyer, who commanded the troops, was away, as was the governor. Troop numbers were low. Any disturbances now and Rehill knew that, without reinforcements, the city would have to be handed over to the people. And that just wouldn't do. Certainly not while he was in charge.

The fact that he had to escort Satyapal and Kitchlew to Dharamsala personally was also a worry. That would leave Plomer in charge at a time of potential conflict. Rehill looked at his deputy and sighed. Plomer was a disgrace – unfit, tiresome and uncouth. Just not the calibre of person required to look after the policing of Amritsar at such a time. But Rehill's orders were to oversee the deportations and he would have to carry them out. Discretion was paramount; the last thing Rehill wanted was for the men waiting in the courtyard to find out what was going on. At least not until after he himself was out of the city. After that, he wouldn't be in a position to be blamed.

'Gentlemen,' Rehill said to the men, 'I really do need you to leave.'

A very dark man with jet-black, side-parted hair and yellow teeth objected. 'Not until we see Doctor Satyapal or Doctor Kitchlew!'

'That simply won't be possible until after they have spoken to Commissioner Irving,' replied Rehill.

'We demand to see them now!' cried an older man wearing a navy blue turban. His beard was as white as snow.

Rehill shook his head.

'*India zindabaad!*' shouted yet another of the men.

One by one they all sat down on the dusty ground, their faces determined.

'We shall sit here until our leaders are brought out,' said the older man. 'We shall commit no crime nor any act of violence and we shall not break any other laws.'

Plomer turned to his superior. 'Should I arrest them, sir?' he asked.

'Arrest them on what charge, Plomer? Sitting down?'

'Doesn't the Rowlatt Act permit us to—' began Plomer.

'Oh, do be quiet, Plomer, and let me think,' ordered Rehill. 'It's that damn act that has caused all this.'

Rehill considered his options. Satyapal and Kitchlew were clever men. They had brought attendants with them in case there was a problem. That way any news could be carried back to the city. If Rehill arrested the attendants too, then no one would return and that would raise its own alarm. Surely it would be better to detain two men rather than eight? As he thought on, Plomer let out a foul smell.

'Sorry, sir,' Plomer said, going red in the face. 'It's this bloody food – I just can't get used to—'

'Yes, yes . . . Is the old storeroom free?'

Plomer nodded.

'Then go and ask the housekeeper to rustle up some tea and perhaps a little food for these gentlemen,' ordered Rehill.

Plomer's simple face showed that his mind was working overtime. 'Food, sir?' he asked.

'Yes, Plomer, *food*.'

'Any particular kind of—?'

'*Just do it!*' barked Rehill.

As Plomer waddled away, Rehill addressed the old man in the turban. 'If you are intent on staying, then may I suggest a more comfortable arrangement?'

The old man stroked his white beard and looked at Rehill intently. 'Comfortable?'

'Yes, sir. Just to show that there is nothing untoward happening here. We have an old storeroom behind the house – there are some chairs and a few tables. My deputy has gone to arrange tea and refreshments . . . Perhaps you and your compatriots would like some?'

The old man shrugged. 'And there is no game being played?'

'No, sir – you have my word.'

The old man turned and spoke to the others in Punjabi. After a few moments he stood and the others followed his lead. Dusting off his clothes, he smiled at Rehill. 'Please do leading the way,' he said.

Rehill smiled back. Now the attendants would be out of the way for a while. And, crucially, they would be at the rear of the house when Rehill brought their leaders out of the front. That would give him a bit more time. Of course, the attendants would eventually discover what had happened and relay news to the city, but by that point Rehill and his prisoners would have a good head start. And once he was out of the city, then it became someone else's problem. Perfect.

10 a.m.

The driver waited patiently for Superintendent Rehill to bring out the prisoners. The sun was already high in the sky, and inside the car, the temperature was stifling. The driver opened his window and sighed as a shiny black beetle worked its way across the passenger seat. Looking out across the driveway to the bungalow, he noticed how well-kept the gardens were. Rose bushes mingled with marigolds and bougainvillea. A freshly cut lawn shimmered. And to the side of the house two banyan trees fought with each other for space, their thick, twisted limbs reaching out across the ground like the fingers of an arthritic giant. The British lived well in their part of the city, away from the overcrowded narrow alleys of the old town.

As he lit a *biri*, there was movement at the front door. Rehill appeared with his deputy, Plomer, at his side. Behind them, looking just a little apprehensive, were Dr

Satyapal and Dr Kitchlew. The driver dropped his smoke to the ground outside his window and stared. What was going on? The doctors were men of influence and power. Why were they wearing handcuffs and where were they going?

The answer came from Rehill, who opened the rear door and spoke to the driver. 'We're going to Dharamsala,' he told him. He turned to the two doctors. 'Gentlemen,' he said, gesturing to the car. 'Please don't make this any more difficult than it needs to be.'

Neither of the doctors replied. Instead they got into the car glumly. Rehill shut the door and got into the front passenger seat.

'Dharamsala, sir?' the driver asked.

'Yes. And do hurry. I want to be away from the city as soon as possible.'

The driver lit another *biri* and started the engine. Just then there was a knock on the passenger window. It was Plomer. Rehill cursed and wound the window down.

'What is it, Plomer?' he asked.

'What do I do with the others?'

'Leave them where they are for an hour and then tell them to go.'

Plomer looked uncertain. 'But what do I tell them about these two?' he asked, gesturing with his head to the prisoners.

'Tell them the *truth*, man,' replied Rehill. 'They'll find out soon enough anyway.'

'But what if there's a problem?' continued Plomer.

'Deal with it,' ordered Rehill. 'If you need help, just send to the fort. There are some troops there, and General Dyer should be back soon.'

'But—'

'And do get a shave, Plomer — you'll end up looking like a bloody Sikh at this rate.'

As Plomer withdrew, Rehill turned to the driver.

'Come along!' he snapped. '*Jaldi, jaldi!*'

Plomer watched the car go through the wooden gates of the compound and then turned back to the house. His insides were gurgling with gas and he felt the need to pass wind again. The sound was so thunderous that he had to look round to make sure there was no one within twenty feet of him. Luckily he was alone, but not for long. As he reached the front door of the bungalow, Lieutenant-Colonel Smith came through it.

'Ah, Plomer — just the chap!' he said cheerily.

'Yes, sir!' replied Plomer, standing to attention.

'Do relax, Plomer.'

'Sir . . .'

Smith looked around the gardens. 'Where are the chaps who accompanied the prisoners?'

'In the storeroom, sir.'

'What on earth are they doing there, man?'

'Drinking tea, sir.'

'Tea? *Our* tea?'

Plomer nodded.

'Well, go and tell them to leave,' ordered Smith. 'We

can't have a bunch of rag-tag Indians about the place. There are ladies due for lunch.'

Plomer sighed. 'But the superintendent told me to wait until later.'

Smith raised an eyebrow. 'Whatever for?' he asked.

'So that they wouldn't take news of the arrests back to the city too soon,' explained Plomer. 'Just in case there's trouble.'

Smith shook his head. 'Nonsense, Plomer. There won't *be* any trouble bar a few insults and the odd effigy being burned. Don't you understand these people at *all*? They are subservient by nature. And whenever they do rise up, we put them down again just as quickly. We are their *superiors*, Plomer.'

'But—' began Plomer, only for Smith to dismiss him with a wave of the hand.

'Run along, Plomer, there's a good chap.'

Plomer acknowledged defeat and walked slowly off to do as ordered. Smith was a pompous, arrogant old man, he said to himself. As soon as news of the deportations hit the streets there would be uproar. Tensions were already high and this would only make things worse. But it wasn't Smith or any of his cronies who'd be in the firing line. Out on the streets it would be Plomer and his men who would have to deal with the mob. The thought made the copious gases in Plomer's stomach bubble and froth. Things were very likely to get ugly, he thought. With no superintendent to turn to and only a handful of troops, if things did go badly wrong, it would be Plomer who took the blame.

'Damn you, Rehill!' he cursed under his breath.

Behind him he heard Lieutenant-Colonel Smith talking to someone. Plomer turned to see who it was. Standing in front of the civil surgeon, speaking animatedly, was a tall man with a shaven head and a beak-shaped nose – an Indian whom Plomer thought he recognized but couldn't place. There was something very familiar about him. The way he stood, with his shoulders square and his feet planted firmly to the ground. Where had Plomer seen him before?

Smith said something in reply to the Indian. When he'd finished, the man turned and left. Smith saw Plomer watching the scene.

'Are you still standing there, Plomer?' he shouted. 'I thought I'd given you a task to perform. An order!'

'Yes, sir!' replied Plomer, turning to scurry away as fast as his stubby legs could carry him.

When he got to the storeroom, one of Commissioner Irving's servants, an old man in a grey turban, was watering a patch of purple, yellow and pink flowers.

'Do you know who the chap at the gate was?' Plomer asked him.

The man shrugged.

'Well?' Plomer tried to put some authority into his voice.

'Me not knowing him, sir,' he replied. 'He not good man.'

Plomer sighed – something he found himself doing more and more. 'Do you know his *name*?'

The old man looked bewildered.

'His *name*,' Plomer repeated slowly.

This time the old man smiled, revealing a mouth devoid of teeth, with blackened gums. 'He very bad person,' he said again. 'Me thinks him calling Hans Raj.'

11 a.m.

Miles Irving felt a sharp pain in his chest. 'Are you absolutely certain, Massey?' he asked.

Captain Massey nodded.

'Dear God!' exclaimed Irving.

The captain said nothing. As the garrison commander of the Somerset Light Infantry, he was used to such reactions.

'Do we know how large this mob is? Are there ring-leaders whom we can detain?'

'I really don't know, sir,' replied Massey. 'I just know they are angry about this morning's deportations and are heading this way.'

What little colour had been left in Irving's face disappeared. His lower lip quivered slightly. Massey allowed himself an imperceptible smile. What had Irving expected after his arrests of Satyapal and Kitchlew?

'Are there men enough to defend us if we are

attacked?' asked Lieutenant-Colonel Smith from the window. The whisky tumbler in his hands sparkled in the sun's rays.

Massey shook his head. 'No, sir. We have enough men to cover the bridge and the railway line, but beyond that, no.'

'So we need to hold them at the bridge then,' said Irving. 'Has anyone contacted Dyer?'

Smith raised an eyebrow. 'Dyer is away in Lahore,' he replied. 'It'll take him hours to get his men back to the city—'

Massey coughed and cleared his throat.

'What is it, man?' asked Smith.

'I took the decision to send a telegram to Lahore last night, sir,' Massey admitted.

'You did *what?*' barked Irving.

'When I heard of the imminent arrests, Commissioner,' explained Massey, 'I sent for reinforcements—'

Irving looked horrified. 'What made you think we'd need reinforcements, Massey?'

Because a senile baboon could have predicted this, thought Massey. He looked over at Smith.

'Well, spit it out, man!' Smith was looking at Massey in a strange way.

Massey gave a quick nod to indicate that he understood. Before sending his telegram the previous evening, Massey had told Lieutenant-Colonel Smith of his fears. Yet here Smith was, refusing to acknowledge that he'd been forewarned. There was something going on, Massey told himself, something political. And it was better to stay out of it.

'I tried to find Lieutenant-Colonel Smith,' replied Massey. 'But everyone was busy and I thought that there might be some kind of backlash. It was just a prediction—'

Irving's face began to go red. 'A *prediction*?' he spat. 'Do you have any idea how this will look, man? We'll look weak!'

Captain Massey glanced at Lieutenant-Colonel Smith. Smith raised his bushy left eyebrow before returning to the view from the window. 'Never mind, old chap,' he said to Irving. 'It'll be over in an hour.'

Irving struggled to contain himself. 'I'm well aware of that!' he shouted. 'I've no doubt that we can contain the mob. It's not going to look too good to the High Command though, is it — junior officers firing off unauthorized telegrams?'

Smith turned and walked over to Irving's mahogany desk — a solid piece of hardwood with sculpted legs as thick as an elephant's. He set down his glass. 'Look — why don't I tell the Governor that sending the telegram was my idea?' he offered.

'I'm not sure how that will—'

'By laying any blame at my door,' said Smith, interrupting, 'that way your authority won't be questioned and Massey here won't get disciplined.

Damn good soldier – we can't afford to lose him over such a trifling matter.'

Irving thought about Smith's offer for a moment. Despite his anger at Captain Massey, he knew that Smith was right. Massey was an outstanding soldier – brave, loyal and respected by his peers. The way things were going in India, the Empire needed solid men, and Massey was as solid as they came.

'I tend to agree with you,' Irving replied finally.

'I thought you might.' Smith smiled warmly.

Irving turned to Massey. 'But be warned, Captain – I won't tolerate any more incidents . . . Do you understand?'

Massey stood to attention. 'Yes, sir!'

'Good. Now go and—'

Suddenly the door was thrown open and Assistant Commissioner Beckett, a junior magistrate, burst in.

'*What the devil!*' Miles Irving shouted.

'*Thousands of them!*' Beckett's voice was full of panic, his face bright red. 'We won't be able to hold them!'

'*Where?*' demanded Massey, his shoulders tense, eyes focused.

'They're streaming out of the city, Captain – heading this way!'

Massey turned to Irving. 'Orders, sir?' he asked frantically.

'Get everyone!' shouted Irving, his voice breaking with anxiety. 'Hold them at the railway. Under no circumstance must the mob cross the railway!'

★ ★ ★

Jeevan watched as Pritam handed the rest of the gang *lathis* and knives at their hideaway. One by one his friends took their weapons, and one by one their faces lit up. Hans Raj, as always, had been correct. The city was rising up; now was the time to fight for the motherland.

'These are for you,' Pritam said to Jeevan as he gave him his weapons. 'The day has come, *bhai* – time for action!'

Jeevan looked at the stout wooden stick and the glistening, freshly sharpened blade of the knife. 'Where are we going?' he asked Pritam.

'The plan is to attack the railway bridge and then to storm the British compound. Tonight Amritsar will again be free.'

Jeevan nodded slowly as Pritam turned to the others. Sucha Singh was grinning from ear to ear like a small child who had discovered a secret stash of sweets. His brown eyes remained fixed. His friend, Bahadhur Khan, was staring down at the floor. When he did look up, Jeevan saw fear in his round face, his beard mere wisps of brown fluff on his chin. For a second Jeevan let himself believe that Bahadhur was weak, but then the words of the soldier, Bissen Singh, rang in his ears.

He recalled sitting on a wall near the police station – the *kotwali* – with Gurdial, barely six months earlier. Bissen Singh had walked by, as he always did – on his way to the post office to collect a letter that never seemed to arrive.

'Did you fight like a tiger, Bissen-ji?' Gurdial had shouted at him.

'A tiger?' Bissen had asked.

'I bet you didn't feel a single ounce of fear, did you?'

Bissen had stopped and stared into Jeevan's innocent eyes. 'In the midst of battle,' he had told him, 'the fool is the one who has *no* fear. *Fear* is what kept me *alive*, son. Fear and God . . .'

Jeevan snapped back into the present and nodded at Bahadhur. Bissen Singh had seemed such a hero only a matter of months earlier – a brave, strong man who had gone to the white man's land to fight for freedom. But then Jeevan had learned the truth from Hans Raj. Bissen was a traitor – a lapdog to his masters. Where was the honour in fighting and dying for the king of another country? Better to fight for your own land than for one that belonged to another. Jeevan looked at Pritam, who was shouting, almost foaming at the mouth.

'. . . our women any more! There will be no more running to satisfy their every whim! Let today be the day when the story of the new India began. Let the imperialist dogs run back to their king with their tails between their legs! *India zindabaad! India zindabaad!*'

The rest of the gang joined in, and after a moment, with Ram Singh's huge hand on his shoulder, Jeevan followed suit.

'Do not spare anyone who gets in our way,' Pritam said as they got ready to leave. 'Any white person you see is a legitimate target, and if some dirty, traitorous Indian gets in the way, then they die too!'

Rana Lal let out a blood-curdling scream and ran into the alleyway – still gloomy despite the sun's height. One by one the rest of the gang followed. Jeevan came last; on his way out he enquired after Hans Raj.

'He will meet us later,' Pritam told him. 'There is something he must do first.'

As Jeevan ran out into the main road, he wondered what was so important that it could keep their mentor away. After all, this was the day Hans Raj had predicted, with such spooky accuracy, for so long. What was it that could be *so* important?

Midday

Captain Massey refused to look at the mob that had gathered on the city side of the two railway bridges. The last thing he needed was to panic. Instead he checked on the men he had deployed to prevent the crowd from crossing the bridges. One was a narrow footbridge: Massey realized that there was no way that they could hold it. He had asked for infantry, but instead of men standing shoulder to shoulder, he had been given a mounted detachment. The horses, scared to death by the approaching mob, whinnied and snorted, their haunches slick with perspiration. They would not stand still. Massey cursed his luck.

He searched out Lieutenant Dickie, the officer in charge of the mounted unit. His mount was rearing up and refusing to follow commands. Massey shouted to him, 'Hold them still!'

Dickie reined his horse in but it was too frightened.

'I'm trying, man!' he shouted back. 'Call for reinforce-ments. Now!'

Massey knew that there were no extra men. He went to his car and took out his spare pistol. He was going to need it. When he next turned towards the bridge, he saw one of the mounted men turn and gallop away from the skirmish. Stones began to rain down on the men who had stayed.

'Who the hell is that riding away?' he demanded.

One of his men told him that it was Beckett, the assistant commissioner.

'Coward!' Massey shouted after him.

But no one heard him. The crowd began to bay for blood and more stones flew through the air, pelting men and horses ferociously. The front line gave way and the crowd surged towards the bridge.

'Good God!' shouted someone from behind Massey.

'*Shoot them!*' screamed Massey as he ran forward.

On the bridge some of the troops took aim and fired. The crowd stopped. People gasped. Several protestors fell to the ground, blood pouring from their wounds. Massey took aim with one of his pistols and fired again. A torrent of blood exploded from a man's chest. He slumped to the floor, dead.

'*Push them back!*' Massey cried out.

More shots rang out; more protestors fell. And then a strange calm descended. For a moment there was silence. In that short space of time, Massey realized that they were in trouble. The crowd was tens of thousands strong. There weren't enough bullets to shoot them all. Then all hell broke loose . . .

Jeevan stood aside as some men carried a body back to the city. The injured man was young, his hair a tight mess of black curls. The front of his shirt was covered in blood and his mouth was open, pink tongue hanging out.

'*BASTARDS!*' shouted the crowd. '*DEVILS!*'

The surge was sudden and seemed to have the force of a thousand horses behind it. Jeevan felt himself fall sideways, but before he hit the ground, the crowd bore him up. He stumbled forward and a powerful hand took his shoulder. Jeevan turned to see Ram Singh at his side again. Behind him, the rest of his gang strained against the tide, trying to stick together.

'Move out to the left!' ordered Pritam. 'We need to get away from the middle!'

Ram Singh led the way, pushing with all his might and parting the crowd. One by one the others followed, until they were free of the mob.

'*To the station!*' ordered Pritam.

Jeevan looked at Bahadhur Khan. 'I thought we were heading for the other side of the bridge . . .'

Bahadhur shrugged.

'The station,' repeated Pritam. 'The British won't let us cross the bridge. We'll take the railway station instead.'

The gang murmured their agreement and moved as

one, quickly and quietly. But before they had even reached the goods yard, just inside the station compound, they had been joined by nearly a thousand others. Jeevan ran for the first shed he could see and pulled open the door. There was little inside, save for some suitcases and trunks.

'Take them out and burn them!' cried a voice.

Suddenly there were dozens of people in the shed. Hammers, axes and swords were used to lay waste to the building. Then someone set fire to it.

'*Run!*' shouted Bahadhur.

Jeevan turned and saw the gang heading for the main part of the station. He followed them. There were people everywhere; destroying anything they could lay their hands on. As Jeevan joined his comrades, Pritam let out a cry.

'*There!*' he shouted, pointing to the farthest shed in the goods yard.

'What is it?' asked Rana Lal.

'A *gorah!*' Pritam spat out. 'Are you ready to begin the revolution?'

'*YES!*' shouted the rest of the gang in reply; all except Jeevan.

Pritam raced for the shed, brandishing his thick wooden club. Jeevan ran after him, thinking that the man in the shed couldn't be a soldier. The soldiers were at the bridge and behind the lines. It had to be a civilian. Pritam set about smashing the shed doors open. One by one, the gang joined in. Very quickly the wood had been splintered and the old, rusting lock smashed.

Once inside Pritam quickly cornered the white man. It was one of the station guards, a harmless-looking man whom Jeevan had seen before. He was on his knees, cowering and crying.

'Please,' he begged. 'For the love of God . . .'

Jeevan's mind began to play tricks on him. He wanted to kill the man and yet he wanted to help him too. Part of him asked what the lowly guard had ever done to hurt Mother India. The other part told him that all white people were enemies. But surely this poor man, this wretched soul . . . surely he couldn't be the—

Pritam sniggered like a madman and swung his club. It caught the guard square on the temple. He slumped to the side and assumed the foetal position. Pritam roared in hatred and swung his club again. The second blow caught the top of the guard's head with such force that it tore his scalp away. Blood – bright, viscous blood – spurted from the wound. Jeevan fell to the ground, waves of nausea overtaking him. He threw up again and again.

'Let it out,' Pritam told him. 'Do not let the fate of this *dog* turn you from the cause.'

Jeevan looked up at his mentor.

'*With us or against us!*' yelled Pritam. 'You decide. This is what being against us will get you . . .' He grinned, his mouth drooling, eyes fixed. 'Let me show you what it means to be a revolutionary!' he whispered.

Before anyone else could move, Pritam began to rain

down blow after blow. The guard's head caved in. Fragments of skull flew off in every direction; his eye-balls popped out; his nose disappeared back into his skull. Only when there was nothing left but a mess of blood and bits of bone did Pritam let up.

'One down,' he spat, his face slick with gore.

He turned and ran for the door, wiping away the blood, eager to find his next victim. Jeevan stood and looked at the guard. Two contradictory voices fought for space inside his head. *Follow your family; they are all you have*, said the voice he most wanted to follow. But then the other voice caught him and held him back.

'What have I become?' he asked.

'A *man*,' replied Ram Singh. 'Now come on!'

Jeevan stumbled after the gang, his heart and his stomach no longer ready for the fight. Only fear kept him going. Fear of what Pritam might do to him if he backed out, and fear of losing his new family.

Zardad Khan, in command of the 54th's detachment, stood at the entrance to the railway station with his men, who held their bayonets and rifles at the ready. The mob had managed to reach the station ten minutes earlier. Khan and his men had arrived very soon after, saving the station master's life. Five minutes later and he would have been dead. Now, having driven the mob off the platform, Khan and his men had to hold the station. If the mob managed to take it, then Amritsar was doomed.

A young soldier, barely eighteen years old, approached Zardad Khan. 'Sir – there is a small gang of protestors circling Mr Pinto's quarters,' he said.

Khan looked across towards the telegraph master's house. He couldn't see anyone. 'There is no one there, Singh,' he told him.

'Perhaps they have gone round to the back?' suggested Singh.

Khan thought for a moment, then turned to his second-in-command, a tall, thin man called Sawar. 'Hold the line here,' he ordered. 'I'm going to check on Mr Pinto with Singh.'

Singh wanted to smile. Zardad Khan was a hard taskmaster. He very rarely took junior soldiers with him when he went on a mission. Only those he deemed worthy.

Sawar nodded. 'Yes, sir!' he replied.

'Come on, Singh,' said Khan. 'Let's go and see what all the fuss is about.'

They ran towards the telegraph master's house, wary of the mob. But the troops of the 54th had done a good job. The people were fifty yards away and the line was holding. Insults and a few stones flew towards the two soldiers but nothing more. As they approached the front of the house, Khan heard the sound of splintering wood.

'*Come on!*' he shouted to Singh.

He raced round to the back, his bayonet at the ready. Singh ran after him. As they rounded the corner, Singh saw a gang of youths running away from the scene;

Pinto was being dragged out by a giant of a man.

Khan ran across. '*Let him go!*' he ordered. '*NOW!*'

Pinto's attacker ignored the command and continued to drag his victim away. Khan let out a cry of rage and ran forward, the sharp edge of his steel ready. He drove the bayonet into the giant's chest, and then into his side. The man let go of Pinto and fell to the ground – though he refused to give up the fight. He went for the blade tucked into his waistband. As Singh approached, he realized that this giant was merely a boy. A boy with a neck as thick as an ox's and hands like spades.

'*Don't do it!*' Khan warned.

But the boy didn't listen. He smirked and raised his knife, ready to strike. Khan said a silent prayer and drove his bayonet in one last time.

As Ram Singh took his last breath, he cried out for his mother.

4 p.m.

Jeevan sat silently as Pritam spat out more words of hatred. The gang had made it back to their little room and everyone bar their leader looked shattered. Ram Singh's death hung in the air like a ghost. No one had mentioned it but it was still there, gnawing at them, making them angry and sad at the same time. Only Pritam seemed to have put it out of his mind. Instead of reflecting on the death of a comrade and friend, he was trying to rally the rest of them.

'Rest a while,' he told them, 'and then let's get back out there and find some more enemies. Amritsar will burn today and there will be no stopping it. Let us rejoice, brothers!'

Jeevan wished to God that he had the courage to stand up and tell Pritam what he really thought. To tell him that he was nothing more than a psychotic madman – a murderer. But courage was something that

Jeevan lacked. It had ebbed away during the day, along with his humanity. As terrible images flashed through his mind – images of things he had seen and things he had done – Jeevan felt himself grow cold. Nothing could save him now. All the lessons he'd been taught – teachings about brotherhood and love – all were gone. All that remained was a vicious, cold-hearted thug; a murderer.

But at least he belonged now, said another voice. Instead of daydreams about his family and fleeting memories of his mother's smile, he had something real, something concrete. Pritam aside, Jeevan had the rest of the gang, the family he had always longed for; and he had Hans Raj, who would surely have stopped Pritam's excesses if he'd been there. After all, he'd promised to look after him, hadn't he? How Jeevan longed for him to appear now, to offer words of wisdom and love.

Pritam told the gang that they were going to drive the white people from the city before sunset. 'By the time we go to our beds not a single *gorah* will remain in our beloved city. Let them take refuge in the fort; tomorrow we will drive them out of there too!'

Rana Lal, Sucha Singh and Bahadhur Khan murmured their approval as he finally mentioned their fallen comrade.

'Ram Singh was a man of honour, a man of courage,' he told them. 'He lived and died for the greater good, just as his father did before him – for the freedom of our beloved mother.'

'We will avenge him!' Rana cried out.

'Yes!' replied Pritam, before turning to look at Jeevan. 'Are you still with us, brother?' he asked.

Jeevan looked up and nodded. What choice did he have but to continue? What could be worse than what he had already done? He looked down at his hands, smelled the kerosene on his clothes and remembered the bank managers . . .

Two hours earlier the gang had found themselves in Hall Bazaar – Amritsar's main street. After Ram Singh's death they had fled from the station and followed the rest of the mob back to the city centre. They had joined in, looting and burning as they went, angered by the death of their comrade. Thousands of protestors had taken to the streets. All around them people raged, venting their anger on the buildings most closely associated with the British. The post offices, missions and churches – all destroyed and set alight. And the banks . . .

Pritam had led the gang into the National Bank, intent on leaving it gutted. Here they had found two Englishmen – the managers. Pritam and Rana set about them, raining down blow after blow, until both men had been beaten unconscious.

'*Take them into the street!*' Pritam had demanded.

Jeevan had hoped not to be involved. He'd tried to stay out of the way. But outside, the two Englishmen were thrown to the dusty ground. A man whom Jeevan didn't know had produced a can of kerosene, ready to set fire to the desks and chairs and files that were being flung out too. Pritam took the can and handed it to Jeevan.

'*Burn them!*' he'd ordered, thrusting a sharp knife in the direction of the two men. 'Let them taste the heat of a funeral pyre.'

Jeevan had hesitated, his hands shaking, his heart thumping in his chest. The sounds and smells of anarchy overcame his senses. His eyes searched frantically, hoping to see policemen or soldiers. But there was no one to rescue the bank managers. No one to stop the madness.

The other rioters began to pile broken furniture on top of the semi-conscious men. The wood was followed by ledger books and papers bearing the details of the bank's customers. From behind Jeevan, someone threw in a painting of the British king. Pritam raised his knife to Jeevan's face. His eyes were filled with murderous intent. They held no semblance of life. Death lurked behind them, waiting . . .

'*Burn them or die!*' threatened Pritam.

'*Burn them!*' insisted Sucha and Rana. '*Remember Ram Singh!*'

'*BURN THE DOGS! BURN THE DOGS!*' sang the mob.

Jeevan looked up to the heavens and begged forgiveness from the cold grey clouds and the sunless, pitiless sky. With Pritam's knife at his side, he doused the two innocent men with the foul-smelling liquid. When the can was empty he dropped it. Pritam produced matches and ordered Jeevan to strike one.

'*Put the British on the pyre!*' he screamed; flecks of saliva flew out of his mouth, as thick and gelatinous as the kerosene Jeevan had poured onto the poor men at his feet.

'*LIGHT IT!*' screamed the mob, united as one, an insatiable predator.

Jeevan, knowing that he would either send the men to their Maker or join them on their journey, lit the match and let it fall . . .

An hour after they had left their little room, Pritam's gang stood by a telegraph pole on the railway line to the west of the city. All along it the telegraph lines were being cut. Amritsar was being closed off from the outside world and they were playing their part. Jeevan watched the skinny Rana Lal as he climbed the pole and began to hack at the wires with a machete. He worked quickly; when he was done, he shouted in defiance: '*India zindabaad!*'

Jeevan turned away.

'You seem troubled, brother,' he heard Pritam say.

Jeevan refused to look at him. 'I'm fine,' he insisted.

'I do not think so. You wear the look of someone who is in shock.'

He shrugged. 'I just don't understand,' he admitted, despite his fear of Pritam. 'What have we achieved today?'

Pritam put an arm around his shoulder. 'No one said it would be easy,' he said. 'The British have forced us into these actions. Do you not think that I would be the first to welcome a peaceful transition?'

Jeevan looked into Pritam's eyes. Had he been wrong about him? Was there, hidden deep within, a heart? The answer was swift and piercing. As Jeevan looked into Pritam's face, searching for some small hint of compassion, he saw only hatred.

'We do not belong to these people,' continued Pritam. 'We are not animals to be bought and sold. We can't be traded or forced to do things that go against our wishes—'

'But we killed innocent men. Men who did nothing to hold us down—'

Pritam grasped Jeevan in an iron grip, fingers digging deep into his flesh. 'There *are* no innocents,' he said with a sardonic smile. 'This is the lesson we must learn . . .'

He let his words hang in the cool evening air for a moment. 'We *must* learn or die,' he finished, once again leaving Jeevan in no doubt as to his choices. 'Do you understand me, brother?'

Jeevan nodded.

'Are you sure? Because I will not tell you again. There will be no more sobbing and crying – that is a child's way. Be a man and stand up for your country . . . your family.'

Jeevan nodded again.

'Stand up or lie down and die, just like you did when

your own mother died,' said Pritam, reinforcing his point and sending a dagger of pain through Jeevan's heart. 'And trust me, brother. If you let me down again, you *will* join the rest of them.'

The shudder that rocked Jeevan seemed to emanate from his soul. It sent wave after wave of electricity up and down his spine. He had been betrayed by Hans Raj. How else could Pritam have known of his mother's death and the despair and helplessness it had caused in his heart? Something snapped loose inside his head and he set himself a new task. He nodded for a third time and forced out his words.

'I won't let you down again,' he lied. 'You have my word.'

'Good, good,' replied Pritam. 'Now, let's get back to the city. The *goreh* will try and rescue their own and get them to the fort. We can't allow that to happen.'

Jeevan stayed at the back of the group, biding his time. He knew now that he *did* have a choice – just one. He had to get away. Everything he had been told, everything that had led him to this day – it had all been lies. Nothing the gang had done would help India to be free. They hadn't killed a single soldier or captain or general. They hadn't taken a single piece of ground the British cared about. All they had done was set fire to their own city and kill innocents along the way.

Jeevan found himself thinking of his friend Gurdial; and of the soldier he had been so quick to judge, Bissen Singh. One was a *real* friend, the other a *real* soldier.

Jeevan realized that he was neither: despite the smiling faces of his so-called family, he was caught in a trap, surrounded on all sides by evil intent. How foolish he had been to believe their honey-soaked words about love and family. His need to belong had led him down a dirty, immoral and dangerous path, and all because evil men had spoken the words they knew he'd wanted to hear. Smiling faces, he told himself, sometimes hid rotten souls.

HMP Pentonville, London,
13 July 1940, 8.55 a.m.

Udham Singh (aka Ram Mohammed Singh Azad)

I can hear them coming. I know their footsteps. Uncle Tom is heavy. His feet fall like those of a stubborn water buffalo and his breath escapes his throat in short, violent rasps. Albert, the other hang-man, is slight and seems to smell of cough mixture. If I wanted I could snap his neck with one hand. But I have no wish to do such a thing any more. I am ready to meet my Maker, and I have done enough killing. I do not want to think of such things in the five minutes that remain to me.

My waking dreams are continually filled with the faces of those who died in the massacre. They do not leave me alone. I see them all – the women, the children. A river of blood flows from the killing field.

The drains are full of bodies. I can see a small child, a girl, wandering through the haze, clutching her rag doll. I want to reach out to her, to hold her, to tell her everything will be fine . . . But nothing will ever be the same again. Not for me. Not for her . . .

By the time I was done helping, no one was left – no dead and no injured. There were bodies in the well but we had to wait until daybreak to retrieve them, and even then we only managed to pull out a few. Those people are nothing but ghosts now. They swim around inside my head and disturb my sleep. They poke me with their bony fingers and scream at me with their disembodied voices. Soon I will join them and become what they became. I too will become one of the ghosts of Amritsar.

When they took me into the orphanage, my eyes were swollen with tears. For many years after she died, I refused to believe that my mother was dead. It took the massacre to make me realize that she was truly gone. And then all I did was replace one with another. India became my mother, and my sole reason for living was vengeance; I let ice fill my soul. I did not wish to become a murderer, but Life and Fate conspired and here I am, awaiting the hangman's noose.

Let no one be mistaken. I go to my end with no fear. I am not about to die. Death is for those who do not believe – let them become food for maggots. When the last breath is gone from my body, my soul will leave this place and return to my home – to the golden land of the five rivers. And finally, after so many years, perhaps I will find my resting place. God knows, it has escaped me until now. I have spent this life trying to find my place. And now I know where it is. Hurry, Mr Hangman, and help me to reach it. I do not wish to wait a second longer.

Part Four

The Soldier

Amritsar, 12 April 1919

Whenever the dreams came, they drenched Bissen Singh in sweat. And this morning was no exception. He sat upright in bed, like a corpse on a funeral pyre, every muscle in his wiry frame taut. His head pounded in time with the gunfire of his dreams. Round after round, shell after shell, a thunderous cacophony of destruction and death, the smell of gunpowder like a phantom in his senses. Perspiration dripped from his brow, and his right leg and buttock throbbed with pain, where the grenade had torn away flesh and shattered bone four years earlier.

The images that haunted him receded to wherever dreams lived. But he could still make out the faces of the men he had killed, and of those who had died alongside him. The final image, frozen in his mind, was like a rose in the early morning English dew. It was her face, her smile, her eyes . . .

★ ★ ★

Two hours later Bissen Singh woke for the second time, the noise of the bustling streets rousing him from yet another dream. He sat up, swung his legs over the edge of his bed and shook his head free of explosions and gunfire. The wailing of dying young men calling for their mothers rang in his ears. And then it was all gone except for the continuous low-level ringing, which he had carried with him from the Western Front, via Brighton and Cape Town, and home again to the land of the five rivers. The air around him was thick with his own smell and that of rotting onions, and it brought back the past once more. He stood up and stretched before bending over and touching his toes as his back popped and cracked. Then he walked across the dirt floor to the wooden shutters and opened them. The world flooded into his small room, making his grey eyes squint.

Out in the street the sun was already beating down, uncomfortably warm for the time of year. Bissen Singh made his way through the narrow lanes of old Amritsar, heading for the post office. More in hope than expectation. The hope of a letter, a note. Something. Anything. All around him traders hawked their wares and people went about their business. Children and animals wandered the mazy paths, not caring where they went. Colours assaulted his eyes; the smell of dung and dust and sweat ate into his nasal lining. Amritsar, the city of his youth. A city that had become alien to him upon his return from the war. He heard the beeping of a horn and stepped aside to let a car pass. Its brakes squealed as a cow walked right into its path.

'Damned animals!' shouted the British officer sitting in the back. He had grey hair and a thick black moustache. On the seat next to him were two rifles and a *lathi*.

Bissen looked at him. The officer, General Reginald Dyer, acknowledged the look, a slight nod of the head – a mark of respect for his exploits on behalf of his king and emperor. At least that's what Bissen tried to believe. The truth, whatever that was, held no meaning for him any more. *His* truth – the thing he wanted to believe in most of all – was thousands of miles away. In another world. In another lifetime perhaps.

'*Chall, chall!*' demanded General Dyer.

The driver, a rotund, red-faced police officer called Plomer, made no reply, but set off down the narrow lane once more, *pap-pap-papping* on the horn as he went. Bissen watched them leave through a cloud of red dust, wondering what they were doing travelling through the streets without an armed escort. Amritsar was in open rebellion, the riots of two days earlier lending an edge of menace to the city. Four *goreh* had been killed and many injured.

But then again, Reginald Dyer was no ordinary British officer. More Indian than English in all regards bar the colour of his skin and the elevated position this gave him, Dyer was arrogantly confident of the respect

Amritsaris had for him. No other British officer would have dared to venture along the back streets at such a tense time. But then no other British officer had such an admiration for Sikhs, as far as Bissen knew.

By the time he had reached the post office he had seen the devastation caused by the riots. The managers of the National Bank had been doused in kerosene and set alight – both dead. Shops all across the city had been looted and destroyed, with people on both sides beaten indiscriminately.

'Such an evil thing, *bhai*,' commented Gurnam Lal, a cloth weaver whom Bissen bumped into outside his shop.

Bissen listened as Gurnam told him what had happened elsewhere in the city – or at least what he had heard.

'These people,' said Bissen, shaking his head. 'They are like dogs that shit in their own basket and roll around in it—'

'*Who?*' asked Gurnam. 'The *goreh?*'

Bissen sighed. 'No, Gurnam Lal-ji – the *Punjabis*. Tell me – how did it hurt the Empire that these so-called revolutionaries burned down their own city?'

'But—'

Bissen shook his head. 'I don't wish to talk of this any more.'

Just then, Gurnam's wife, a delicate, petite woman called Gian, came out of their open-fronted shop. '*Sat-sri-akaal*,' she said to Bissen.

'*Phabbi-ji*,' offered Bissen, smiling.

'Tell me, young man,' she teased. 'How old are you now?'

'The same as I was yesterday and the day before that and the one before that too,' he replied.

'Twenty-four,' said Gian. 'And yet you have no wish to take a wife? Who will make your food for you, Bissen Singh?'

'I have my mother and my sisters,' he told her.

'But they have returned to your ancestral village. From what I hear you are alone here in the city.'

'How do you know so much of my business?' asked Bissen.

'Why,' replied Gian, winking at her husband, 'you are the talk of the young women of Amritsar – despite your limp.'

Bissen half smiled and then thanked Gurnam for all the news. 'I must be on my way,' he said. 'Much to do . . .'

'Will we see you at the Vaisakhi festivities tomorrow?' asked Gurnam.

'Undoubtedly,' replied Bissen.

As he continued down the lane, the images flooded back into his head. Gian's mention of his limp had set his mind racing. And talk of wives had brought *her* back too. Bissen hurried back to his room, thankful that he had a small amount of *pheme* left. Tomorrow he would visit the priest at the *gurdwara*, and talk of dreams and sins. Today he longed only for the arms of Morpheus . . .

Neuve Chapelle, France,
9 March 1915

Bissen Singh's unit, the 1/39 Garwahl Rifles, reached the forward lines at nightfall, by which time he was exhausted, cold and dirty. Three days had passed since his last opportunity to wash, and his feet were blistered from having to wear boots a size too small. All around him his companions, part of Lahore Division, attempted to rest. Some cleaned their weapons while others began eating their meagre provisions. The trenches weren't particularly deep but the water had surfaced anyway, seeping through the rotten duckboards that had been put down. Rain added to the misery of their surroundings, particularly when it turned into a light snowfall. But Bissen had grown used to such discomforts in his time with the British Expeditionary Force. The trenches were hellish and only two avenues provided an escape – death or serious injury.

Bissen stepped around a large rat that sat up imperiously on one of the duckboards, seemingly unfazed by the arrival of the men. It nibbled at a scrap of discarded food, eyes shining in the growing darkness. Bissen moved further along the trench, keeping his head low so that an enemy sniper wouldn't spot his turban. He found a dugout, shallow but relatively safe, and sat with his feet hanging down to the floor, his back arched, neck straining. Putting his Lee Enfield .303 rifle to one side, he searched the pockets of his jacket for cigarettes. Constantly aware of any danger, he turned towards the rear of the dugout and lit it quickly. Days earlier he had seen what happened when a Tommy enjoyed his smoke too openly. The bullet had entered the boy's head dead centre and blown his brains out of the back of his skull before his second drag.

Once he had finished his cigarette, Bissen turned and moved towards the front wall of the trench, below a thick line of sandbags. His eyes, growing more accustomed to the gloom, searched out the nearest fire-step. He crept across and, placing a boot on the three-foot ledge, peered quickly over the edge. In that instant he made out nothing except broken tree trunks and lines of barbed wire. He listened carefully for sounds from across the open ground but he heard only a few whispered words from his comrades and the squeaking of rats.

He made his way back to the dugout and was just sitting down on the damp earth when two of his friends, Jiwan and Bhan, joined him.

'Do you have a cigarette, *bhai*?' asked Jiwan, a young man of nineteen years. His beard was not yet more than a few wisps of golden-brown hair and his turban seemed far too big for his head.

'Saleyah – don't you know it is forbidden for Sikhs to smoke?' teased Bissen, smiling.

'I doubt God is watching us here,' laughed Jiwan.

Bhan Singh clapped the boy across the back of his head, cursed, and then turned round to light his own cigarette. 'God watches over us wherever we go,' he told the lad.

'I was only—' began Jiwan, but Bhan cut him off in a show of authority – authority based on the fact that, at twenty-five, he was one of the oldest men in the unit.

'I know what you were saying, you son of a goat herder: here we are in this man-made hell and God will forgive us our small acts of sin.'

'That's exactly it,' replied Jiwan.

'Three days ago I killed a boy younger than Jiwan,' said Bissen. 'He was crying and wore no boots.'

'*Bhai*, that is just what we have to do,' Bhan reminded him.

Bissen appeared not to have heard his words. 'I took my bayonet and I cut through his guts until they spilled out into the mud,' he continued, his eyes glazed.

'There will be much worse to come in the morning,' Bhan Singh told him. 'Much worse . . .'

For the next few minutes they crouched in silence. It was Jiwan who eventually spoke up.

'Do we know what the plan is?' he asked Bhan.

'I do,' replied Bhan. 'They gave me a map.'

'A map?' Bissen looked surprised.

Bhan Singh pulled a scrap of paper from one of his pockets and showed it to his friends. 'It even has coloured lines on it; targets for the battle.'

202

Battle plans on paper were rare. In fact Bissen had never even seen one. He took the map from Bhan and peered at it more closely. Their position for the start of battle was clearly marked. They would begin to the right of the British First Army, under the direction of James Willocks, commander of the Indian Corps. He looked at the position of the German trenches. They seemed so close, the first line sitting in front of the village.

'Are we to take the village?' he asked Bhan Singh.

His friend nodded. 'And there will be a surprise for our enemies,' he whispered.

'What surprise?' asked an excited Jiwan.

Bhan shook his head. 'I cannot say,' he replied as three huge rats slid across Bissan's boots and into the water at the base of the trench.

Bissen kicked out and caught rodent flesh. A shriek pierced the air. 'Damn rats!' he said. 'It's a wonder they don't try to eat us as we sleep.'

'*Sleep?*' asked Bhan Singh. 'I wish I could remember what that means . . . How I long for the village of my birth. Instead, here I am fighting a white man's war.'

Jiwan glanced at Bissen. When Bissen refused to return his look he shook his head. 'We are fighting to keep the world free, *bhai-ji*,' he told Bhan.

'For king and emperor – to help maintain this British Empire. I was there when Willocks made his speech too. It means nothing to me.'

'But that is mutiny,' whispered Jiwan. 'Court-martial . . .'

'However I am killed,' replied Bhan Singh, 'it will be here, fighting for these people so that they can continue to keep our motherland in shackles. Or perhaps I'll die running away? Wherever it is, it won't be for the good of my own country.'

'I think you need to rest, *bhai-ji*,' said Jiwan, his brown eyes darkening with concern. Bhan Singh was one of the most courageous and loyal men he had ever met. For him to be speaking of such things could only be explained by lack of sleep. Why else would he risk being court-martialled?

'Rest will come when I am back in my own land,' said Bhan. 'Not until then. And if that means never, then that is the will of God.'

Bissen turned and lit another cigarette, thankful that the trenches they occupied were still so fresh. No battle of any consequence had taken place, which meant there were no rotting corpses for the rats and maggots to feast on. There was only the vile, putrid odour coming from the latrines, which were just deep holes covered with planks of wood coated in urine and faeces.

He thought about the impending death that dawn would bring. The lottery of leaving the trenches and charging with bayonet fixed at a line of enemy guns. Of not knowing how many seconds you had left on this earth. Of praying with the depths of your soul that the God you had learned to worship since infancy would indeed be waiting for you when you went to meet Him. Not the empty, lonely void of perpetual nothingness but a true heaven, angels and all.

'I have not even kissed a girl,' Bissen said to himself absent-mindedly.

'What's that, *bhai-ji*?' asked Jiwan, taking the cigarette Bissen offered him.

'Nothing . . .' Bissen scratched the back of his head, where lice were nestling against his unwashed and flaking scalp.

Before he could say another thing, before he could move, Jiwan had lit his cigarette. The bullet was just a noise, a movement of air. Jiwan fell forward, dead before he hit the ground. The other members of the unit ducked even lower, one of them scrambling along the duckboards towards Bissen.

'What happened?' asked the man, a sturdily built Muslim called Atar Khan.

'Get that body out of the way!' a hoarse whisper ordered, this time in perfect English. It was one of the senior officers, crouching some ten feet away, eating from a tin can.

'Yes, sir!' replied Atar.

'He didn't turn round,' said Bissen.

Atar Khan shook his head. 'At least he won't feel his stomach churn in the morning,' he said. 'Won't have to spend the entire day walking around with breeches full of shit—'

'I should have done something.'

'*Allah* chose not to give him a brain, *bhai*. What could *you* have done?'

Between them they dragged Jiwan's body along the trench and round a traverse. They found a hollow and pushed the body into it. It was makeshift but it would do. The rats would eat well that night, Bissen Singh thought as Atar Khan began to chant.

'*Allah hu Akhbar*,' the Muslim whispered over and over again.

'*Satnam Waheguru*,' replied the Sikh.

About five feet from where they crouched, Private James Burton, aged eighteen years, tried to stop crying.

'*Our Father who art in Heaven . . .*' he sobbed.

10 March 1915

Dawn brought with it a damp, muggy mist, which made it difficult to see what was going on. Although not quite a fog, in places it was dense enough to obscure anything more than ten yards away. Bissen Singh had been ready since four in the morning, along with his unit and the rest of the Indian Corps. To their immediate right were the massed troops of the First Army, under the command of General Sir Douglas Haig. Beyond them were the 7th and 8th Divisions of the IV Corps. Along the length of the two-thousand-yard-long front sat 342 guns aimed at the first line of the German defences. And up in the skies the Royal Flying Corps were on recon missions, preparing to bombard German reinforcements along the roads that led to Lille, some fifteen miles to the north-east.

In the short briefing Bissen's unit had been given, they were told that their job would be to take the enemy trenches before moving on into the village of Neuve Chapelle itself. Once this was secured, they would assist in gaining the low ground to the east of the village while the rest of the troops attempted to gain the strategic foothold of Aubers Ridge. When Bissen had asked how high a vantage point the ridge was, the officer had shrugged and changed the subject. Now, as he peered through the early morning light, despite patches of thick, swirling mist, Bissen knew that there was no visible ridge beyond the village. He knew because an English Tommy called Charles had told him.

'They want us to risk our lives to take a twenty-foot-high ridge,' he'd complained as he passed Bissen in the trench.

'Twenty foot?' Bissen had asked with his ever-improving English. He was shocked.

'Twenty damned foot!' repeated Charles. 'Absolute folly . . .'

Before Bissen had a chance to ask him anything else, the Tommy had gone. He turned to Bhan Singh. 'When do we go?'

'The *sahib* didn't say,' replied Bhan. 'I hope it's soon though. I am getting very cold standing here.'

'Have you cleaned your rifle?' asked Bissen.

Bhan gave him a dirty look. 'That is all I did last night. Over and over again. My rifle won't be getting stuck. Not like the rubbish those Germans are using—'

'Mausers,' said Bissen.

'Twelve rounds a minute I'll fire at the enemy,' boasted Bhan. 'Just as we were trained to do. Let's see where the enemy gets with his five-round magazines.'

'Just be careful, *bhai-ji*.'

Bhan Singh shook his head. 'Let us be victorious,' he replied. 'Let the *German* be careful.'

Bissen wondered what had occurred overnight to turn Bhan Singh back into a loyal servant of the emperor. Perhaps he had finally been able to get some sleep, as Jiwan had suggested. Bissen shuddered at the thought of his dead friend. And then shuddered some more, knowing that more of his fellow Rifles would be dead by the time the battle was over. He looked around at faces that had become so familiar, wondering which of them he would see again in the evening; which of them would join Jiwan as food for the rats. He realized how fleeting all his relationships had become, here in hell; how nonchalant his attitude to death and loss. There would be other Jiwan Singhs – lots of them. The trick was not to become one too.

Turning to face the back of the trench, he lit a cigarette, its harsh smoke coating the back of his already dry throat. But he held in the coughing fit that followed, letting his eyes water and barely making a sound. In the briefing they'd received they were told that there would be a long barrage of gunfire and shelling before the infantry attack began. The English officer had been bursting with pride when he'd described the new tactic.

'A predetermined number of guns will concentrate on one target for a set period of time,' he'd said. 'Then they will be raised and begin firing at target number two. At this point the infantry will attack the first target, which should by then be blown to smithereens. Any questions, men?'

Before anyone had been able to raise a hand, the officer said, 'Jolly good!' and scuttled away. It was left to an Indian *subedar*, a sergeant, to explain in full. Not that Bissen had needed any further explanation. His English was good enough to understand what the officer had told them. And he realized that, if the bombardment worked, the battle itself would be less dangerous than anything he had previously engaged in.

As he awaited the first round of shelling, Bissen sneaked another look across no-man's-land. The German trenches were different to theirs. They were not deep and were built up some four feet high from ground level, with a thick layer of sandbags. Any direct hit would send sandbags and earth in every direction, showering the men behind them. Bissen breathed a sigh of relief. The less gunfire they had to run into, the better. As he crouched back against the wall, Atar Khan joined him.

'*Bhai*, I've heard a rumour that we will attack at seven-thirty a.m. – that is barely ten minutes away . . .'

Bissen Singh had learned early on that Atar Khan's rumours were usually as good as direct orders. He was one of those people who always seemed to know more than he should. Bissen steadied himself and gave his weapon a final once-over.

Atar nodded towards the enemy lines. 'When we go, stick close by. That way we can help each other,' he suggested.

Bissen Singh nodded but cleared his mind of all thoughts by praying to himself. At precisely seven-thirty the shelling started.

It lasted for thirty-five minutes, the guns and howitzers pummelling the German defences. Shells shrieked and whistled through the air; guns were being fired in rapid bursts. Wave after wave hit the enemy and the noise became cacophonous, jarring, discordant. It thundered and raged all around. Smoke began to merge with the damp mist and visibility waned. Bissen Singh tried to keep his mind focused but the noise was like nothing he had ever heard. And the ground on which he stood vibrated and shook, encompassing him. For a while he was back in Amritsar, washing himself in the pool that surrounded Harmandirsahib – the Golden Temple that he had loved since he was a child. Pilgrims flocked to the temple; multi-coloured doves sailed past in the sky, cooing and purring. The sound of tabla and harmonium combined to form sweet melodies in his ear. A strong, earthy woman, no more than twenty years of age, walked past and smiled at him, her eyes a shimmering, sparkling green. As he watched her go, he found himself lost in the hypnotic rhythm of her hips as they swayed to and fro, to and fro—

Something crashed, something thundered – deep, sonorous, booming. He snapped back to the present, readying his Enfield .303. Noticing that the other men were standing and walking about freely, he stood too. The barrage was providing cover from sniper fire. He looked out into the wasteland, unable to hear anything but the bombardment, unable to see through the smoke but knowing that the first line of the enemy's defence would be obliterated. If they were still able to fight, where were the sniper's bullets, the return fire and the counter attack? Confidently he lit a cigarette, coughed freely and savoured its taste. This was too simple, too easy . . .

The infantry attack went wrong. By the time Bissen Singh had reached the German trenches, expecting them to be smashed to pieces, it was too late. After the battle he learned that the rest of the bombardment had worked brilliantly. It was only the spot *his* company had charged that the bombs had missed. The Second Battalion of the Garwahl Rifles was the first to be affected by the blunder. Bissen's unit followed on behind. The smoke and the noise had created havoc. No instructions were being received, no messages were getting through. The soldiers simply charged the enemy line and killed everyone they could find. Or were themselves cut down with bullets and bayonets and bombs.

Bissen charged over the trench walls behind someone he recognized as Rifleman Gobar Singh Negi, who ran towards the enemy, bayonet at the ready. Before Bissen could blink, Gobar Singh had killed two attackers and rounded the first traverse. As he prepared to follow, other soldiers overtook him. Atar Khan was one of them. Remembering what Atar had said about sticking together, Bissen fell in behind his friend. He trampled over dead young men, some of them with scorched entry marks where bullets had splintered and smashed through bone. Others lay wailing and moaning, their lives ebbing away slowly as their insides spilled out onto the foreign soil in a tangled mess of guts and blood. Bissen saw movement as he rounded a traverse. Sensing the danger, he rushed in with his bayonet, spearing the German soldier through the left temple with a force so brutal that the blade emerged on the other side of his head. The dead man, his rifle poised to shoot down Atar Khan, slumped into the mud, blood gushing in torrents from his wound, dousing the rats that scurried all around.

Next to him sat another young German, not much older than Jiwan Singh had been. The same wisps of teenage hair grew from his chin and cheeks. His face was smeared with grime and mud, and his pleading blue eyes showed mortal fear. Just a boy. Bissen saw that he was unhurt. He readied his bayonet as the German shouted above the thunderous cacophony that continued all around them:

'Halt! Bitte nicht schiessen! Ich ergebe mich! Ich ergebe mich . . .!'

Bissen realized that he had to think quickly. He had to move. Death came swiftly to those who stood still in the heat of battle. Emotions raged inside his chest as he recalled the teachings of the Gurus. Every man is your brother, every woman your sister. Shouting, explosions, whistles and gunfire – all seemed like a dream. A nightmare, during which time stood still and Bissen's eyes closed momentarily.

It was the screaming that snapped him back to reality. Opening his eyes again, Bissen saw that he had speared his brother through the heart. Without thinking, without knowing. The boy's eyes remained open. They looked up in shock and amazement, locked in the instant of death. Bissen found himself wondering what the boy's mother looked like. What his name had been; his sweetheart's. He gazed at the Enfield in his hands, asking himself what he had become. Why hadn't he let the boy live? Shivering with guilt, he moved on. Round the next corner he found yet more broken and twisted bodies, lying in the stinking filth of an exploded latrine.

Germans, Englishmen and Indians, covered in shit, not glory, and all equal in death.

His left foot slid from beneath him and he fell against the earthen mound of the trench. He turned quickly and lifted his bayonet, knowing instinctively what was coming. The German soldier's bayonet pierced his right shoulder and a searing pain racked his body. Bissen screamed. Stabbed and hacked out with his rifle. The German screamed back, collapsing onto him. Bissen cried out and pushed him off, before slashing at him again and again. He felt his humanity ebb away as he cut his enemy's face into ribbons of ruby-coloured fat and gristle. Then an arm pulled him away. It was Bhan Singh.

'Come on!' he shouted. 'Bissen!'

Bissen let himself be led away, trampling bodies and limbs underfoot. He refused to succumb to the pain in his shoulder, concentrating instead on the next turn in the maze, the next enemy soldier. As they rounded the third traverse in a row without meeting resistance, they saw the reason: Gobar Singh Negi lay there dead, his eyes still open, his turban still in place. All around their comrade were dead Germans. Gobar Singh had obviously put up a courageous fight. Both Bissen and Bhan Singh said a swift prayer for their fallen friend, lifting him out of the mud and propping his body against the side of the trench before moving on.

Bissen stooped to pick up a pistol. It was a Webley Mark IV – standard issue to British officers. Bissen wondered how far the man had managed to get before being killed. The answer lay ten feet further on. Lieutenant-Colonel Ernest Wodehouse lay face down in the mud, his legs blown away and half his head missing. Bissen stopped and turned what was left of the dead man over. He remembered a smiling, jovial Englishman, always ready with jokes and stories about buxom village girls with loose morals. Bissen pulled him to one side and pushed his body into a dugout, clear of the filthy, stinking mud. Then he went on, slowing down as he realized that the trenches had finally been taken. The few Germans who were unhurt had surrendered. As he rounded the next corner, a misdirected shell exploded above the dugout where he had placed Ernest Wodehouse's remains, removing all trace of the officer's body for ever.

11 March 1915

The crucifix stood alone. It was simply made, of two thick poles, the wood weathered, darkened by time. The statue of Christ crucified was untouched by the chaos, dirt and blood of the battle. All around, buildings had been turned to rubble and ash, their timber-framed roofs blackened and charred. Some still smouldered – and in one or two places fires burned. Bissen Singh wandered through what had once been someone's courtyard, his rifle poised and ready, even though the enemy was long gone. After the previous day's fighting, the German front line had retreated from the village, to an area of flat ground called the Bois de Biez. Bissen had no idea what this meant. He had merely heard an officer calling it this. Not that it mattered. Not now.

The battle had been a disaster. Reports were reaching Bissen's *subedar* of successes along other parts of the front line, but Bissen had scoffed at these so-called victories. The indiscriminate slaughter that he had taken part in should have achieved three objectives. The enemy were to have been driven back a great distance; the village was to have been retaken; and finally the high ground of Aubers Ridge should have fallen into Allied hands. The enemy *had* fallen back, but only by just over a mile. The village *had* been taken, but it remained a village no longer. The homes of its people had been shelled and fired on and flattened. Its orchards and trees and flowers had been destroyed. The town square resembled a quarry: great piles of rubble and stone lay where artists had once sat with easels, and where couples had walked arm in arm past pavement cafés. And Aubers Ridge remained in enemy hands.

Bissen edged through a small door that hung by one rusting hinge. He'd entered a small storeroom. It was pitch black inside and smelled of rotting onions, damp and mildew. A scratching noise came from his left. Then a hissing, snarling sound, followed by a click and more hissing. He stood there, breathing quietly, the throbbing in his shoulder a constant, nagging companion. Realizing that it was only a cat, he left the storeroom and made his way back across the courtyard. Three of its walls were gone. The fourth stood alone, a solitary hanging basket attached to it. No flowers.

The ringing in Bissen's ears had faded since the barrage of the previous morning. All night, as he sat hunched against a damp wall, listening to Atar Khan talking of the Punjab and attempting to sleep, his ears had buzzed. Nothing gave him respite from the insistent drone. Not closing his eyes or listening to Atar's words, or the morphine he had been given to ease the pain in his shoulder. The wound had been cleaned and treated by the field doctor; a short, slight, fair-haired man who wore wire-rimmed glasses and had the breath of an alcoholic. Bissen had thanked him in his best English, a courtesy that seemed to shock the doctor.

'Not many of your lot speak English,' he'd said to Bissen.

'At school,' Bissen had tried to explain. 'I learn from early. From a boy—'

'Good on you,' the doctor had replied. 'At least one of you has made an effort. I can't make head or tail of what them other ones are talking about. I just nod and say yes.'

'You are from where?' asked Bissen.

'I'm sorry,' replied the doctor. 'James Cromwell. From a village called Church Langton in Leicestershire. Pleased to meet you.' He held out a hand, which Bissen shook.

'Bissen Singh. From Amritsar, Punjab.'

'Like I said,' Dr Cromwell went on. 'Good to meet one of you who I can talk to. Did you lose many?'

'More than half of unit,' replied Bissen sadly. 'Two my best friends gone . . .'

Dr Cromwell shook his head and placed a hand on his shoulder. 'I'm sorry. This war is brutal.'

Bissen nodded.

'I'll give you a spare bandage and some morphine, Singh,' the doctor told him. 'It's not much but it should help until this battle is won. Then we'll get you properly treated.'

'Thank you,' Bissen said, their eyes meeting.

'And good luck.'

Bissen got up off the wooden board propped between two chairs, which had been acting as a makeshift treatment table. 'You too,' he told the doctor, before making his way back to what was left of his unit.

* * *

Now, as he stood in the courtyard of some Frenchman's home, he wondered why he was so far away from his own. What had made him leave his beautiful homeland for the horror and savagery of war? A war in which the main protagonists looked exactly the same. A war in which fat, overfed, red-faced commanders ordered young men to go and die for the sake of a mile of land; land that was charred and smoking and soaked in blood and guts. A war in which young men had to kill other young men or face being shot for desertion by cowards who hid well behind the front lines.

He shook his head, trying to clear his thoughts. Trying to find the focus he needed. According to the officers in charge, the village had been cleared of German soldiers, but that didn't mean that it was actually clear. The German trenches his unit had attacked *should* have been obliterated by the barrage; blown to smithereens, as the briefing officer had put it. But that hadn't stopped Bissen and his comrades from running straight into a fortified defensive line, had it? It hadn't prevented the deaths of so many of his fellow Rifles either. The only answer, it seemed to Bissen Singh, was to follow his own instincts. There were too many hiding places in amongst the ruins of Neuve Chapelle, too many dark holes and cellars and storerooms. All it would take was one confused, angry, frightened German, and Bissen would find himself dying in a stranger's land, thousands of miles from home. And that was something he would not allow to happen.

He turned to look at the crucifix once more, still amazed that it had remained standing when everything around had been reduced to nothing. He wondered at its significance – if it meant anything at all. As far back as he could remember – in his native village – his half-crazed grandmother had told him tales. There were signs of God in everything, she said: in the warmth of a stranger's smile, and the flight of birds and the taste of a mango. In the waves of butterflies that erupted during the spring, and in the fat, life-giving droplets of rain that soaked you to the skin and made the gulleys and paths run with water. But she hadn't meant this literally. The crucifix was supposed to be a sign of God. It was literal.

'When a man is happy,' his grandmother had told him, 'he will not seek God. He will not see God, nor will he listen to his teachings or abide by his signs. But when a man is in strife, when he is in peril, then God will seek that man out. He will show him his signs, make them clear . . . Do you understand, little one?'

Bissen recalled shaking his head in confusion.

'Man does not always have faith in the Lord,' his grandmother had explained. 'But our Lord will never lose his faith in Man. One day, when you are older, you will understand. Man is the lover who takes his wife for granted. God is the wife, forever holding onto her faith in Man—'

'What nonsense are you teaching the boy?' Bissen remembered his grandfather shouting.

'What would *you* know?' his grandmother had yelled in reply.

'God is the *wife*? That kind of blasphemy will send you to hell, you foul hag.'

'Better a foul hag than a demented fool,' his grandmother had countered.

Bissen smiled to himself as he recalled her words. The crazy, wizened old woman who had always carried the odour of rotting onions and sour milk – the stench of a death not yet met, she'd called it, and . . .

Rotting onions . . .

Bissen heard the blast before he felt it. A grenade, launched by hand, from the storeroom where the cat had been hiding. It sent him hurtling onto a mound of rubble. He landed awkwardly, and the right side of his body went completely numb. The ringing in his ears returned. Blood thumped in his head . . .

The German was upon him quickly, sobbing and screaming. He stabbed down at Bissen with his bayonet. Again and again . . . Bissen felt nothing. There was no pain. This must be what death feels like, he told himself. From somewhere he heard the muffled report of a rifle, and then another. The German stopped screaming and slumped to the ground. Bissen heard other voices, shouting in Punjabi. He felt a hand on his head. Heard Atar Khan's voice . . .

As Bissen Singh faded, his grandmother's voice rang loudest in his head and told him again about signs from God . . .

Part five

The Journey

Amritsar, 12 April 1919

Gurdial sat on an upturned wooden crate in the centre of the market, searching the faces of everyone who passed by. It had been nearly two months since Sohni's father had set him his task. Two months, and he was no nearer to discovering what the most valuable thing in India was. And if he didn't know what it was, how could he possibly know where to look? Now he was desperate – and fully aware that, on the eve of Vaisakhi, he was about to fail. There was no time left in which to do anything at all. All he could do was sit and stare at the crowds – a sad, solitary, pathetic failure.

All around him Amritsar seethed with tension and rage. The anti-British protestors were agitating for all they were worth and the British were responding in kind. But as the revolutionary tumult gathered pace, Gurdial could only sit and wonder. He had not seen Sohni for over two weeks, heeding her warnings about them being discovered, and he missed her. His chest felt hollow and his head frayed around the edges. He slept when he was hungry and ate when he felt tired and nothing seemed to fit into anything else.

And added to all that was an unshakeable feeling that something was wrong with the world. Deep inside, he sensed that there was a great evil at large, an evil so powerful that it would destroy all that it touched. But through the long, lonely hours when he should have been sleeping, he couldn't work out what that evil was or where it was coming from. It was just there, and it was coming closer.

Darshana watched the Chinaman as he swirled water around a wooden bowl in the early morning light. They had been in the garden watching the water go round for more than fifteen minutes and Darshana was becoming increasingly impatient.

'What do you see?' she asked again.

'Ssshhh!' replied the Chinaman. 'I must concentrate.'

'You've been saying that since you began!' spat Darshana.

The Chinaman grinned at her. 'There is much that you must learn about the dark arts. You cannot rush these things.'

He began to rotate the wooden bowl once more as Darshana looked at his long, bony fingers and claw-like, yellowing nails. This time, within seconds, he began to see something. 'It's coming,' he told her.

'Hurry up and tell me what you see!'

'Trees . . . I see trees and a clearing. A stream . . . They are both there.'

Darshana peered into the bowl and saw nothing but water. 'Sohni is there?' she asked.

'Yes,' he replied.

'And the boy?'

'He is there too – I can see him clearly . . .'

Darshana peered in again. 'What are they doing?'

The Chinaman cackled. 'They are doing what all animals do in the springtime. What you once did, long before you were married, with more than one man—'

'How dare you speak to me like that!' she shouted.

'I dare because I can,' he told her quietly. 'I dare because you asked me to help you with your troubles. If I can see into the souls of your husband and your step-daughter, then I can see into yours too.'

'I was young,' she said, attempting to excuse her past.

'It is of no consequence. You do not pay me to judge you.'

Darshana nodded. 'What else do you see?' she asked.

'I see butterflies coloured like the summer sky,' he continued, 'and toads sitting by the stream—'

Suddenly he cried out in horror and threw down the bowl. It hit the ground and smashed into three equal pieces.

'*What?*' demanded Darshana.

The Chinaman looked up at her, his face pale.

'What did you see?' she asked again.

227

He shook his head slowly. 'Danger,' he told her.

And then, without another word, he took a knife from his pocket and used it to cut two straight lines into his left forearm. They began to ooze blood immediately.

'What on earth are you doing, you crazy old dog?' asked Darshana.

'Protecting myself,' he replied. 'And you too . . . Trust me.'

Darshana shook her head and went back inside, ignoring the old fool. She had much to tell her husband.

Gulbaru was standing at the entrance to the kitchen sucking an orange.

'It is as you feared,' she told him.

'What are you on about, you stupid woman?'

She ignored him and thought about the day she would be free of him; a day that was fast approaching. 'Your daughter has been cavorting with the orphan,' she told him with a sneer. 'That which she should have held onto has been given away . . .'

The orange dropped from Gulbaru's hand and rolled away across the dusty floor. 'You are sure?' he said in a whisper.

'The Chinaman has just seen it with his own eyes,' she replied, without explaining how.

Gulbaru felt the rage as it began to swell inside him like a tornado. His eyes glazed over and his cheeks began to burn. He threw out a fist and knocked his wife sideways.

'*She dies!*' he yelled as Darshana steadied herself.

'I'll do it,' she offered, tasting the blood he had drawn with his punch. And then, she thought to herself, as you sleep I'll cut your throat from ear to ear.

Gulbaru looked at her and shrugged. 'And when you've finished with her, get rid of the Chinaman too.'

'But he is helping us,' she replied.

'He's helping his own pockets,' Gulbaru insisted. 'No more!'

'As you wish,' said Darshana.

But there was no way she was going to kill the Chinaman. He was her most loyal ally. She resolved instead to rid herself of Gulbaru and inherit his wealth.

'The bitch first,' she said out loud.

'Did you say something?' asked Gulbaru.

'No,' she told him. 'It was nothing.'

The marketplace was packed as usual, buzzing with people. The woman stood by the fruit stall with Mohni. She was watching Gurdial as he made his way along the street.

'Things are beginning to come to a head,' she warned the old man, 'and there will be danger.'

'I understand,' replied Mohni. 'What would you have me do?'

The woman took his hand. 'You have always been my father – even when I *had* a father. Now you must be a father to Sohni.'

Mohni shrugged. 'I am that already,' he said softly.

'They plot to kill her today,' she told him. 'It will be the witch and the Chinaman who come for her . . .'

The colour drained from Mohni's face and his hands grew cold. 'Are you certain?'

'I am *absolutely* certain,' the woman reiterated. 'They will do it this evening. I will be back before then but in the meantime you *must* protect her.'

'I shall,' replied Mohni. 'No harm will come to her – you have my word.'

'I knew I could trust you. But you are in grave danger too, and you must watch your own back as well as Sohni's.'

Mohni nodded. 'I promise.'

'I will not be long.'

'Don't worry,' said Mohni. 'Sohni is the only reason I have for being alive and I will honour the promise I made to her mother.'

A tear fell down the woman's left cheek – a tear so bittersweet that it would have tasted of ginger root and sugarcane juice. 'You have been good to Sohni and good to the memory of her mother. You are truly one in a million men.'

'No, no,' replied Mohni. 'I am just an old goat with too much time on his hands.'

'I will return as soon as I can,' the woman said. 'Now go – keep watch till I return . . .'

Mohni waved goodbye and turned to go back to the house. He had to find a way of getting Sohni out of there. When he looked round for the woman once more, she was gone. And further into the marketplace, the boy had vanished too.

The woman stood in front of Gurdial and waved a mango in his face. The fruit looked ripe; its skin orange and red with patches of yellow. Gurdial studied it before staring into the woman's face. How could she have a ripe mango at this time of year?

'It looks delicious, doesn't it?' she said to him.

Gurdial nodded. The woman had pale skin like that of a white woman. Her eyes were amber jewels and her smile made Gurdial long for his mother. She wore a white *salwaar kameez* and a black shawl over her head. There was an air about her – a sense of calm. Gurdial found himself smiling at her.

'Would you like me to cut you a slice?' she asked, returning his smile.

Gurdial nodded and watched as she produced a small knife from nowhere. His eyes searched her clothes for pockets but found none. The woman cut away a juicy wedge of mango flesh and held it out to him.

'Here,' she said. 'Take it.'

Gurdial took the slice. The sweet juice ran through his fingers and dripped to the ground. He held it up and bit into it. The tasty sap flooded into his mouth – so much nectar from such a small piece of fruit . . . He looked up at the woman and wiped his lips on his forearm. She mocked him gently with her smile.

231

'It is the best mango I have ever tasted,' he told her truthfully. 'Where did you get it?'

She shook her head. 'It's not about where it came from,' she said mysteriously. 'It's about how much you wanted it . . .'

Gurdial gave her a quizzical look. 'I don't understand . . .'

'Mango is your favourite fruit. You always long for the new season to begin, do you not?'

He nodded in amazement. How had she known?

'Perhaps then, if you were to say what the most precious thing in the whole of India is, for you it would be a mango?'

Gurdial got down from his perch with a start. 'But how do you—?' he began, only for the woman to interrupt him.

'There is *much* that I know,' she told him. 'And very much more that *you* do not, Gurdial.'

As the poor boy's eyes bulged from their sockets, the woman smiled, clicked her fingers and made the marketplace vanish.

Gurdial saw that he was standing on a beach. Not that he knew it was a beach, for he'd never seen one before and did not know what it was called. He looked out to sea and saw small boats moving towards the shore, their sails puffed out with the breeze. The sun rode high in the sky and its heat made Gurdial feel light-headed. He turned, sensing that the woman was close, and found her sitting on the sand with the mango still in her hands. For some reason, instead of feeling panic, Gurdial felt calm, as though some inner peace had descended upon him.

'Where are we?' he asked the woman.

'In Kerala. The fishermen are coming in with their catch.' She nodded towards the boats.

'But I don't understand. How have we managed to end up here?'

This time the woman did look up. She smiled warmly. 'Best not to ask questions that I can't answer,' she advised. 'Now take another look at the mango.'

She held it up to him as bright sunshine made the white sand grains glisten like millions of minute diamonds. Gurdial took the fruit and studied it.

'What do you see?' the woman asked.

'I see a mango – the same one that you cut a piece from in the market.'

'See how beautiful it is?'

Gurdial nodded.

'Take a bite,' she told him.

Without questioning her he did as he was told. He should have been scared or at least intrigued by what was happening, but the feeling of tranquillity that had come over him prevented it. The mango tasted even sweeter than it had done in the market and he took another bite.

'Does it still taste as good?' asked the woman.

Gurdial began to nod but stopped as soon as the

bitter, acrid taste hit his senses. The mango had become rotten. He spat it from his mouth and looked at what was left in his hands. He had bitten right down to the stone, a pitted, brown husk, and as he watched, tiny yellow maggots began to appear in the remaining flesh, wriggling and squirming. He dropped the mango and retched.

The woman laughed. 'Even the most beautiful thing in the world can hide ugliness within,' she told him.

Gurdial wiped his mouth before asking her what she meant.

'I'll let you decide that,' she replied.

She got to her feet and told him to follow her. She turned and walked quickly across the burning sand towards a fishing village about half a mile away.

'Where are we going?' asked Gurdial.

The woman didn't reply.

The village was quiet when they arrived. There were a few women around; women with skin as dark as ebony and almond-shaped eyes and rounded, hardened bodies. They wore brightly coloured clothes in yellow and red and orange, and their children played in the sand, most of them naked. Gurdial had never seen people with skin so dark and he found himself staring at them as he passed. He followed his companion through the village towards the small wooden jetty.

'Are these people Indian?' asked Gurdial when he caught up with her.

'Yes,' she replied. 'Much more so than you or I. Our ancestors are both Indian and something else. Some of them were pale-skinned, with yellow and brown hair and proud noses—'

Gurdial frowned. 'I have no idea what you are on about.'

'The reason why we do not look like these people is well documented,' she explained. 'The lands to the north were conquered long ago by white men who came from the west; Macedonians and Greeks who followed their king and took over vast areas of the world. Many of them stayed behind.'

'If that's true,' replied Gurdial, 'why have I never learned of it in school?'

The woman smiled. 'Education is a funny thing. Ask yourself who is teaching you, what they are schooling you in and what reason they have for doing so.'

Gurdial was still confused.

'The British want to teach *their* history,' she explained patiently, 'and the Indians want to teach *theirs*. No doubt it is the same the world over. But do you really learn the truth or simply another person's version of it?'

Gurdial shrugged. 'I learn what I am told to learn,' he admitted.

'Well, next time you learn something, ask yourself why you did so and in whose interest.'

Gurdial turned away from her and gazed out at the incoming boats. 'Why are we here?'

'You want to find the most valuable thing in India, don't you?'

'Who *are* you?' Gurdial asked. 'And how do you know of my search?'

The woman removed her shawl and used it to wipe the sweat from her forehead. Her hair fell down in long waves of silver and yellow. Gurdial gasped when he saw it. He studied her eyes and her mouth.

'It's not possible!' he gasped.

The woman smiled and put a finger to his lips to quieten him. '*Anything* is possible,' she told him. 'Now let us ask the fishermen what they think the most valuable thing is.'

The urge to speak was strong but the sense of calm that the woman had bestowed on Gurdial kept it at bay. He felt as though his thoughts and actions had been wrapped in silk and soaked with honey. Nothing worried him, nothing fazed him. He looked at the woman and grinned.

'You can ask me later,' she promised. 'You can ask me after we've spoken to the fishermen.'

The fishermen seemed to know her. Their skins were as dark as those of their women but much less smooth, as though someone had washed their faces in rock salt and left them to dry in the midday sun. Some of the men had broken and missing teeth; others were missing the odd finger or thumb. All were short, their bodies wiry, with tightly packed muscles. The first to speak had a thick welt of pink scar tissue arcing from his left shoulder down to his belly button. He seemed pleased to see the woman.

'It has been a long time,' he said.

'Very long,' she replied.

'And who is this you have with you?'

Gurdial knew in his bones that he should not have been able to understand what the man was saying. The language he was speaking was a million miles removed from the Punjabi he had been taught, yet it made perfect sense. How it could be so clear, Gurdial failed to understand, but once again he could not ask.

'He is a friend,' the woman explained. 'He searches for something of great value and wishes to ask you about it.'

The man looked into Gurdial's eyes. 'What is it you seek?' he asked.

Gurdial heard himself answer the question; the fishermen began to laugh. The man with the scar across his chest spoke up.

'The most valuable thing in India is whatever suits you,' he replied. 'For me it is the boat in which I go out to sea, for without it I would not be able to fish and I would starve.'

'And for me,' answered another voice, 'it is the nets I cast to catch the fish, for without them what *use* are the boats?'

Gurdial nodded as a third voice rang out.

'But what good are the boats *or* the nets without the

sea itself? The *sea* is the most precious thing in all existence.'

The woman took Gurdial's hand. She thanked the fishermen for their help and began to lead him away.

'Won't you stay for supper?' asked the first fisherman.

The woman shook her head. 'Not today,' she replied. 'We still have much to do.'

'Perhaps another day then . . .'

'Perhaps.'

'And I hope we have been of some assistance to you,' the man said to Gurdial.

But Gurdial had no time to answer, for as soon as he opened his mouth to reply, the woman clicked her fingers and they were gone.

He found himself sitting in a dense forest in the dark. He spun round to look for the woman but she wasn't there. But far from feeling panic, he was relaxed and accepting. The night was full of strange sounds – shrieks and whistles from animals and the buzzing of insects. From somewhere close by came a hissing sound. He peered through the blackness but failed to see anything. Not that he needed to. The hissing could only be a snake – from the sound of it, a very big one. Still he felt no fear.

The vegetation to his right rustled and the woman reappeared. She crouched by his side and pointed through the bushes. 'The snake catchers,' she said.

Gurdial followed her gaze, and suddenly the gloom

lifted. His eyes hit on a clearing. Several men stood in a circle; they were holding sticks – and three also had empty cloth sacks hanging at their sides. They were attacking something inside the circle but Gurdial could not see what it was. Suddenly one of them stepped aside and a second emerged from the centre, grinning as he held up the longest cobra that Gurdial had ever seen; he grasped it just behind its huge head with one hand, the other hanging onto its tail. Another man quickly opened a sack and the serpent was dropped inside, the neck of the bag twisted shut and tied with string.

'Where are we?' Gurdial asked the woman.

'It's not important,' she replied.

'And who are the people?'

'The wretched of the earth. Come on . . .'

She made herself known to the men, and once again they greeted her like a long-lost sister. Gurdial followed her into the clearing. The men looked him up and down before greeting him.

'The boy seeks riches,' explained the woman, 'to help him prise a daughter from the hands of her father.'

The man holding the captured snake smiled. 'We have no riches,' he replied, 'except for our hands and our brains.'

'And our ginger tea,' added a second man. 'You are most welcome to come and enjoy a cup with us, back at our *motta*.'

Without waiting for a reply they led the way back to their village.

The girl who brought Gurdial his tea was not much older than him. She smiled as she poured it out. Her skin was the colour of mango wood and just as smooth, and her hair jet-black and shiny. He took the cup and thanked her.

'A real beauty,' said the man sitting next to him on the dirt floor of a dung-brick single-storey dwelling.

The woman smiled at him and urged him to try the tea. 'It is very special,' she told him.

Gurdial took a sip and savoured the tingling sensation of the spicy drink in his mouth. 'It's delicious,' he agreed.

The man who had carried the snake back to the village coughed before speaking. 'So how can we help you, young man?'

Gurdial shrugged. 'I have been set a task,' he explained. 'I must find the most precious thing in all of India . . .'

A few of the others laughed at his reply.

'And you think that we can help you?' asked the first man.

'I don't even know how or why I am here,' he admitted.

'He's on a journey he cannot understand,' the woman told them. 'A test, perhaps, to ensure that he is worthy of the love that he craves.'

For the men this seemed to make perfect sense, and one or two of them nodded their understanding.

'I wanted you to show him that riches are not always what they seem,' she went on.

The first man scratched his chin. 'We are the Irula,' he told Gurdial. 'We are known as the snake catchers, and for many generations we have helped our fellow countrymen stay safe as they wander through the fields, the forests and the jungles. Our skill is in catching the deadliest serpents.'

Gurdial nodded. 'One of the teachers at my school told us about you.'

The man lit a thin cigarette and puffed on it before continuing. 'We have saved rich and poor with our skills,' he said. 'But we are still the lowest of the low in this society. Our standing is no greater than that of the snakes we catch. Indeed, we are deemed to be lower than those too.'

Gurdial was about to say something but the woman read his mind and told him to remain quiet.

'Many years ago,' continued the man, 'my great-grandfather was approached by a powerful rajah from Madras. The rajah had all the wealth in the world but still he was not satisfied. His wish was to be the wealthiest, most powerful ruler in India. He asked my great-grandfather to find for him a sacred thing.'

The other men sat in hushed reverence as he told his story. Outside, some of the womenfolk had also gathered.

'What did he ask for?' said Gurdial.

'The cobra is a sacred serpent,' the storyteller

explained. 'The king of these serpents is said to carry within it an element so precious that it bestows wealth beyond imagination on any human who can possess it. The rajah asked my ancestor to find for him this element. It is called a *nagmani*. My great-grandfather agreed, but only on the understanding that his tribe, then owned solely by the rajah, be allowed to leave his kingdom once it had been delivered. The rajah agreed readily and told him that he would also give him a chest full of gold pieces. But my great-grandfather refused. "Just give us our freedom," he said to the rajah, "for that is the most precious thing we could hope for." The rajah, although perplexed, said that he would.

'The tribe spent the next two months catching and trapping snakes. It is a dangerous job that we do, and after the two months had passed, several of my great-grandfather's tribe had died. But they had also managed to catch three King Cobras. My great-grandfather took all three into a hut and proceeded to find a *nagmani* for the rajah. For three days and three nights he stayed alone inside the hut, and on the morning of the fourth day he emerged holding a cloth sack. Inside it was the precious element. But no one else was allowed to look at it, on the orders of the rajah. My great-grandfather told his people to pack their belongings and make ready to leave. They did so at once.

'The *nagmani* was taken to the rajah at his palace. Upon seeing the sack, he fell to his knees and touched the feet of my great-grandfather, something unheard of

– for my people are said to be the lowest of all castes. The rajah told him that he would give him anything he desired. My great-grandfather asked for nothing save that the rajah only put his new power to use *one full day* after the tribe had left. The rajah agreed. My great-grandfather thanked him and hurried home.

'The tribe walked for more than twenty-four hours, through the night and well into the day, before daring to rest. And once they had rested, they walked for another full day. They repeated this for two weeks, until finally they came across a jungle clearing and sat down. It was here that they started to build their new *motta*.'

The man cleared his throat and asked Gurdial what he thought happened to the rajah.

'I don't know,' replied Gurdial. 'Part of me thinks that the rajah became as rich as he desired, and part of me thinks that it was a trick – for why would he be asked to wait until the tribe had left before opening the sack?'

The storyteller smiled. 'Your suspicion serves you well,' he said. 'But you still cannot see the point clearly enough. My great-grandfather did not trick the rajah. That old fool cheated himself. Remember, we, the Irula, are snake catchers without compare. Each day we catch snake after snake. But no matter how many snakes we catch, we remain at the bottom of the well and our people still die trying to save the lives of others. What does that tell you about the rajah and his request?'

Gurdial shrugged. 'I don't know.'

'*Look* at us!' demanded the man. 'We build houses

with dung and wear the clothes of our parents; our children cannot read or write and often we have no food to eat.'

Gurdial thought hard but it was no use.

'If the *nagmani* truly existed,' the storyteller said, exasperated, 'wouldn't the Irula be the most powerful and wealthy people on earth?'

The other men in the room burst into laughter. Outside the hut their women followed suit. Even Gurdial's guide smiled.

'The rajah was a fool,' said the storyteller. 'Don't let yourself become one too.'

Gurdial looked across at his guide. She smiled warmly and told him that they had to leave. 'Finish your tea,' she added.

'Are we going back?' he asked her.

She shook her head. 'Not yet. There is more that you need to see.'

This time they did not suddenly appear at their next destination. The woman took Gurdial to Madras by elephant, bullock-drawn cart and train. From there they caught another train, this one full to the rafters with people, and headed north towards Delhi. The journey took them across the vastness of India, and along the way they made frequent stops. Each time they broke their journey it was to speak to yet another group of people about Gurdial's quest. The woman told Gurdial to listen carefully.

'But I don't understand,' he complained. 'Why are you taking me to all these places?'

'To show you,' replied the woman. 'To help you to understand.'

'Understand what?'

'Life.'

They met rich people and poor people and asked them about the nature of wealth. They spoke to farmers and merchants; young people and old. At one stop the woman took Gurdial to meet a Buddhist monk who lived beside a Hindu holy man. Neither of them really helped Gurdial. Instead they spoke to him in riddles that he had neither the intellect nor the patience to unravel. He learned about money, wealth, fame and love but still found nothing concrete that he could take back for Sohni's father.

On their arrival in Delhi they made their way to a tenement where three children lived in a one-room shack with their desperate mother. The children were thin with hunger and their bones showed beneath their dusty skin. They spent much of their time playing in the open sewers, chasing away rats and stray dogs. And each evening their mother would feed them what little food she had bought and then sing them to sleep. The woman – at times barely able to stand – cared nothing for herself. Her only concern was the welfare of her children.

Gurdial's guide asked him what he thought of the children's mother.

'She is a saint,' he replied without hesitation. 'The love she gives to her children is so pure, so true.'

She nodded. 'Do you know how she earns her money?' she asked him.

'How can I? I don't know her.'

'She is a whore,' the woman revealed. 'Each day, as soon as the children have left the house, she begins her work. Each night, after they have gone to sleep, she continues. There is no limit to the number of men who have sought something from between her thighs. They abuse her and beat her, and when they are done, she begs them for more because she needs money to feed her brood. She is also very, very sick; within a year she will be dead.'

Gurdial's face fell.

'Is she still as pure and true in your eyes now?' asked the woman.

He shook his head. He didn't know what to say. The smiling, caring, selfless mother was also a cheap whore. It was yet another riddle to grapple with.

'Will Karma dictate that she returns in the next life in better circumstances?' added the woman. 'Or will they be worse?'

'I do not know,' admitted Gurdial. 'I just want to find the thing I need to win Sohni's hand.'

'The most precious thing in India is a mirage,' the woman told him. 'It is whatever a person wants it to be. For you it would be the hand of Sohni, would it not?'

Gurdial nodded. 'Yes,' he replied. 'There is nothing more precious to me.'

The woman clicked her fingers and transported them through time and space to a Punjabi village. Gurdial found himself looking in on a Sikh couple and their son. He felt a surge of energy flow through his body, from his toes to the top of his head. He felt warm, as though he had been wrapped in a woollen cocoon.

He turned to his guide. 'Where are we now?' he asked her.

'Look around, Gurdial,' the woman replied. 'See what you can see; feel what you can feel.'

The house was small – two rooms and a courtyard encircled by a low mud wall. All around the perimeter stood shrubs, their flowers resplendent in pinks and purples and blues. At the far end of the courtyard he saw two water buffalo tethered to a gnarled wooden post. The couple were doting on their baby son; the mother rubbing his pale skin with citrus-scented oil, the father telling him how big and strong he would grow. It was an idyllic scene; a dream of happiness that Gurdial had often had. That was when he realized where the woman had brought him. He was the baby and the couple were his parents.

'Would you give up Sohni?' asked his guide. 'Would you give her up for a mother's love?'

Tears burst uncontrollably from Gurdial's eyes as he fell to his knees. He turned to the woman, took hold of her legs and began to sob and wail. For a full ten minutes he continued until at last she pulled him to his feet and embraced him.

'I can never have them back,' he said to her. 'They are gone for ever . . .'

'Yes, they are,' replied the woman, soothing him. 'But their love will never die. And nor will your love for Sohni. That is why I brought you on this journey: to test you. You *know* why I have to make sure that Sohni is truly safe with you.'

Gurdial nodded.

'Life, Fate – they will do as they please,' she added. 'My task is to make sure that you look after the girl.'

'But I cannot have her,' Gurdial cried. 'It is too late and I have missed my deadline. I was due to meet Sohni's father on the day of Vaisakhi.'

'Oh yes . . . that,' replied the woman dismissively. 'Don't worry; we'll get you back there.'

Gurdial threw up his hands to the heavens. 'But we've been gone for too long! We've missed Vaisakhi.'

'You haven't missed a thing,' she told him. 'Take a look.'

Gurdial raised his head from her bosom and wiped his eyes. He saw the familiar sights of Amritsar's market and heard the voices he had known since he'd arrived in the city.

'You haven't even been gone,' the woman told him. 'This is the exact time at which we met, on exactly the same day. Vaisakhi is tomorrow and you can still meet your deadline.'

Gurdial looked down at the upturned wooden crate on which he'd been sitting. The woman was right: even though it felt as if they had been gone for an age, they were right back where they'd started.

'I know who you are,' he told the woman.

'Yes,' she replied. 'I'm aware of that. But do you know what to *do*?'

Gurdial nodded. He did not know how or when the realization had dawned, but it had. He knew clearly what his task would be. The woman bent down and pulled something from behind the crate that Gurdial had been using as a seat. She handed it to him.

'You know what to use this for?'

'Yes,' he replied. 'I know . . .'

The woman smiled.

'What will *you* do?' Gurdial asked her.

'I have an old foe to catch up with.' She smiled.

Gurdial scratched his head. 'How is it that I know everything about you and yet you never once told me?'

The woman laughed. 'The magic — when you can *feel* it, when it flows right *through* you, then you do not need to be told. You just *know* . . .'

'Thank you,' Gurdial whispered.

The woman hugged him and he closed his eyes to savour her touch. 'No need for thanks,' she told him. 'What else would a mother do?'

Gurdial felt her let go. He waited a moment and then opened his eyes. The woman was gone, and in her place, fluttering about his head, was a small blue butterfly.

Darshana Kaur sat in her kitchen and dreamed of ways in which she could take her husband's life. As she did so, she used a smooth grey stone to sharpen the edge of her dagger. It was a fine weapon with a gilt-edged handle set with blue and red stones – the same knife she'd used to kill her daughters in their infancy. How apt then that it should also take the life of Gulbaru's daughter, Sohni, followed by his own. She smiled to herself as she remembered their early years together, before her teeth began to rot and her body took on a foul stench.

For two years Gulbaru had been loyal to his wife, Heera, and eventually she gave birth to Sohni, as beautiful a child as Heera was a woman. But the birth had been complicated. After pulling Sohni from her mother's womb, the midwife watched helplessly as the womb followed in a torrent of blood. While Heera lay in that curdled mess, Gulbaru was busy drinking with his friends, prematurely celebrating the birth of his first son. Upon returning home he found that he had been too hasty and flew into a rage. Not only had he been given a daughter but his wife lay stricken and unable to bear any more children.

Gulbaru's rage did not subside for nearly five days, all of which he spent drinking and gambling and cavorting with whores. It was on the final night of this marathon of sin that he met Darshana. Very quickly they became inseparable, the cloth merchant and his beautiful lover. Darshana had shone back then; a true gem, rivalled in looks only by Heera herself. But whereas Heera's heart was pure, Darshana was a schemer, just like Gulbaru. Together they cooked up their plan to remove Heera, marry and live with the riches that Gulbaru would inherit after the death of his wife.

And so it was that Darshana found herself hiding in the very same kitchen in which she now sat. It was a cold night and the stars were bright in the sky. As she waited in the dark, Gulbaru ushered his unsuspecting wife towards her doom. As soon as Heera entered the kitchen, Darshana pounced, using a knife she'd been given by Gulbaru to slit her rival's throat. Once Heera was dead, the two of them cut her body into pieces, and little by little, over the next week or so, took them out and fed them to the stray dogs that roamed the streets.

The only piece of Heera that they saved was her left hand with her wedding band on it. Gulbaru took this with him to the police station to report his wife's murder. She had been set upon and kidnapped, he told the officers. A ransom demand had been made and money paid. But the kidnappers had killed her anyway and left her hand at the front door as proof. The police officers had believed every word, and soon the rest of Gulbaru's neighbours and friends accepted the story too. And throughout the whole drama, it had been Darshana who had comforted Gulbaru and helped look after his only child.

They had been so successful in fooling everyone that, six months after Heera's death, when Gulbaru married

Darshana, there were only one or two dissenting voices; one of them had been Mohni, the old servant whom no one listened to anyway. Darshana and Gulbaru began their new life together. And that was when Darshana's body began to fall apart.

'But I'll outlast them all,' she said to herself just as the Chinaman walked through the door.

'I'm ready, mistress,' he told her.

'Good,' she replied. 'The bitch should be back any-time now.'

Mohni hurried across when he saw Sohni arrive at the gate. He wanted to reach her before Darshana did but he wasn't quick enough. She ushered the girl into the living room with a sly smile.

'I've left some clothes in the kitchen,' she told her stepdaughter. 'And there are dishes too. Make sure everything is done before you go to bed.'

Sohni nodded and went wearily into the kitchen. When she saw the pile of clothes to be washed, she sighed. It would take her all night. She sat down and wondered where Gurdial was and what he was doing. Just then, there was a knock at the back door. Sohni got up and opened it, smiling when she saw Mohni stand-ing there.

'The old witch has given me a mountain of chores,' she said.

'Never mind!' whispered Mohni. 'We don't have time for that.'

'But why are you whispering?' asked Sohni.

The old man put a finger to his lips. 'S*shh!* We must get you away from here!'

Sohni was about to question him further when the door burst open and the Chinaman appeared, his eyes blazing. He wore his evil intent openly: in his left hand was a large knife. He shrieked at Sohni in his own language before lunging at her. He was quick but Sohni managed to dart through the door and slam it behind her.

'*This way!*' shouted Mohni. '*Hurry!*'

He pulled her along the garden path towards the back gate and the dark alleyway beyond. He threw it open, and urged Sohni on. But Darshana had already cut off their escape route. She stood in the alley, dagger at the ready. Before Mohni could blink, she slashed at his face, catching his cheekbone, tearing through the flesh. He screamed but still managed to push Darshana aside as Sohni came out into the alley, stumbling through the overgrown weeds. Mohni followed her and the Chinaman gave chase.

Sohni was quick-footed but Mohni's old body betrayed him: his right knee gave way and he fell to the ground. Sohni turned to see him looking up at his attackers. She watched in horror as the Chinaman let out a blood-curdling cry, dropped his knife and pounced on Mohni with his claws. The old man stood no chance: his attacker was like a tiger tearing apart its prey. Within seconds the Chinaman had dug out

Mohni's eyes, torn off his ears and bitten away his nose.

Sohni attempted to scream but found herself voiceless. The Chinaman looked up at her, a chunk of Mohni's flesh hanging from his blood-soaked mouth. He smiled for a moment and then stood up.

'Now,' Sohni heard her stepmother say, 'it's her turn. Leave her breathing. I want to cut out her heart while it still beats.'

Sohni, unable to utter a word, froze to the spot as the Chinaman pounced.

Gurdial watched as Gulbaru Singh's assistant left for the day. Moti-Lal did not notice him as he walked off down Amritsar's main street. Once Gurdial was sure that he would not return, he stepped into the doorway. Gulbaru was behind the counter, writing something in a ledger. Gurdial coughed to get his attention. Sohni's father looked up, and for a moment failed to recognize Gurdial. But then a sneer spread across his face.

'What do you want?' he spat out.

'I've come to claim my wife,' replied Gurdial calmly.

Gulbaru snorted. 'Would you like me to give you my money as well?' he asked sarcastically.

Gurdial edged forwards. In his right hand he carried a small white bag; inside it was a piece of blue stone. He held it up. 'I've brought you what you asked for,' he said.

Gulbaru looked from the bag to Gurdial and back again. 'What is *that*?' he asked. 'I *asked* you for the most precious thing in the whole of India—'

'What is more precious than this?'

'Are you *mad*? I don't even know what you have, so how can I know if it's precious?'

'The bag contains a stone,' explained Gurdial. 'And the stone will give you anything you want. Anything . . .'

Gulbaru's sneer disappeared. He looked at the bag once more and Gurdial saw the interest in his eyes.

'A *stone*?'

Gurdial nodded. 'Yes. A *nagmani* . . .'

The cloth merchant's eyes lit up. 'Never!'

Gurdial threw the bag to him and told him to see for himself. Gulbaru opened it quickly and pulled out the shiny blue element. He held it up to the light and examined it.

'You expect me to believe that this is the legendary *nagmani* itself?'

Gurdial smiled. 'So you've heard of it?'

'Prove it,' Gulbaru said, challenging him.

'I know what you want more than anything in the world,' Gurdial told him.

'How can you possibly know that?'

'The stone . . . It shows you things . . .'

Gulbaru looked unimpressed.

'All right . . .' continued Gurdial. 'Get a large bowl of water and put the stone in it.'

Gulbaru thought about it for a moment before replying. 'No,' he said. 'I am not the pauper here. *You* get me a bowl.'

255

'As you wish,' answered Gurdial.

He went into the back room and took a large wooden bowl down from a shelf. He carried it back to Gulbaru and asked where he could get some water. Gulbaru pointed to an earthenware jug sitting on the opposite side of the shop. Gurdial thanked him; he poured some water into the bowl, then set it down in front of Gulbaru.

'Now what do I do?' the man asked.

'Put the stone in the water,' replied Gurdial. 'Slowly . . .'

Gulbaru looked into Gurdial's eyes. 'If this is some sort of trick, I will kill you,' he threatened. 'And count yourself lucky that you are not already dead. I know that you have taken my daughter's honour.'

Gurdial felt himself blush but he kept his nerve. His journey had turned him from a boy into a man; now was the time to show it. 'Just put the stone in the water,' he demanded.

Gulbaru looked at the stone in his hands. What if the boy *was* telling the truth and it really *was* a *nagmani*? He studied it closely. He had no idea what a *nagmani* would look like; it was a myth, a legend. But what if it really was what the boy claimed? Finally, after a little more deliberation, he dropped the stone gently into the water. Then he stood back, expecting something to happen instantly. But the stone simply sat where it was, and the ripples it had created on the surface of the water subsided.

'Nothing is happening,' he remarked, his eyes glued to the bowl.

'That's because you haven't asked it to show you anything.'

Gulbaru said nothing.

'Let me,' suggested Gurdial. 'I know what it is you seek . . .' He moved closer and bent down so that his lips were only a few inches from the surface of the water. Gently, he blew on the stone and then whispered to it: 'Gulbaru Singh wishes for nothing more than a son. Show him . . .'

Gurdial prayed that the old woman's magic would work; that Gulbaru would see what he wanted to see. He remembered the story that the Irula had told him – the rajah who had fooled himself. But the water in the bowl remained calm and the stone did nothing.

'What is this?' Gulbaru demanded.

For a moment Gurdial lost his faith in the old woman. But then something remarkable happened. Gulbaru gasped as the water around the stone began to bubble, slowly at first, then faster. Suddenly the stone lit up, its heart burning with blue flames. The light within it pulsed on and off many times before a picture began to emerge at its core. The picture grew and grew until it became crystal clear. It showed a woman holding a baby boy and crying.

Gurdial looked at Sohni's father. 'Do you know that woman?' he asked.

Gulbaru stood in shock and awe. His bottom lip

began to tremble as he fought to hold back tears. He fell to his knees and sang praises to the Gurus, his eyes never leaving the picture before him. How did the boy know what he dreamed of? How could the stone show him such things? It had to be . . .

'Do you know who she is?' repeated Gurdial.

'Yes,' sobbed Gulbaru, his resistance gone. 'It is my wife . . .'

It took Gurdial ten minutes to calm Gulbaru. When he'd stopped sobbing, Gurdial told him the rest.

'Your wife is with child,' he revealed.

This time there was no hatred in the reply he received. Gulbaru needed no more proof that the boy had indeed brought him the mystical *nagmani*. What else could explain the miracle he had just witnessed? He nodded.

'But she plots to kill Sohni,' continued Gurdial.

He watched as Gulbaru's brain registered his words and his face betrayed his shock. For a moment Gurdial felt anxious that he wasn't with Sohni himself but then he calmed down. There was no way the woman would let anything happen to her; she had promised. And after all that he had seen, Gurdial had complete trust in her powers.

'The *nagmani* knows all,' he said. '*You* ordered Sohni's death. You killed your first wife. On your hands too are the stains of infanticide. From this truth you cannot hide. But be warned, Gulbaru Singh, if your wife succeeds in her evil act, your son will join his sisters in the next life before he has ever taken a single breath in this one—'

'*No!*' shouted Gulbaru.

Gurdial fixed him with a steely glare. 'Yes,' he replied. 'The only hope you have of saving your unborn son is to save your first born too.'

Sohni closed her eyes and let out a scream, bracing herself for the Chinaman's attack. But it never came. Instead she heard a powerful, commanding voice.

'*STOP!*'

Sohni opened her eyes to see the Chinaman frozen in mid pounce and Darshana rooted to the spot. Her brain failed to understand what she saw. She turned towards the source of the voice. It was a woman, short in stature but with a regal air. She wore a black shawl over her head and a white *salwaar kameez*. By her side sat a black dog with powerful jaws and a thick neck. Its eyes seemed to burn like fire. The woman held her left arm up in the air; she smiled at Sohni, and then let it drop. As soon as it returned to her side, the Chinaman fell to the ground. Sohni watched as he turned over and sprang to his feet again. Darshana remained frozen, as did the dog.

'You know who I am,' the woman said.

The Chinaman wiped away the remnants of blood from his lips before nodding slowly.

'Then you know what will happen. Your days of sorcery and murder are at an end.'

The Chinaman smiled. 'It must come to us all,' he said sadly. 'I have lived a long life – I look forward to the next.'

Before anyone could move, the woman clenched her right hand into a fist. As she did so, Sohni's attacker fell to his knees, his hands clutching at his throat; rasping sounds came from his mouth, his cheeks turned red and his eyes rolled back in his head. The woman held out her fist and clenched it tighter still. The Chinaman fell forward, his face now purple, the mouth set in a silent scream. His legs thrashed around for a few seconds, his eyes began to bleed, and then, with one long exhalation, he died. Only when he had stopped moving did the woman let her hand relax.

Sohni looked past the woman to the end of the alley. She thought about making a run for it, but her saviour stopped her.

'Take heart, child. I am here to protect you . . .'

The woman crouched down and took what was left of Mohni in her arms. His blood soaked into her white clothes. She whispered softly, 'You stupid old goat. I told you to be careful . . .'

Then she stood up and turned to Darshana, her eyes blazing. She snapped her fingers, let her shawl fall to the ground and began to laugh.

'Who are you?' asked Darshana, stepping closer to take a better look.

'You know who I am.'

The darkness receded just enough for Darshana to see the woman's face. '*No!*' she screamed.

The woman shrugged. 'Nothing is ever what it seems. Your actions taught me that . . .'

'B-b-but—'

'Don't worry' – the woman's voice was suddenly comforting – 'I only came back to bring you good news.'

Darshana's eyes widened as rivers of sweat ran down her body. 'What news?'

'You are with child, Darshana. A son.'

Darshana shook her head slowly. 'No,' she whispered. 'I cannot be with—'

The woman smiled at her. 'Feel your belly,' she said. 'Go on . . .'

Against her will Darshana found herself following the woman's instructions. She raised her right hand and pressed it to her belly. Within seconds something began to move inside her. It felt like tiny limbs pushing at her womb, aching to get out. She looked down at her stomach and then back up to the woman. 'You are a demon,' she managed to spit out. 'You cannot be . . .'

'Yet here I am, Darshana,' answered the woman. 'You should thank me: Gulbaru always wanted a son, and now that you have one, perhaps he won't kill you.'

The kicking and wriggling inside Darshana grew more intense. She clutched herself with both hands. There was yet more movement in her belly; it seemed to seethe and turn. She felt herself grow tense inside. Suddenly, she heard the sound of people running.

'*Stop!*' she heard Gulbaru cry.

She turned to see him racing down the alley with a young man. He came and threw his arms around her. 'You are pregnant!' he told her.

Darshana began to shake her head. She looked beyond her husband to the woman, who was still talking to her; Darshana could hear her voice clearly, but it was only in her head. She didn't see her move her lips once. Confusion and fear gripped her. The woman before her had died many years earlier, so how could she be standing there, talking? It had to be magic; dark magic that was much more powerful than the Chinaman's.

Gulbaru pulled her closer still, his stomach pushing her hands further against her belly. The wriggling within grew stronger.

'Good evening, Gulbaru,' said the woman.

Gulbaru's face turned white with shock at the sound of her voice.

'Like a maggot-ridden mango, evil eats at us from within,' she continued. 'Behold the fruit of your loins . . .'

He stepped away from his wife to face her. He tried in vain to speak. Darshana cried out in agony: her stomach had begun to twitch and spasm.

The woman smiled at Gulbaru. 'Don't you want to see what you have created?' she asked him.

Gulbaru spun round just in time to see his wife's belly erupt with blood; deep, dark, purple blood — and after the blood, small black rats — thousands and thousands of them — dropped to the floor, surging over his feet until they had disappeared into the night. Darshana's body slumped wearily to the ground. Her single thick black brow twitched once, and then she was gone.

The woman looked at Gurdial. He had taken Sohni by the shoulder and stood in a protective manner, shielding her from the terrible sight.

'Take Sohni into the house,' she ordered. 'I have something to finish here . . .'

Gurdial nodded and led Sohni back into the garden. He moved quickly, not once turning his head to see what was happening in the alley. He had already seen enough.

The woman waited until they were gone before turning to Gulbaru. 'You have no time left,' she told him.

'But we *killed* you,' he whispered in reply, his voice breaking.

'Yes, you did,' replied Heera. 'But Love stopped me from dying.'

Suddenly Gulbaru's face changed. His eyes clouded with rage, his temples pulsed with anger and his heart pounded in his chest. He drew a knife from his waistband.

'Well, this time not even the Gurus themselves will save you,' he spat.

He leaped towards her, ready to cut her into tiny pieces for the second time, but he found himself slashing at thin air, then lost his balance and landed in a pool of blood and gore. He turned round to find her standing above him, holding back the snarling and salivating dog. It looked into his eyes for a moment, then drew back its lips to reveal a fearsome set of fangs. Heera let it go and stood back. The dog howled into the darkness of the night and a hundred mangy, hungry strays emerged from the shadows.

'Feast well,' whispered Heera before heading back to the house.

The dogs waited a moment before pouncing.

'Who *are* you?' asked Sohni, her eyes full of fear, her hands trembling.

Heera smiled. She looked across to Gurdial, who nodded. It was time. 'I am your mother,' she revealed.

Sohni shook her head vigorously. 'No!' she cried out. '*No!*'

'Yes,' replied Heera.

Sohni looked at Gurdial, searching his face for the truth.

'It's true,' he told her.

She looked back at her mother. 'How can you be *alive?*'

Heera shrugged. 'I'm *not* alive. I'm a ghost.'

Gurdial caught Sohni before she fell to the floor. He helped her into a chair, then took hold of her hands and whispered soothing words, calming her down.

'I came back to help *you*,' continued Heera. 'To watch out for you and protect you from your father.'

A sudden gust of wind threw open the kitchen door

and Sohni turned in fear, half-expecting to see her father at the threshold.

'He won't be coming back,' Heera told her daughter. 'You are safe now.'

Sohni nodded. 'I don't believe in ghosts,' she said.

'Well, you should, my daughter. Amritsar is full of ghosts, and there will be many more to come.'

'But—'

'Both of you know at least one other like me, I can guarantee it,' Heera insisted.

'How long have you been . . . ?' Sohni began, only to realize that she didn't know how to finish her sentence. What was she supposed to say to a woman she knew to be dead but was standing in front of her, looking alive and well?

'Many years,' Heera told her. 'Mohni told me everything about you.'

'He knew?'

Heera nodded, looking down at her blood-soaked clothing for a few seconds and remembering the old man's smile. A smile she hoped to see again very soon.

Gurdial cleared his throat to speak. He let go of Sohni's hands and crouched beside her, running a hand through her hair.

'Where do we go from here?' he asked Heera.

'Wherever you wish, my son,' she replied. 'Tomorrow is Vaisakhi – the dawning of a new life for both of you.'

'But what about you?' Sohni asked. 'I don't know anything about you . . .'

Heera smiled. 'I will be around.'

'But what if I need you? What if I don't want you to go?'

Heera sighed. 'I can't stay for ever, *beteh*,' she told her daughter. 'As much as it breaks my heart, one day I will have to leave. But until then, just stand in the garden and call out my name and I'll come.'

'There are so many things I want to ask you.'

'And you will be able to ask me them all,' replied Heera.

Gurdial frowned. 'What about Gulbaru and Darshana?' he asked. 'People will want to know where they have gone.'

A dark cloud seemed to pass over Heera's face. She waited a moment before replying. 'Tomorrow there will be a gathering at Jallianwalla Bagh,' she told him. 'By the time the sun has set you will know how to explain their absence . . .'

Gurdial wondered what she meant and Heera saw the question in his eyes.

'You must trust me,' she ordered. 'Whatever you do, do *not* go to the Bagh, I beg you.'

'Why?' asked Sohni.

'I cannot tell you. Life and Fate must play themselves out. There is so much I wish I could say but I can't. Just heed my words, and when things become what they must become, *remember* that I couldn't tell you.'

Gurdial, who had become used to Heera's cryptic words, nodded his acceptance, as did Sohni.

'I must go,' Heera told them. 'But if you need me, just call to me and I'll come.'

'As you wish,' Gurdial replied.

'Oh,' added Heera. 'I nearly forgot . . .' She pulled out an envelope and handed it to Gurdial. He studied it carefully. It was addressed to Bissen Singh.

'What is this?' he asked, shocked. 'And how do you know of my friend?'

Heera smiled. 'You should know me by now, my son,' she joked. 'The letter is a gift for your friend. Make sure he gets it tomorrow – but do not tell him where it came from. The poor soul has been searching for happiness for so long that he deserves to find it before . . .'

'Before what?' Gurdial asked.

'Nothing.'

Gurdial nodded. 'A gift from whom?'

'It is from the ghosts. Please make sure he gets it – and look after my daughter.'

'I will,' he promised.

Heera walked over to Sohni and took her hand. 'You grew up to be such a beautiful woman,' she told her. 'I wish I could have told you sooner.'

Sohni raised her face, her eyes filled with tears. 'Don't go,' she pleaded.

'I must. But I'll return soon – I promise.'

With that she let go of her daughter and left the house without looking back. Behind her the scent of mangoes and cream lingered long into the night.

Part Six

The Soldier and the Nurse

Brighton Pavilion, 12 September 1915

Bissen Singh was woken by the sound of a young soldier crying out for his mother. He sat up in bed, forgetting for a few moments the injury that had nearly destroyed his right leg. But immediately the intense pain returned. He bit down on his tongue, closed his eyes and let the convulsion pass. As soon as he could bear it, he opened his eyes again and looked around. The hospital ward was in darkness, save for a light at the far end. He gazed up at the intricately carved ceiling and wondered for the umpteenth time how the British could use such a beautiful building as a hospital. Was the country he had fought for so rich that such wondrous rooms could be turned into wards for the sick and the dying?

The soldier whose cries had woken Bissen now sobbed quietly. He was three beds away. Bissen's own bed was at the end, as far from the doorway as it was possible to be. Not that Bissen minded; he couldn't walk unaided yet and wasn't likely to want to take a stroll in the gardens. And besides, his bed was right next to a large window with a view of the east lawns of the pavilion. He could watch the Muslim soldiers praying, and beyond them the steady streams of curious English people come to have a look at the darkies.

Bissen had been in the hospital for many weeks: he had arrived from the battlefields around Neuve Chapelle in a morphine-induced fog with most of his right buttock blown away and his leg in a bloody, twisted mess. Yet very quickly he'd realized just how lucky he had been. Although the grenade had taken off chunks of his flesh, it hadn't done enough to destroy his leg entirely. As the Hindu doctor had told him, he was very, very fortunate.

'Last week I had to remove both the legs of one soldier, *bhai*,' he'd said. 'The poor bastard cried and cried all night. The next day his friend gave him a revolver with which to blow his brains out.'

Small beads of sweat appeared on Bissen's brow as he wondered how many more of his fellow Indians had lost limbs. He knew of three on his ward alone. Then there were the blinded and those who'd lost all reason and fallen into madness. One man who had been in the bed next to Bissen's for two weeks and seemed fine had suddenly started smearing himself with his own dirt and babbling like a baboon. He had not returned. Bissen's thoughts dragged him back to France and to the moments before the explosion. He thought about the devastated village, empty of civilians, and the scratching sound he'd dismissed as a cat. And then, for some reason he couldn't fathom, the image of the church settled in his mind. It had been utterly destroyed, yet in the middle, like a beacon, the tall wooden cross had remained untouched. He remembered thinking of it as a sign of God and smiled to himself.

A low moan broke into his thoughts. It was coming from the next bed: its latest occupant was a Muslim called Gauhar Ali.

Bissen called out to him, 'Do you need something, *bhai*?'

Gauhar coughed before speaking. 'I'm fine,' he replied. 'It's the pain . . .'

Bissen told him to try and sleep. He understood very well the dull, throbbing, insistent agony; he'd been through it himself and it hadn't got any better. It just became easier to deal with. 'Tell the doctor in the morning,' he advised. 'He'll increase your morphine dose.'

Gauhar thanked him and fell silent. Bissen listened to his breathing for a few minutes before settling down and closing his own eyes.

The following morning Bissen watched Dr Chopra making his rounds. He lay still, having finished his breakfast of bread, jam and tea. The doctor was a portly man with a balding head and a large, jowly chin covered in shaving cuts. His eyes were huge and he reminded Bissen of an owl. Accompanying him were two nurses and an English officer called Peters, who was in charge of the patients. As Bissen was the last patient on the round, he picked up a three-day-old copy of *The Times*, given to him by Dr Chopra, and tried to make sense of it. His spoken English had been passable when he'd joined up and was now better. But reading the print and making sense of it was still a struggle.

The first story to capture his attention concerned a

thirteen-year-old boy who had attempted to kill himself. Wilfrid Sidney Thomas had jumped into a river in Maidenhead, only to be rescued by a passing Belgian. Bissen had trouble making out the Belgian's name but read on anyway. From what he could understand, the boy had written to the police beforehand, blaming his mother. He was now being charged with attempted suicide. The next story was about a naval deserter who had jumped from a train near a town called Nuneaton; above that, an African donkey was being advertised for sale. As his thoughts wandered from the boy to the donkey and then on to the deserter, Bissen wondered about the country he found himself in. The boy was being charged and would probably face jail; the deserter, if caught, would no doubt face the firing squad. Was this really the country he had almost given his life for? And what exactly was an African donkey doing in England?

Dr Chopra's cough brought Bissen out of his daydream.

'And how are you today?' the doctor asked in his thick accent.

'Getting along,' replied Bissen, in his even thicker accent.

Dr Chopra turned to the nurses. 'Check the wounds and change his dressing,' he said.

Bissen looked at the nurses, both of them English. One of them was tall, only a couple of inches shorter that himself, with blonde hair and strong, chiselled features. The other was shorter, with wide hips and brown hair. They seemed surprisingly young. Bissen had only ever seen older women in such roles, both here and in India. As Dr Chopra spoke to Captain Peters, both nurses paid close attention, neither of them looking at Bissen. But as soon as the doctor had finished speaking, the shorter woman looked up. Something sent Bissen's heart into a pounding frenzy. He had seen many nurses since arriving at the hospital but none of them had charmed him. This one, however – she shone out. He looked away and then back again, unable to help himself. Her eyes were bright blue, shimmering like the waters that surrounded the Golden Temple in Amritsar on a sunny day. Her lips were full; her face perfectly symmetrical, almost feline.

'Hello,' she said.

Bissen coughed and went red. He waited a moment and cleared his throat. 'Hello,' he replied.

'And what's your name?' asked the nurse as her companions walked off.

'Bissen Singh, madam,' Bissen said, a bit too quickly.

The nurse giggled.

'Something is funny?' asked Bissen.

'It's just that you called me madam. I'm just a miss.'

Bissen apologized.

'No need to say sorry,' she told him. 'Now, let's take a look at those dressings . . .'

She asked Bissen to turn carefully onto his left side. The right leg of Bissen's pyjama bottoms was slit from his hip to his ankle, which allowed the medical staff to treat his wounds without undressing him.

'They look like they should have been changed days ago,' she said. 'Let's hope there's no infection.'

She pulled a pair of scissors from the pocket of her dress

and began to cut away the bandages. Bissen winced as she did so.

'I'm sorry,' she said, stopping immediately, her face full of concern.

'Its not your fault,' Bissen reassured her. 'Just the pain . . .'

The nurse smiled before continuing more carefully. 'There we are,' she said once she was done.

Bissen closed his eyes as she used her delicate fingers to examine the welts of traumatized flesh at the top of his right leg. At one point a stabbing sensation made the leg twitch.

'That looks very tender,' she told him. 'I think I'm going to have to clean out the wound – there might be some infection.'

She explained that she was going to get Dr Chopra to take a second look. 'Don't go anywhere,' she joked.

Bissen felt himself smile. 'What your name?' he asked her without looking up.

'Lillian,' she replied. 'Now lie still until I get back . . .'

That night Bissen dreamed of rotting onions and explosions. One minute he found himself standing in Amritsar; the next he was talking to his fallen friend, Jiwan Singh, in a trench in France. Jiwan smoked a cigarette while blood poured from a bullet wound in his forehead. The blood was soaking the cigarette and running through his fingers but Jiwan seemed unconcerned and continued to smoke. Bissen tried to stop him, but then he was gone, replaced by a young German soldier whose head Bissen had cracked open with the butt of his rifle. The German spoke to him in some unintelligible language. Then he too disappeared and Bissen was back in

Amritsar, sitting in the marketplace, watching the traders. A strange presence loomed behind him; long nails stroked the back of his neck. He turned to see a woman standing there, smiling down at him maternally. It was his mother. He reached out so that she might take his hand, but she disappeared, to be replaced by Lillian. When he eventually woke up, sweating and shivering, in the deepest part of night, it was the nurse's face that remained.

14 September 1915

Lillian returned two days later when Bissen was taking a nap. She made her rounds with the doctor, then set about her tasks for the day. Once again Bissen was the last soldier she came to. He was sound asleep, his chest rising and falling in time with his breath. She watched him for a while, fascinated by his turban, the thickness of his beard and the way his proud nose curved like an eagle's beak. His skin was as light as hers and his forearms covered with black hair. Beads of sweat lined his brow and his lips moved occasionally, as though he was having a conversation in his dreams. His hands lay by his sides, thick-fingered and strong-looking – the hands of a man who had worked hard all his life. She wondered what he had done before becoming a soldier; most of the other patients were the sons of farmers. Was Bissen also a farmer, or was there something more exotic about him? Maybe he was a prince. She smiled and wondered what her friends would think about the way she was sizing up an Indian man.

Eventually she woke him up and told him that she needed to check on his wounds once more. Bissen sat up gingerly and asked her how long she'd been at his side.

'A little while,' Lillian admitted.

Bissen nodded and looked away. The young nurse seemed flustered. How long had she been there? For a fleeting moment he thought she must have been watching him sleep, but then he realized how silly that was. Why would she watch him? When he turned to look at her again, she was smiling at him.

'You make fun of me?' he asked.

'No, no,' replied Lillian. 'I was just wondering about your beard – it's very thick—' Instantly she felt herself blush. 'I'm sorry, I didn't mean to—' she began.

'It's all right,' Bissen reassured her. 'I have never shaved. My religion forbids it.'

She nodded, relieved that he didn't seem offended. 'You aren't one of the Mussulmen,' she said matter-of-factly. 'I see them praying out on the east lawn.'

Bissen shook his head. 'I am Sikh,' he told her. 'Not like the Muslim . . .'

'Are you from India?'

'Yes – from the Punjab.'

'Punjab,' repeated Lillian. 'Is that very beautiful?'

Bissen nodded. 'Beautiful like rose,' he said.

Lillian smiled again. 'I've always wanted to visit far-off countries. My uncle lived in India for a while . . . He said it was the most amazing place he'd ever been to.'

'Was he a soldier?' asked Bissen.

Lillian shook her head. 'A surgeon,' she replied. 'He helped with the wounded and set up a clinic for the poor in Delhi.'

'Many English in my country,' said Bissen.

'And now,' added Lillian with a big smile, 'many Indians in England.'

'I want to see more of England,' Bissen told her.

'And perhaps you shall. Once this wound is healed we'll get you outside and walking around – you'll see.'

'Hoping so. I see roses from the window. I would like to smell them . . .'

'Do you like roses then?' asked Lillian, wondering why she was blushing.

'Very much,' said Bissen. 'They are like a gift from the *Waheguru.*'

Lillian frowned. 'I don't understand,' she said.

'*Waheguru* mean God,' he explained. 'And God send you—'

She broke into a giggle.

'It is true. You are helping me and I like . . .'

Lillian blushed again before telling Bissen to turn onto his left side. 'Let's get those wounds seen to,' she told him, changing the subject.

Later that afternoon one of the other nurses brought Bissen another copy of *The Times*. This one was more recent, printed the day before, and Bissen set about trying to read the stories. As he flicked through the pages, his eyes lit upon a list of fallen soldiers. He read through the names to see if there were any Indian Corps mentioned but there were none. On the next page he read about the death of one Herbert Thomas Steward at the age of seventy-six. Mr Steward was described as a famous authority on rowing but Bissen could not work out what that meant. Was the man adept at arguing or making a nuisance? Or was this another of those English words with more than a single meaning? He decided that he would ask Lillian when he saw her.

The next story he read concerned a soldier who had been shot and killed accidentally on a street in Glasgow. The poor man, Private Simon Lawson, had caught a bullet in the back; the guilty party was another soldier who had been alighting from a tram when his rifle accidentally went off. Bissen put down the newspaper and thought of all the men he had seen killed on the battlefield. At least they had died during a war; Private Lawson was on home leave and had probably been looking forward to seeing his family. What an awful twist of fate, to die in such a manner after surviving the horrors of the Western Front.

This story sent Bissen into a depression from which he didn't recover for the rest of the day. By the time his evening meal arrived, he wanted nothing more than to sleep. The pain was back and Bissen found himself longing for a dose of morphine strong enough to send him to sleep. But instead he let the pain wash over him until he could close his eyes. He lay like this for an hour or so until an ear-splitting scream rang out through the ward.

Bissen sat upright, a stabbing sensation coursing its way up and down his body. He looked towards the source of the scream and saw a short, shaven-headed man convulsing in his bed. His arms and legs seemed to have taken on a life of their own and blood poured from his mouth. Bissen moved his legs across, ready to try and get out of bed. Gingerly, he placed his left foot on the floor, taking his weight. Then he tried to do the same with his right, but the agony was too much to bear. It felt as though his right leg was on fire. He stopped and called out for help instead.

As the rest of the patients began to wake up, two guards ran to the man's bed and held him down, waiting for Dr Chopra, who arrived within seconds, holding a syringe with a long, thick needle and enough morphine suspension to pacify a water buffalo. Quickly he plunged it into the man, pressing down until the syringe emptied. The man began to froth at the mouth, little pink bubbles emerging from his lips. Then he lay still. The patients closest to the drama began to whisper to each other. Bissen watched as Dr Chopra checked the man for a pulse and then shook his head sadly.

'It's no use,' he said. 'He is gone.'

Later, when the dead man had been taken away and silence had returned to the ward, Bissen found himself thinking of Neuve Chapelle once more. He recalled the briefing about Aubers Ridge and the importance placed on its capture by the officers. He remembered the shock on the faces of his fellow soldiers when they'd found out that the ridge was little more than a mound of earth. And he winced as he saw again the first wave of German gunfire cut down those who had gone over the top. But at least death had been quick. The poor man who had died earlier that night had suffered weeks of agony in the hope of being cured, and yet had died anyway. Surely a bullet to the head would have been better? If Fate had brought Bissen to the hospital, only to kill him at some later stage, he realized that he would rather have died with his comrades during the battle. But then again, Fate did as she pleased and all men were subject to her vagaries.

17 September 1915

The man in the next bed, Gauhar Ali, told Bissen that the dead were taken to two places.

'My fellow Muslims are buried somewhere,' he said in Punjabi, 'although I don't know where.'

'And the rest?' asked Bissen.

'To a place they call Patcham – that is where the cremations are carried out.'

Bissen nodded. 'Where were you fighting when you got injured?' he asked Gauhar.

'In France somewhere,' he replied. 'I don't know exactly where because I do not understand English very well.'

'I was at Neuve Chapelle,' Bissen told him.

The Muslim nodded. 'I know – one of my brothers told me. He was at the same battle. Your English is very good, isn't it?'

Bissen nodded. 'I learned it back in Amritsar.'

'I saw you talking to the young nurse. She is very pretty.'

Bissen shrugged. 'Is she?'

'Be careful, *bhai* – the *Engrezi* will not want you messing with their women,' warned Gauhar.

'But I am doing no such thing. We just talk about things, nothing more.'

'As you wish, *bhai* . . .'

Bissen could see in the man's face that he didn't believe him but he let it lie. There was no point in arguing – there was nothing to argue about. Bissen couldn't even walk, let alone chase after some white woman. At least that's what he told himself. Had he been able to get out of bed it might have been a different story. There was something about Lillian – a warmth and tenderness – that he desired. And each time he looked into her eyes, something in his heart moved. He told himself that it was simply because he was bed-ridden and had too much time on his hands, but that was a lie. There was much more to it. Bissen knew that it was dangerous too: the white men would not allow such a thing. In any case, who was to say that Lillian herself felt the same way? Why would a beautiful white girl be interested in a crippled Indian soldier?

Lillian arrived in the ward after lunch and Bissen waited patiently for her to reach him. When she did, he glanced across at Gauhar Ali, who was smiling mischievously. Bissen turned away.

'Hello!' said Lillian in her bright, melodic voice. 'How are you feeling today?'

Bissen shrugged. 'Pain was bad last night,' he told her. 'I didn't much sleep.'

Lillian placed one of her hands on his. 'Perhaps we should

increase your dosage,' she said. 'Let me get the wound cleaned out and we'll see.'

Bissen remembered the article he'd read about rowing. 'What is the meaning of rowing?' he asked her.

'Rowing?' she repeated.

'Yes.'

She smiled.

'I read in newspaper and not understand,' explained Bissen.

'I'm not surprised,' replied Lillian. 'On the one hand, if you pronounce it *rowing*, it means to have an argument or disagreement. But if you pronounce it *rowing*, it means propelling a boat down a river or across a lake.'

'Propelling?'

'Moving. They use oars – long wooden paddles – to push through the water and move the boat.'

'I see. So that story about boat rowing, not argument.'

Lillian shrugged. 'I didn't see the story,' she told him. 'But I'd guess that you're right.'

Bissen smiled.

'What's so funny?' she asked.

'You speak very fast,' said Bissen. 'Like my sister.'

'You have a sister?'

Bissen nodded. 'One sister, two brother, back in Punjab. You?'

Lillian shook her head as she turned him onto his left side. 'I am an only child,' she told him. 'And my parents passed away when I was young. My uncle brought me up.'

'I sorry,' replied Bissen.

'No need for that. You weren't to know. It must be lovely to come from such a large family.'

Bissen laughed.

'What is it this time?' she asked.

'Most Indian have big family,' he told her. 'My father have six brother and five sister; all my uncle live next to us in our village.'

'Good heavens! I bet Christmas at your house is lovely.'

'No,' said Bissen. 'I know of Christmas but we Sikh. Not celebrate the Christmas.'

Lillian stopped what she was doing and smiled. 'I love Christmas,' she told him. 'And you've never had one? Of course you haven't – how silly of me!'

'No. Not silly . . .'

'Well, that'll change soon enough. I don't think you'll be leaving until next year at the earliest, which means you'll see England at its best over the festive season.'

'I very much like that,' said Bissen.

'Me too,' said Lillian. 'Now, let me get this done and then I have a treat for you.'

Bissen's face lit up. 'A treat?'

'Yes . . . Doctor Chopra and the other medics want you to get some fresh air. I'm taking you outside.'

'But I cannot walk,' Bissen reminded her.

'If Mohammed won't go to the mountain . . .' joked Lillian.

'What?'

'Never mind,' she said. 'All will be revealed.'

Ten minutes later she returned with a wooden chair on

wheels and two Indian hospital guards. She had placed two cushions on the seat.

'Your transport has arrived!' she said.

'Oh.' Bissen didn't know what else to say.

He had seen many of the other men in such chairs but had never sat in one himself and he felt excited. It had been a long time since he'd been in the open air and the thought of it made him giddy.

'Can you please help Mr Singh into the wheelchair?' Lillian asked the guards.

'It is your lucky day today,' one of them said to Bissen in Punjabi.

'*Bhai*, with my injury, every day is a lucky day,' replied Bissen as they helped him out of bed.

Progress was slow and painful; the extra painkillers that Lillian had given him made Bissen feel weak. But eventually, with the help of the guards, he was sitting comfortably in the chair, although there remained a dull ache in what was left of his right buttock. Once she was sure he was ready, Lillian thanked the guards and began to wheel Bissen out of the ward. As they passed the other patients, Bissen said a few greetings. Most were returned in kind but one or two of the men scowled at him. Bissen guessed they were too caught up in their own worries to care about him. It was only natural, he told himself; he knew they meant no harm. Once he was out of the ward, he soon forgot them.

'The light will feel bright,' Lillian warned him. 'Just let your eyes get used to it for a while . . .'

She wheeled him past yet more guards, then through the ornate lobby and out into the gardens. She was right –

the light was blinding, but any discomfort soon passed and Bissen looked out on a lovely, sunny late summer's day.

'Where would you like to go?' Lillian asked.

'I do not mind,' replied Bissen. 'It is so very good of you to do this for me.'

'You're welcome. You looked so pale indoors. The fresh air has already brought colour to your cheeks.'

Bissen inhaled deeply. 'It is wonderful,' he said.

'Let's go round the outside of the pavilion,' suggested Lillian. 'That way you can see where you've been staying. And you can see how beautiful it is too.'

Bissen nodded. 'I would like that.'

'And then I'll take you out into the public gardens and maybe even find you a view of the sea.'

'Yes, please.'

For the next hour or so Lillian wheeled Bissen around until her arms began to ache. When finally she needed to rest, she stopped next to a large rose bush and plucked one of the flowers for him. Bissen immediately held it to his nostrils. It had delicately scented pink petals.

'Isn't it wonderful?' asked Lillian.

'It is,' said Bissen. 'I have loved roses since I was a child.'

'Me too,' replied Lillian. 'Just think: we are about the same age, we grew up at different ends of the earth, yet both of us grew to love roses.'

Bissen nodded at her, then smiled, handing her the flower.

'For me?' she asked, her face beaming.

'I like this you do for me,' he said.

'Well, it's all part of the service, sir. The doctor feels you need more fresh air.'

Bissen wondered whether to say what was on his mind. He didn't want to offend the nurse or upset her in any way. Maybe he was just being silly but he had to ask.

'Will you be bringing me again?'

Lillian looked into his pale-grey eyes and nodded. 'I'd love to,' she replied.

'Me too.' He grinned from ear to ear.

Lillian blushed and looked away. She wondered again what her friends would say. There was something so sweet, so wonderful about Bissen. And he was truly handsome, just like she'd always imagined a foreigner. She recalled her Uncle Bertie telling her of the Sikhs he'd met while in India. Proud, fierce and utterly loyal; true warriors, and so charming, her uncle had said, they'd give the French a run for their money.

'You'd fall at their feet, Lillian,' he'd joked.

And he had been right. Here she was, her heart all a-flutter. She decided to go and see her uncle, and tell him, perhaps, of her Sikh soldier.

20 September 1915

The night air carried a chill that cut through to the bone. As Lillian walked along the promenade, every now and then she looked out at the darkness over the sea. The sky was almost black, but in places the clouds lightened to shades of navy and marine blue with touches of steel grey. Lillian shivered, wishing that she had worn a warmer coat. Luckily she was only five minutes away from the small subterranean bar where she'd arranged to meet her uncle.

Uncle Bertie stood as she approached his table, smiling warmly. He was a tall, distinguished-looking man with a full head of grey hair combed back with brilliantine cream. His pale blue eyes were mischievous and his nose proud. Despite his age, he carried not a single ounce of fat and regularly attracted the attention of women young enough to be his granddaughters. Not that Uncle Bertie noticed, Lillian thought to herself as she sat down.

'Good evening, darling Lillian,' Bertie said, his eyes sparkling. 'You look absolutely radiant.'

Lillian shook her head. 'I look dreadful,' she replied, 'but you're very sweet.'

Bertie sat down and introduced his dinner companion, Max, even though Lillian had known him for years.

'I do believe my dear uncle is beginning to show his age,' Lillian joked to Max.

'Aren't we all?' said Max. 'Just the other day, I closed my eyes after a rather splendid lunch and did not wake up until well after supper.'

'Perhaps the wine played some part...?' suggested Bertie.

The two men smiled at each other.

'We haven't ordered yet,' Bertie told Lillian. 'Would you like to take supper with us?'

'That would be lovely.'

Max stood up and excused himself. He wore an elegant grey three-piece suit with a crisp white shirt. His dark hair and moustache were immaculate, but his face was flushed and his brown eyes glazed.

'It seems to me that Max has been at the wine again,' said Lillian as she watched him walk away.

'He had a meeting in London,' Bertie told her. 'And then he came down to see me. We've been tasting reds.'

'I see...'

Bertie summoned a waiter to pour Lillian a glass of wine, then asked her what was on her mind.

'Oh, nothing much,' she said.

'Come, come, my dear, I know you too well.'

Lillian smiled. 'When you lived in India—'

'India?'

292

'I was wondering about it . . .'

'*Wondering?*'

'Yes. I was talking to someone the other day, a friend, and I happened to mention your time in Delhi and I started to wonder what it was like.'

Bertie took a sip from his wine glass. 'It was wonderful,' he said. 'It was like nothing else on earth. The colours, the smells, the sounds . . . But I've already told you all about it, Lillian; why the renewed interest?'

'No reason,' she lied.

The room was dark and almost empty. It had once been a smugglers' cave with a concealed entrance, connected to a network of caves that stretched along the seafront and back into the town. The walls were bare and had been given a colour wash of orange and red. The ceiling was panelled in the same oak that had been used to make the bar. Thick cobwebs hung in every corner and the air was dense with minute specks of dust and the slightly sweet, musky aroma of damp. As Max returned, Bertie clapped his hands together.

'Shall we order?' he suggested.

After they'd eaten and their plates had been taken away, Bertie poured Lillian another glass of wine.

'So,' he said, putting the bottle down on the table again, 'this friend – is he Muslim or Sikh?'

Lillian's eyes widened and she looked away.

'I think I've hit a nerve,' Bertie said to Max.

'She *is* blushing rather,' agreed Max.

Lillian composed herself and turned to her uncle. 'How

could you know?' she asked him. Uncle Bertie had always been the cleverest person she knew, but surely even he wasn't that clever.

'Despite my love of Sherlock Holmes stories,' he replied, 'this particular deduction was rather less than elementary . . .'

'What do you mean?' said Lillian.

Bertie grinned. 'You work at the Royal Pavilion as a nurse,' he pointed out. 'The only patients you treat are Indian soldiers, and the vast majority of those Indian gentlemen are Sikhs, with a good scattering of Mussulmen thrown in; as I said, rather *less* than elementary.'

Max looked confused. 'What are you two talking about?'

'I think my niece may have fallen for a handsome young soldier,' explained Bertie. 'Tell me, my dear, is he tall?'

Lillian felt herself blushing even more as Bissen's face came to mind. 'He's just a friend,' she replied. 'We talk sometimes . . .'

Max and Bertie shared knowing smiles.

'Yes, but is he tall?' repeated Bertie.

Lillian nodded. 'As tall as you, dear Uncle. And he's a Sikh.'

Bertie walked Lillian back to her lodging house after dinner. Max had made his excuses and left them to it, eager to catch the last train back to London in order to attend an important meeting the following day.

'What is it that Max does?' Lillian enquired.

'You've been asking me that same question for years,' Bertie reminded her. 'He works for the government, as you know.'

'But what exactly does he do?'

'Something at the Home Office. He doesn't tell me because when we meet he'd rather forget about work and enjoy himself.'

Lillian decided not to question her uncle any further. His relationship with Max was complicated, she knew, and she had no desire to push him.

'All these questions are merely a deflection,' added Bertie. 'Tell me more about this soldier.'

Lillian shrugged. 'There isn't much to say ... He was injured at Neuve Chapelle by a grenade blast. His right leg is a mess and he'll limp for the rest of his life.'

'At least he's alive,' Bertie said thoughtfully. 'So many young men have died during this awful war and it shows no sign of ending.'

'We talk about things ...' Lillian went on.

'But you must talk to lots of patients,' said Bertie. 'You rarely tell me about them. What makes this one so special?'

Lillian wondered whether she should tell him about the way her heart fluttered when she was about to start a shift at the hospital, knowing that she'd see Bissen. Should she admit that her dreams were filled with images of his smile and his eyes?

'Dear God,' Bertie exclaimed when Lillian failed to reply. 'You really are in love!'

'Do you disapprove?' Lillian asked, concerned.

He took her hand and shook his head. 'Your happiness is my only concern,' he told her. 'If you are taken with this chap then I am happy for you.'

'But nothing has happened between us and I don't know

what to do,' she admitted. 'Part of me thinks that I should tell him how I feel.'

'Does he feel the same?' asked Bertie.

'I'm not sure . . . I think so. Sometimes the way he looks at me . . .' She tailed off. What if she was wrong?

He gave her a hug. 'Well, at least we know he has good taste,' he said.

'But even if he does feel the same, there are too many dangers.'

Bertie squeezed his niece's hand. Despite her tender years, she had a great deal of common sense. She understood that any relationship between a white girl and an Indian soldier would be frowned upon by most of society.

'Well, do keep me informed of any developments,' he said as he took his leave of her. 'You'll work it out, I'm sure. Are you coming for lunch on Sunday?'

Lillian nodded. 'I wouldn't miss it for the world,' she replied. 'Goodnight.'

22 September 1915

Lillian sat on a bench in the pavilion gardens; Bissen sat facing her in his wheelchair. His pale skin was rosy from the sharp wind and he had a distant look in his eyes.

'Is something the matter?' she asked.

Bissen shook his head. 'No. I am just thinking about my family. I have not written to them since I left France and I have no idea if they know of my injuries.'

'But surely the authorities have informed them,' said Lillian, looking concerned. How awful for Bissen's mother – not knowing if her son was alive or dead.

'I must ask,' said Bissen. 'I will check with the doctor when I see him. He is good man.'

'Yes, he is,' replied Lillian. 'I can post a letter for you, if you write one.'

'Thank you. You are very good to me.'

Lillian patted the parcel that sat on her lap.

'What is that?' Bissen asked her, watching a fat pigeon pecking around behind the bench.

'A treat,' she said, smiling at him.

The unseasonably cold weather meant that there weren't many people in the gardens, which suited Lillian. She had chosen a seat at the far end, by a second gate that led to a side street. Several tall bushes and some trees obscured much of the pavilion, affording them a degree of privacy.

'What is the smell?' asked Bissen as his stomach rumbled slightly.

Lillian smiled again as she unwrapped the newspaper from around the parcel. Bissen looked down and saw food.

'Fish and chips,' she said triumphantly.

Bissen gave her a quizzical look.

'It's a seaside speciality,' she explained. 'Fish fried in batter, with chipped potatoes, smothered in salt and vinegar.'

'Which fish is this made from?' he asked.

'I don't know. It's probably cod but I didn't ask. It might be a bit lukewarm too. I got it before I started my shift.'

Bissen studied the food and spotted a couple of onions hiding under the potatoes. 'I like onions,' he said.

'These have been pickled in vinegar,' Lillian told him. 'They're delicious.'

Bissen nodded. 'You bring these food for me?' he said, instantly annoyed with his bad English. 'I'm sorry – I mean *this* food.'

'Don't apologize, Bissen,' said Lillian. 'Your English is marvellous; far better than my Punjabi!'

'May I try some?'

'Of course you may.' She opened out the wrapper a little more.

Bissen reached across and took a chip. It felt soft

in his fingers and only slightly warm. He looked at Lillian.

'Go on,' she said. 'It won't kill you.'

When he placed the chip in his mouth his taste buds went wild. The potato melted and the tang of the vinegar made him screw up his nose. The salt bit into his tongue. The combination of flavours made him want more.

'Do you like it?' asked Lillian.

'It is delicious. I've never taste anything like it.'

'I knew you would,' said Lillian. 'Or at least I hoped you would when I bought them for you. Here, try one of the onions.'

She handed Bissen one of the pickles, which he placed whole into his mouth. At the same time he felt a little flutter in his stomach. Something was going on between them.

'You're supposed to take a bite,' she teased.

Bissen crunched down on the onion and his eyes lit up. It was even more tangy than the chip – incredibly good. Lillian waited for him to swallow it.

'I've been thinking about you . . .' she said as she broke a piece of battered fish off for him.

'About me?'

Lillian nodded, wondering whether to continue. During the night she had resolved to tell Bissen exactly how she felt about him. But since breakfast a nagging doubt had troubled her. She was making an assumption – she really had no idea whether he felt the same way about her. There was every chance that she could ruin their friendship. But it was a chance she was prepared to take. No man had ever made her feel the way Bissen did. She thought about him day and night, smiling to herself when his face or his voice came to mind.

'About *you*.' She gazed into his eyes.

Bissen looked away. Inside, his stomach performed a somersault. Could it be that this beautiful woman, this *goreeh* nurse, actually liked him? What if he was wrong and she was just being good to him as a friend? Suddenly he saw the face of Jiwan Singh, eyes open, gaping wound in his forehead. *Life is too short*, a voice inside told him. *Seize the moment.*

Bissen cleared his throat. 'I think about you too,' he told her, praying he hadn't made a big mistake.

Lillian handed him the piece of fish. 'Here,' she said. 'Try this too.'

He took the fish and ate it. Although it tasted wonderful he had suddenly lost interest in the food. He was totally focused on Lillian.

'I like to spend time with you,' she continued.

Bissen's face lit up and a surge of nervous energy coursed through his body. His scalp began to prickle. She was saying the words he'd longed to hear since the moment she first spoke to him.

'I like to—' he began, only for Lillian to stop him by placing an index finger to her soft cupid's-bow lips.

'Please,' she said. 'I've been practising this since last week. If I get it wrong I'll be mortified.'

Bissen nodded. The surge of nervous energy had become a tidal wave of emotion.

'The time we spend together is special,' continued Lillian. 'It isn't about your injuries or my being your nurse. I can't stop thinking about you and—'

Bissen took her hand, interrupting her. 'I not good at these things,' he admitted, 'but since I meet you no rose is beautiful as much as you.'

He searched her eyes, desperate to find out if his broken English had conveyed what his heart felt. Lillian took his other hand, looked around, then leaned over, kissing him gently on the lips. When she pulled away, Bissen was wearing the biggest smile she had ever seen.

'I love it when you smile,' she told him. 'You look so alive, so radiant; you are *so* handsome.'

Bissen blushed.

'Listen to *me* . . .' added Lillian. 'You must think I'm so silly.'

'No,' said Bissen. 'You are wonderful.'

She picked up the second pickled onion and bit into it before handing what was left to Bissen. As he ate it, she ran her fingers down his face, praying that she had done the right thing.

Lillian made her way towards Bissen's bed at the end of her shift, hoping to have a few more words with him before she left. The hours had passed so quickly since she'd told him of her love. She wanted something to take with her: another smile perhaps, or the sparkle in his eyes, so that she might sleep soundly.

'Hello, Private Singh,' she said to him as a warm feeling grew inside her.

Bissen glanced around. None of the other patients were looking in their direction so he held out his hand. Lillian gave it a quick squeeze before letting go.

'We need to be careful,' she told him in a whisper.

Bissen nodded.

'Being together will be difficult,' she added. 'Not only because of your injuries . . .'

'I know,' replied Bissen. 'I am Indian.'

'I don't care that you are Indian. But when you are well they'll send you away and I won't be able to bear that.'

'I could stay in England,' he suggested, knowing that it would be impossible. Once fit enough to leave, he would have only two choices: back to the front or home to the Punjab. That was the law.

'You'd have to desert to stay,' she replied. 'And they might catch you.'

Bissen shook his head. 'Do not worry over this,' he told her. 'Today is a great day. Let us go to sleep with smiles on our faces.'

Lillian shook off her doubts and smiled at him. 'You're right. I'm just being silly. I had better go before they suspect something.'

Bissen held out his hand once more, savouring her brief touch. 'I see tomorrow?' he asked.

She nodded. 'In the morning I'll take you outside after my shift ends.'

Bissen said that he would look forward to it. As Lillian left, he watched her, his heart pounding. Once he could no longer see her, he closed his eyes and thought of her face, praying for sleep so that the new day might come sooner.

1 December 1915

Bissen wondered how far he could get without the guards calling him back. He was in the pavilion gardens, by the bench where Lillian had kissed him for the first time, leaning on a pair of crutches. Walking, although at times uncomfortable, was at least possible now, and Bissen wanted to get stronger. But the wounded were not allowed beyond the gardens and he knew that he would have to ask for permission to reach his intended destination: the seafront. Deep, charcoal-coloured clouds were coming in from the sea and there was a chill in the air, but Bissen didn't feel it. He was too busy thinking about what lay beyond the gardens. Lillian had told him many things about Brighton, but hearing and seeing were very different things. Bissen longed to get closer to the sea, to take a walk along the promenade.

A tall Sikh in a sky-blue turban named Hurnam Singh came to stand beside Bissen.

'*Sat-sri-akaal*,' he said in greeting.

'*Sat-sri-akaal, bhai*,' replied Bissen.

'How are you today?'

Bissen shrugged. 'I am still alive,' he said.

Hurnam Singh had suffered shell shock: every few seconds his dark brown eyes twitched – outward signs of the damage his mind had suffered. His left ear was missing and scar tissue scaled the left side of his neck, thick and red. His beard was flecked with grey and white.

'This place is like a convict station,' he said.

'A *convict* station?' repeated Bissen, unsure that he had heard correctly.

Hurnam sighed. 'I know they feed us well and make sure we are clothed. They tend to our injuries and hope to make us well but we still cannot come and go as we please.'

Bissen thought about his ambition to visit the seafront and nodded.

'I long to visit the rest of this town,' added Hurnam. 'Pay a visit to London even . . .'

Bissen laughed. 'We'll be lucky to see London Road, and that is just across the gardens.'

'You see my point then?' Hurnam asked him. 'This is a prison . . .'

Bissen had to admit that he was right. Why else would there be barbed wire around the perimeter and sentries posted at every door?

'We have fought and nearly died for these people,' complained Hurnam. 'What harm could there be in allowing us to walk about as free men?'

'Perhaps they think we will run away,' suggested Bissen.

'*Run?* Where would we run to? Give me passage on a

ship bound for my motherland and I might just try to escape, but to stay *here*?'

'We are not free men, *bhai-ji*,' Bissen told him. 'When we signed up we gave our freedom away.'

A fire started to burn in Hurnam's eyes. 'No, *bhai*,' he said. 'We had no freedom to begin with. We were merely their chattels – the same dogs who ruin our country; these are the devils we fought for . . .'

Bissen, wary of starting a debate about their colonial masters, asked Hurnam if he knew when he would be allowed to leave the hospital.

'When *they* say so,' he replied, his face twitching.

'You must have *some* clue . . .'

'Two months, according to the doctor. I am to be assessed, and if I can fight on, I'll be sent to the Eastern Front or back to France. If I cannot lift my rifle in defence of my emperor, I will be sent home. God willing, it will be the latter.'

Bissen nodded. 'And what will you do when you get home?'

'In all honesty?'

'Yes, *bhai-ji*,' said Bissen.

'Take up my gun and help to chase these devils from my land,' vowed Hurnam, his expression as hard as granite.

Bissen nodded again but said nothing. His own dream was very different and it involved *staying* in England. But that would be difficult. Becoming an accepted part of Lillian's life would be harder still. She had spoken to her Uncle Bertie and certain wheels had been set in motion, but there was no guarantee of success. The laws against desertion and immigration were harsh, and Bissen would have to circumvent or ignore both in order to have his dream. Not to mention putting both Lillian and her uncle at risk.

Lillian arrived later that afternoon, her face pink from the cold breeze, her eyes sparkling. Over her uniform she wore a red coat and a matching woollen hat. Bissen was still in the gardens and she came to find him straight away. Looking around to make sure that no one was watching, she gave him a peck on the cheek.

'I missed you,' she told him. 'Two days is too long to wait to look at you and hold your hand.'

Bissen smiled. 'It is the same for me. I dream of you when you aren't here.'

'Is that very terrible for you?' she asked jokingly.

'It is lovely,' replied Bissen. 'But is better when you *are* here.'

They talked about Lillian's day and then the subject turned to her Uncle Bertie.

'He came to see me yesterday,' she informed Bissen. 'There is a problem.'

His face fell. He understood what she was telling him. 'There is no legal way?'

'No. You could gain employment with some rich family, but even then they will stop you. You are a soldier, and if you don't return to the front you'll be charged with desertion.'

'I see,' said Bissen.

'And I won't allow you to pay such a penalty,' added Lillian. 'Not for me.'

Desertion incurred a simple penalty: death. Lillian's eyes

began to water at the very thought of it. To find her love and lose him would be unbearable.

'Please not cry,' said Bissen, taking her hand. 'We will find a way.'

Lillian wiped her eyes. 'That's the other problem. I'm being transferred from here next week—'

'No!' replied Bissen, his face falling.

She nodded. 'Someone has complained about me. I'm to go back to the main hospital.'

'Who complain?'

'Someone who objects to our friendship. I was admonished over it yesterday.'

'Because I am a Sikh,' said Bissen. 'I know.'

Lillian shook her head. 'Let them say what they want,' she said defiantly. 'No one can tell me what to do with my own life.'

'But you get trouble.' Bissen was concerned.

'You are worth it.'

He turned his face away as a tear made its way down his cheek.

'You are so special,' Lillian said, taking his face in her hands and wiping the tear away.

'I don't know why I cry,' said Bissen, feeling slightly ashamed.

'No need to say anything,' she replied.

After her shift had ended, she took Bissen out in a wheel-chair. They gazed out into the darkness.

'It feels as if it might snow,' said Lillian.

'I would like that,' replied Bissen.

She cleared her throat. 'My uncle has a plan,' she told her lover. 'He thinks he can get you out of here and hide you at his house.'

'Is this possible?' asked Bissen, suddenly excited.

'Yes. Your wounds are healed and there is no more chance of infection. But it will mean danger and sacrifice and it must happen this week. We can't take the chance that they might discharge you and send you away. And I won't be able to keep an eye on things when I move to the main hospital.'

Bissen smiled. 'I am ready to do anything for you,' he promised.

Lillian frowned. 'You'll have to stay locked away, as you are here . . .'

'Very well.'

'And you may have to shave . . .'

Bissen swallowed hard. His hand went involuntarily to his beard, then his turban.

'I'm sorry,' said Lillian. 'Truly, I am—'

'No, no.' Bissen shook his head. 'For you I will do.'

Lillian put her hands to his face. 'Are you absolutely sure?'

'Yes . . . Tell your uncle I will come . . .'

Bissen took her hands and squeezed them gently. The turban and beard, he told himself, were not what made him a Sikh. It was what he held in his heart that made him who he was. And besides, if God's laws would not allow him to fulfil his dreams, then he would have to find new laws that did. It was this thought that kept him awake well into the small hours, long after Lillian had left.

He *had* to leave the hospital. If there was no other way

to be with Lillian than to become a deserter, then he would do it. *Seize the day*, his inner voice demanded. He had been loyal to his emperor, prepared to lay down his life. But now his emperor would have to forgive him, as would his God. What did the firing squad or eternal damnation matter if he couldn't have his freedom? What was the point of breathing if he couldn't take in the aroma of Lillian's perfume or feel the heat from her breast? Whatever she and her uncle had planned, he was ready to do it.

3 and 4 December 1915

Lillian's uncle strode confidently into Bissen's ward at just after seven in the evening. Bissen smiled to himself: Bertie was on time, just as she'd said he would be. A tremor of excitement ran through his heart; all being well, he would soon be a free man. The guard at the door asked Lillian's uncle what his business was. He snorted with contempt and produced a letter from his pocket before replying.

'Government business!' he said, his voice reverberating around the room.

'Oh,' replied the guard, looking slightly confused.

'It appears that you have a person of interest on this ward.'

Lillian's uncle wore the uniform of a top ranking military officer and the guard deferred to it. He glanced at the letter for a moment, noted the government seal, then handed it back to his superior.

'Is everything to your satisfaction, young man?' asked Uncle Bertie.

'Yes, sir!' replied the guard. 'Which of the men do you wish to see?'

Bertie coughed. 'I don't wish to see him, you buffoon! The letter states that I must interrogate the man over an alleged incident in the trenches. This is a delicate matter, Private . . .'

'Yes, sir.'

'There may be a court-martial at the end of it.'

The guard frowned. This was a serious situation. 'I see, sir,' he said.

'It's the man at the end there,' added Bertie, nodding towards Bissen.

The guard walked quickly back to his desk and picked up a sheet of paper. On it was a bed plan with the name of each patient.

'The man you want is Bissen Singh, sir,' he told Bertie.

'Yes, yes. I know who he is — just get him out of bed and into a damned wheelchair. I don't have all night!'

The guard did as he was told, and within five minutes Bissen was being wheeled out of the ward by Bertie.

The guard followed behind. 'I need to make a note of where you are taking the patient,' he said.

'To London,' replied Bertie. 'And he is no longer a *patient*, Private. The man is now a prisoner.'

The guard nodded. 'Excuse me for asking, sir, but where exactly in London are you taking him? Only, my orders—'

'Your orders are to *follow* orders, Private!' shouted Bertie. 'And *my* orders supersede anything you have been told thus far. Is that *clear*?'

The guard nodded.

'I'm with Military Intelligence and the man is being taken to the Defence Ministry.'

'Thank you, sir,' said the guard.

'An officer explaining himself to a private . . .' muttered Bertie. 'The world's gone mad . . .'

The guard thought about replying but changed his mind. He'd pushed his luck as far as it would go. And he had no desire to upset anyone from Military Intelligence – not over an Indian. 'Shall I see you out to your transport, sir?' he asked instead.

Bertie shook his head. 'No thank you,' he replied curtly. 'I have a man waiting for me. Back to your post, Private . . .'

The guard nodded as he watched the officer wheel his prisoner out of the building. He walked back to his desk and sat down. Picking up a pencil, he crossed out Bissen Singh's name and wrote: *Removed to MoD for interrogation by Colonel Smythe.*

The bored-looking guard at the gate let 'Colonel Smythe' and his prisoner pass without any fuss. Bertie thanked him and wheeled Bissen towards a van parked by the kerb. It was black with white stencilled writing on the side. Bissen couldn't make out what the letters said. Another man, also dressed in uniform, jumped down from the driver's seat, walked round to the back of the van and opened the doors. His hair was black as night and his eyes a deep, dark brown. From the man's skin tone, Bissen realized that he wasn't English. He looked like he came from the East.

'This is Hamadi,' Bertie explained. 'He is from Egypt and he works for me.'

Hamadi smiled at Bissen, and then he and Bertie helped him into the back of the van. There were two wooden benches on either side. Bertie took the cushions from the wheelchair and gave them to Bissen.

'The seating might be a little uncomfortable,' he told him. 'Use the cushions.'

'Thank you, sir,' replied Bissen.

'No matter, dear fellow. Just hang on as we drive; the ride is rather bumpy, but we'll only be half an hour or so ...'

Bissen nodded before Bertie closed the door and left him in darkness. Within a minute, Hamadi had started the engine and they were off. The wheelchair stayed where it was, waiting to be discovered.

The ride was as uncomfortable as Lillian's uncle had warned. By the time the van came to a stop, Bissen could feel his wounds biting. But the pain passed quickly, and once the door was opened and he had been helped outside, he was more than happy. In front of him stood an enormous stone house with a grand doorway framed by intricately carved pillars. The house seemed to be sitting in the middle of nowhere, surrounded by trees and open land.

'Welcome to my home,' said Bertie with a smile. 'No one will think to look for you here ...'

Bissen nodded and wondered how rich he was to own such a wonderful home.

'Do come in,' Bertie went on. 'It's bloody freezing out here.'

He turned to Hamadi and said something in a language Bissen didn't recognize but guessed was Arabic. Hamadi nodded, jumped back into the van and started the engine. As Bissen and Bertie entered the house, the van disappeared into the darkness.

Bissen was led up a grand stone staircase and into a large, well-lit bedroom. Over by the window was a bed much bigger than anything he had ever seen before. It had four corner posts; soft swathes of cream-coloured fabric were draped between them. On top of the bed were countless pillows, in white, cream and red, and on a bedside table sat a silver teapot, a cup full of steaming tea and a plate of bread and jam.

'Get some rest,' Bertie told Bissen. 'Lillian will be here in the morning and we have much to discuss.'

'Thank you,' said Bissen. 'You are very kind to me.'

Bertie smiled. 'Nonsense. My Lillian is all I have left in the world. Nothing is too much . . . Now eat a little and try the tea – it's been spiced. Probably not authentically Indian but as close as I could get.'

'Yes, sir.'

Bertie shook his head. 'There are no superiors here, young man,' he told him. 'Just human beings . . .'

The following morning Bissen sat in the drawing room and read the paper. Bertie had gone out after waking Bissen, showing him the amenities and telling him that there was breakfast waiting for him in the kitchen. It turned out that Hamadi was not the only person who worked for Lillian's uncle. In the kitchen Bissen found a plump, friendly white woman called Nora, who fed him boiled eggs and toast and gave him some more of Bertie's spiced tea. Bissen had eaten well before exploring the house and finally settling in one of its many rooms – one with large French doors and views across a well-kept lawn that led down to a stream and, beyond it, dense woods. Bissen was reading about the war when Lillian came into the room.

'Look at you!' She ran across and threw her arms around him. 'You look like the lord of the manor . . .'

Bissen dropped the paper and embraced her, taking in her scent and the warmth of her body. 'Thank you,' he told her.

Lillian let go and admired Bissen's grey eyes and his smile. 'I can't believe we did it,' she said. 'That you are actually here.'

Bissen nodded.

'Uncle Bertie said it would be easy but I didn't for a moment believe him. I thought it would be far more difficult.'

'He dressed like colonel,' Bissen told her. 'He looked like real thing.'

Lillian laughed. 'My uncle has many friends,' she explained. 'Most of them in high places too. I don't know what tricks he pulled to get you out, and frankly, I don't care, just so long as you are here.'

She took his face in her hands and kissed him over and over. 'Just think,' she said. 'We'll be together for Christmas – your first!'

'Yes . . .' Bissen's eyes glazed over.

'Oh, this is like a dream! A wonderful, wonderful dream!'

They spent much of the day in each other's arms, no longer able to hold back what they felt. The first time they made love it was awkward, but as passion took hold they overcame their nerves. Lillian was careful not to aggravate

Bissen's wounds, but for his part, he forgot all about his leg. The sensations he felt – her touch, her taste, the heat that came from her skin – more than compensated for the pain. It was just as he had imagined it; no, it was better. When they were finished, Bissen lay with his head against Lillian's breasts and fell soundly asleep.

By the time Bertie returned that evening, they were sitting by a warm fire in the drawing room, holding hands and talking of their future.

'It's been a long day,' Bertie told them. 'I'm ready for a drop of Scotch . . . Anyone else?'

Lillian nodded and asked Bissen if he would like one too. He shrugged. He had only ever tried alcohol once, when he was fourteen. Back them it had made his stomach churn and his head ache. He had never touched it since, and as a Sikh, that was what was expected.

Bertie realized as much and grinned. 'Lillian knows very little of your religion,' he told him. 'Sikhs don't drink, do they?'

'But one drink not hurt,' he replied, smiling broadly. 'I have a little . . . please.'

Later, as Lillian squeezed Bissen's hand tight and whispered her love to him, he closed his eyes and prayed that he was not caught in some fantasy inside his own head; that Fate was not playing some awful trick. He realized that he couldn't recall the last time he had felt so happy.

10 December 1915

The temperature had fallen to below freezing and remained there. As Bissen sat in the drawing room, he shivered from the cold. A fire burned steadily in the grate but the window frames were old and let in a draught that ate at his bones. Lillian, who'd moved back into Bertie's house the previous evening, had gone to work, leaving Bissen to his own devices. There was little to do except read the newspaper or study one of the thousands of books that Bertie had accumulated over a lifetime. Not that Bissen minded. Books were such an amazing gift, allowing him access to new people and countries. He sat with a copy of *The Hound of the Baskervilles* by Sir Arthur Conan Doyle in his lap, intrigued by the plot and the descriptions of English life. The detective, Sherlock Holmes, was a popular character, according to Bertie, and Bissen was enjoying the novel immensely, despite his difficulty with some of the language.

Just as Holmes had decided to head back to London, leaving Dr Watson to hold the fort, there was a knock at the door. Bissen, unsure what to do, did not answer. A second knock followed, this one louder. He stood up, laying the book face down on a side table so as not to lose his place. He walked slowly over to the door and opened it.

'May I come in?' asked Bertie from across the threshold.

Bissen nodded, wondering why he needed to knock to enter a room in his own house.

'Didn't want to disturb you, old chap,' explained Bertie, sensing Bissen's surprise.

'Please come,' replied Bissen, walking back to his chair and sitting down.

Bertie followed him and perched on a window ledge. 'How are you finding life outside the hospital?' he asked Bissen.

'Very good,' Bissen replied. 'I must thank you.'

Bertie dismissed his gratitude with a wave of the hand. 'Nonsense,' he said. 'You are more than welcome – there really is no need to thank me . . . What are you reading?'

Bissen held up the novel.

'Ah!' Bertie exclaimed. 'One of my absolute favourites.'

'You tell me about this yesterday,' Bissen reminded him. 'So I read.'

'A very good choice . . . I was wondering if we might have a talk, you and I.'

Bissen nodded. 'Please,' he said.

Bertie came and sat down by the fire. 'That's better,' he said. 'Those windows are damned draughty. I shall have to get the workmen to take a look at them . . .'

Bissen put the book back down on the table and waited for Bertie to continue.

'I want you to know,' he said, 'that I'm perfectly happy with your being here. Lillian is very taken with you and I can see that you are a good chap.'

For some reason Bissen found he was waiting for the 'but'. When it came, however, it wasn't what he'd been expecting.

'But there are many dangers that we may have to face,' said Bertie. 'You are officially a deserter and I'm afraid that if you get caught, the firing squad awaits you.'

Bissen nodded. 'I know this when you take me from the hospital. I happy to take my chance that you give.'

Bertie smiled. 'And I know how much my niece means to you,' he said. 'I can see it in your face when you look at her. Lillian is my only family, young man. Her parents died when she was very young and I took her in. To be honest, I thought it might be a mistake; that it might hinder me in some way. I have a rather unconventional lifestyle . . .'

Bissen wondered what he meant but said nothing.

'I was wrong. Lillian turned out to be the most precious thing I have ever been blessed with,' continued Bertie. 'I want her to be *truly* happy.'

Bissen nodded his agreement. 'You wish to know if I will look after her,' he said, beginning to understand.

'Yes,' Bertie replied. 'I feel rather foolish in asking; as if I were some overprotective father interviewing potential suitors.'

'No,' Bissen reassured him. 'It is correct that you ask me these things.'

Bertie smiled. 'I'm pleased that you think so, Bissen. I can see why Lillian is so enamoured of you.'

Bissen frowned. 'What is the meaning?' he asked.

'Of *enamoured* . . .? How much she *adores* you.'

'I see.'

Bertie coughed and cleared his throat. 'I think I'd like a little drink; how about you?'

'Yes please,' said Bissen.

Bertie went to pour two large brandies. He handed one to Bissen before retaking his seat. 'Lillian is very sensible,' he said, swirling the amber liquid around the glass. 'But she is also quite prone to flights of fancy. I don't mean that she is unrealistic. It's only that she is a romantic at heart.'

'I understand.' Bissen took a sip of brandy.

'Her feelings for you are so strong,' Bertie told him. 'If you ever did get caught, I'm not sure how she'd cope.'

'It could happen. There is a chance.'

'Yes, there is. You and I need to be prepared for the worst. We must protect the woman we both love. I can see that you are a decent man, Bissen Singh, and I want you to know that I would welcome you into my family. But many of my countrymen have strange prejudices towards people from the East.'

Bissen took another sip of brandy before replying. 'Some English will not like Indian man with white woman.'

'Exactly my point,' replied Bertie. 'I just hope that you can be strong enough to cope with that. God knows, Hamadi has had enough trouble in town over the past few years.'

'But not all white men are the same. In France some of the *Engrezi* would not talk to us or share their sleeping quarters. They call us savages and heathens. But then there are many more who give us cigarettes and tell us jokes.'

'It must have been such a strange experience,' Bertie said. 'To be Indian and fighting in France, I mean.'

'I did not understand why white men fight other white men,' Bissen admitted. 'But I wanted to do my duty.'

'Is it as awful as they say in the news reports?'

He frowned. 'It is worse,' he replied. 'The English talk of hell: that is what it is. So many men killed for nothing. At Neuve Chapelle my comrades died all around me. I still see their faces when I dream.'

'What about India?' Bertie asked. 'Do you not wish to return?'

Bissen shook his head. 'I did when I first arrived at hospital, but Lillian change that. If I'm not with Lillian then nowhere can be my home.'

Bertie drank down the rest of his brandy. 'But if you *had* to be together in India,' he said, 'would you be able to cope with the prejudices of your own countrymen?'

'Yes,' replied Bissen. 'My only wish is to be with Lillian; nothing else. The world is a big place, *Uncle-ji*.'

Bertie grinned. 'When you call me *ji,* that is a mark of respect for your elders, is it not?'

Bissen nodded. 'You know Indian language?' he asked.

'From my time in Delhi,' explained Bertie. 'I picked up little bits. I loved your country: the people, the climate, the food. I would have remained but I had to come back for Lillian. Not that she is aware of that; I've never told her. When her parents died I was still out there. As soon as I got the telegram, I returned to look after her.' His eyes glazed over as his memory took him back to long-gone days. 'I left *so* much behind,' he continued. 'But it was worth it.'

321

Bissen nodded his understanding. 'I won't tell her,' he said.

'Thank you, Bissen. Now, would you care for another drink?'

Bissen shook his head but Bertie ignored him. He poured two more large measures, inspecting the liquid before handing one to Bissen.

'Far too cold,' he said. 'Now, tell me what you think of Sherlock Holmes.'

24 December 1915

It had snowed overnight; in the morning, Lillian and Bissen woke to find that a white blanket had covered everything in the gardens. They washed, ate breakfast and then decided to take a walk. They spent all morning out in the snow, walking around the gardens and then exploring the rest of estate. Bissen felt as excited as a child. He had never seen snow before: when he picked it up, it froze his hands before melting away into nothingness. He savoured the sensation, picking up handful after handful, until his fingers were red with cold and Lillian told him to stop.

'You'll give yourself frostbite,' she warned. 'And then where will you be?'

The look on Bissen's face told her that he didn't understand so she explained herself before fashioning a snowball and throwing it at him. It glanced off his turban and fell down his face. Lillian giggled and ran as he gathered up some snow to throw back at her. His face was red and the tip of his proud nose was frozen. The snowball he threw missed its target by a distance and he lost his footing, slipped and fell into the snow. He grinned at Lillian when she ran over to see if he was all right.

'I'm fine,' he told her. 'Happy. Very happy.'

'Let's get you inside,' she replied. 'We need to give you some painkillers.'

They trudged back to the house, where Hamadi was waiting with a worried expression.

'Is something the matter?' asked Lillian.

Hamadi nodded. 'Your uncle has been questioned by police,' he told them. 'This morning . . .'

Lillian's face fell. She gripped Bissen's hand tightly. 'Is this to do with us?' she asked, although she already knew the answer.

'They ask about Bissen,' replied Hamadi, confirming her worst fears.

Bissen felt his heart sink like a stone. Deep inside he had known that their perfect world could not last – not without something getting in the way; but for them to find out so soon? It felt as though the ground was falling away beneath him.

'Your uncle is returning soon – he say to tell Bissen that beard and hair must go,' added Hamadi. 'I bring you scissors and razor.'

Lillian turned to Bissen and tried to smile. 'I've always wondered what you would look like without your beard and turban,' she joked.

Bissen nodded, hiding the sadness in his eyes. 'For you,' he told her, 'I will do.'

'How could the police know about him?' she asked Hamadi. 'He's been nowhere since you helped him escape.'

Hamadi shrugged. Two weeks earlier some men had been at the house, working on the gardens and rebuilding a fallen stone wall, he explained. They had been kept well away from the main residence, but who was to say they hadn't seen Bissen?

'Your uncle will know,' he told Lillian. 'Until then you do as he say.'

In the bathroom opposite Bissen's room, he stripped to the waist and began to unwind his turban. His hair fell halfway down his back in thick, shiny waves.

'Such beautiful hair,' murmured Lillian. 'What a shame to lose it.'

Bissen shrugged. 'It is no matter. Hair can grow again.'

Lillian picked up the heavy scissors Hamadi had given her and began to cut off Bissen's thick locks. She worked on small areas at a time and apologized repeatedly. Bissen stopped her at one point and gave her a kiss.

'If this I need to stay with you,' he told her, 'then it is of no matter.'

Very soon his hair lay on the floor around them and Lillian turned her attention to his beard.

'I'll cut away what I can with the scissors,' she told him. 'Hamadi can shave the rest.'

Bissen nodded. 'Will you still like me,' he joked, 'when I look like other man?'

'Your eyes will stay the same,' she replied. 'And your smile too ... I'll get Hamadi to give you a proper haircut – you look like a scarecrow the way it is now.'

Bissen asked her what a scarecrow was and Lillian told

him as she cut off his beard. When she was done, she called for Hamadi, who grinned when he saw Bissen.

'Is something funny?' she asked.

Hamadi nodded. 'He will look like Egyptian,' he replied.

Lillian realized that he was right. Once Hamadi had shaved him, Bissen would look totally different. The authorities would be looking for a Sikh man. They would never recognize him once he was shorn of his beard and no longer wore a turban. At least she hoped they wouldn't.

'I'm going downstairs,' she told them. 'I'll see you when you are done.'

Uncle Bertie arrived half an hour later; the expression on his face told Lillian that things were not good.

'It's all over town,' he told her. 'There was nothing for a few weeks after we helped Bissen escape – the army kept it hidden – but then a newspaper reporter found out and ran the story. Now it's the talk of Brighton.'

Lillian sighed and shook her head. 'What does this mean for us?' she asked.

'I don't know, Lillian,' he replied. 'I've spoken to some friends – they think everything will be fine, but someone has mentioned my name and I don't know who it can be.'

'How could anyone know? Bissen hasn't left the estate since he arrived.'

'There were some workmen here,' Bertie told her. 'Perhaps they saw something. I don't know . . .'

'Did they actually see Bissen?'

'I don't think so. But perhaps one of them came into the house while I was out.'

'What did the police ask you?'

Bertie shrugged. 'They said that someone had reported a foreigner living at this address and I told them about Hamadi. But he's been here for three years and has papers. Anyway, once I'd explained, they seemed to accept my word and left it at that.'

'Bissen is shaving,' Lillian told him. 'He should be down at any moment.'

'Good, good,' replied Bertie, taking her hand.

'I'm so worried, Uncle . . .'

'No need, my child,' he reassured her. 'Once the fuss has died down, it will all be fine.'

'I hope so,' answered Lillian. 'I don't know what I'd do if Bissen were caught. They'd court-martial him for desertion and then—'

'Try not to think about it, my dear,' said Bertie. 'If it came to the worst I'd find him passage on a ship to the East – I won't let the authorities capture him, I promise.'

'What ship?' Lillian asked.

'There are some Persians who live in Hastings,' he explained. 'They can take Bissen to London or Dover and put him on a ship.'

'But then I would lose him just the same,' she pointed out.

Bertie shook his head. 'No – you'd just have to wait and then go to him. The world is a big place, Lillian. If you can't be together in England, then perhaps you can be together somewhere else. Like India . . .'

Lillian stopped and thought about what her uncle was saying. She knew him too well: he wasn't just theorizing – he was talking about an *actual* plan that he had formulated.

'You've already arranged things, haven't you?' she said.

Her uncle nodded. For now he would let her believe that things weren't too serious. No point in her getting upset just yet. Not until it was time . . . 'Just a fail-safe,' he replied. 'I have to cover all eventualities.'

Lillian nodded. Her uncle had been a rock in her life for so long that she didn't think she'd be able to cope without him. Thank God she didn't have to. If anyone could help her and Bissen, it was Bertie. 'You are a wonderful man,' she said.

'If the authorities get too close, then my friends will step in – they are only a telegram away . . . Until then, the newly shaven Bissen should be fine. And if not, there are plenty of rooms in which to hide him here.'

Lillian gave her uncle a warm hug just as Bissen came in. Uncle and niece turned to look at him and Lillian's breath caught in her throat.

'Well, well!' said Bertie. 'You really are a splendidly hand-some chap!'

Bissen shrugged and looked into Lillian's eyes. 'You still like?' he asked self-consciously.

Lillian nodded, unable to speak. She studied his high cheekbones and the pallor of his skin; the sculpted perfection of his jaw line; his striking grey eyes. She felt her-self blush as a warm, tingling sensation gathered in her belly and worked its way lower. Without thinking, she walked over to Bissen and took his face in her hands.

'You are beautiful,' she told him.

4 January 1916

Christmas passed without further incident. It was a bitter-sweet time, with both Lillian and Bissen trying to forget the trouble that loomed over them. Lillian wanted to make Bissen's first Christmas as special as possible; after all, it might turn out to be his last. She had gone out of her way to create a seasonal atmosphere, with a tree and presents and decorations. But on the day before New Year's Eve the police had arrived.

Bertie had done what he could to protect his niece and her lover but it wasn't enough. Various meetings with Max and other friends had made it clear that his position was untenable. He hadn't told the whole truth when Lillian had asked him about things on Christmas Eve. The workmen had spotted Bissen through the drawing-room window, reading the paper by the fireside. And they had reported him to the police when the story of the missing Indian broke in Brighton. It was his own fault, Bertie told himself. He should have made sure Bissen remained hidden while the work

329

was being carried out. And now he simply had to go – an outcome that tugged at Bertie's heartstrings.

Hiding him, which is what Hamadi had done when the police arrived, was a temporary measure. He could not stay locked away indefinitely. At some point he would have to come out – otherwise why rescue him from the prison of the hospital ward in the first place? A free man couldn't spend his life in confinement. It just wouldn't do. And when Bissen did appear, the police or any other eagle-eyed observer would soon realize who he was. The description given in the news reports was very accurate – and exactly how many eastern-looking chaps were there wandering around Brighton? No, Bissen would be a sitting target. And the police *would* return; Bertie had that on the best authority.

There was also the issue of Max – who had furnished Bertie with the false letter he'd used to spring Bissen. If Bissen were found on the estate, Max would be easily identified as the insider: he was the only person Bertie knew with the authority to forge a letter; he was a junior government minister. They were known associates and fellow club members – not to mention clandestine lovers. And it was Max who had clarified Bertie's options at dinner on New Year's Eve.

'Just won't do, old chap,' he'd said. 'If they rumble us, I'll be for the chop – and I've been in this business for far too long to let it slip now.'

'Damn,' Bertie had replied.

'You know I love Lillian as much as you, but we have to watch ourselves. We've held onto our secret since we were

330

young men. We even gave up our idyllic existence in India and survived. Now is not the time to let the cat out of the bag.'

Bertie reached across the table and gave Max's hand a little squeeze, careful not to let anyone else in the club see. 'I'm ever so sorry,' he replied sadly.

'It's not your fault. But we both have far too much to lose.'

'I'll deal with it, Max.'

'Poor things,' said Max. 'To be torn apart in such a way. Sometimes I feel deeply ashamed of my country. What harm could it do if Bissen stayed? The man nearly lost his life defending our so-called freedom, for God's sake!'

Bertie wiped away a tear and poured another glass of wine.

Now here he was, four days into the New Year, about to break his niece's heart. He waited until Lillian and Bissen had finished breakfast before summoning them to his office, a large square room with floor-to-ceiling windows and an extensive library. When they arrived, he told them both to sit.

'I have some terrible news,' he said immediately, not wanting to sugar the pill. They deserved much more than that.

'*Please . . . no!*' gasped Lillian, realizing what this meant. Her hand clutched Bissen's thigh and the colour drained away from her face.

'I'm sorry, my dear,' replied Bertie. 'Truly I am . . .'

Bissen watched the conversation between Lillian and her uncle impassively. He had known since the day the police had come that things were over for him in England. But everything he'd felt – the despair and the agony – he had kept inside, not wishing to burden Lillian with it. Instead he had let her enjoy their final few days together, blissfully unaware of their impending fate. Or perhaps entirely aware and hiding from it. Now, as that fate became apparent, he nodded silently.

'I've arranged things with the Persian chaps,' added Bertie. 'They are arriving this evening, under cover of darkness—'

'*No!*' cried Lillian, unable to come to terms with what was happening.

'There is no other way,' Bissen told her. 'I cannot get caught – *Uncle-ji* will get much trouble.'

'But we'll run away!' insisted Lillian. 'To that place in north Wales by Porthmadog, Uncle Bertie; the place where we used to go for holidays. No one will look for us there.'

Bertie shook his head. 'Bissen will stand out wherever he goes until the war is over. The authorities treat desertion as a serious matter, Lillian. They won't let it rest.'

Tears flowed freely down her face, salty and warm. She looked at Bissen and stroked his face until her belly began to spasm. She sobbed uncontrollably, from her very core, and threw her arms around him. Bissen held her, pulling her close.

'I'm so, so sorry,' Bertie said to him. 'I really did think it would be all right – if only I'd considered those blasted workmen!'

Bissen shook his head. 'What you do for me, for us, no other man do. You are a good man, *Uncle-ji*,' he told him.

He looked down at his lover and nuzzled her hair, taking

in its familiar scent. But then, as he closed his eyes, the smell changed. Suddenly he was back in Neuve Chapelle, and there was the stench of rotting onions all around him. He opened his eyes with a start, trying to banish the memories, but the smell remained. Why the smell? he asked himself. Why now? A flashing image came to him: gunshots and screaming, blood flowing across a dirt floor. He found himself thinking of a marketplace in Amritsar, as a woman tried to sell him fragrant oranges. Her eyes tried to tell him something but he couldn't work out what. And then came more gunshots and the faces of countless dead men lying at the bottom of trenches, inches deep in rainwater.

Two hours later Lillian was still crying with her head resting on Bissen's right shoulder. They were lying on his bed, talking very little, as their situation sank in. There was no other way around it, that much was certain. Bissen would be gone by the end of the day and their brief, sweet time together would be at an end. He caressed Lillian's back and told her everything would be fine.

'You come to India. There we can be together.'

Lillian looked up at him and nodded. 'I will go anywhere to be with you,' she replied.

'It will not be long.'

'Uncle Bertie will find a way for me to come to you,' she promised. 'And I'll write to you every week.'

Bissen shifted so that her head rested on his chest. 'Perhaps I come back too,' he said, 'when the war is over.'

'Yes,' sobbed Lillian. 'When these stupid people stop making up horrendous rules. You can come here like

Hamadi did and work for my uncle. And I'll make sure that everyone knows how much you gave for this country; that you're a hero!'

'We will see,' replied Bissen. 'Whatever comes, we will be together.'

They spent the afternoon there, talking and making love and planning for a future together somewhere – anywhere. As dusk began to fall, Lillian grew inconsolable. They made their way down to Bertie's office; she clung to Bissen for all she was worth and refused to let him go. It took Bertie to gently prise her away. She began to sob again, this time on her uncle's shoulder. Bissen felt his own eyes welling up; he wiped away the tears as soon as they fell. He looked over to Bertie.

'I'm afraid the time is here, Bissen,' said Bertie. 'Hamadi and the Persian gentlemen are outside.'

Bissen nodded.

'They are good men. I trust them implicitly. They tell me that the passage may be difficult, but only until you reach the ship. Once you're aboard, you'll be fine.'

'Does the ship go to India?' asked Bissen.

Bertie shook his head. 'Afraid not, old chap. It docks at Cape Town in South Africa. From there you'll be met and put aboard another ship bound for India. But I don't know where in India exactly.'

'It is not a problem,' replied Bissen. 'Once in India I can get home.'

'I've packed you some things,' Bertie told him. 'Not much – just a few books and things. Please feel free to take whatever food you'd like from the kitchen.'

334

'Thank you,' said Bissen.

Lillian looked up from her uncle's shoulder and tried to smile. 'You can give me a rose when I get to India,' she said to Bissen. 'Like the ones you told me about.'

'Yes,' he replied.

'And show me the Golden Temple and your father's village and the hills of Anandpur and—' She ran to Bissen and threw her arms around him. 'I'm so sorry!' she cried. 'I wish I could change things . . .'

Bissen held her for a few moments and then, at her uncle's signal, let her go.

'Through the kitchen and out the back – quickly!' ordered Bertie. 'We have no time to lose.'

Lillian watched as he left the room, closing the door behind him. He did not stop to look back, fearing that if he did, he might not be able to leave. She continued to stare at the door, her mind and heart in a state of shock. Not since the death of her parents had she felt so numb.

'Goodbye . . .' she whispered.

Outside it was cold and wet. Hamadi introduced Bissen to the two Persians but he didn't catch their names. They were both short, squat, powerful-looking men with thick mono-brows, light skin and broad shoulders, and Bissen realized immediately that they were brothers. One of them spoke quickly in a thick accent.

'Come, come,' he said. 'We must quick!'

Bissen climbed into a van that was similar to the one in which he'd escaped from the hospital. Inside, the air was foul with the stench of dead animals. One of the brothers told

Bissen that no one was likely to look inside and pointed to a blood-soaked blanket in the corner.

'If they look,' he said, 'get under that.'

Bissen nodded as the man closed the doors and joined his brother. He heard them say something to Hamadi, and then they were away, off into the dark Sussex night. Bissen sat on the floor of the van and cursed his luck. How quickly things had changed, he told himself, from bliss to despair. He closed his eyes and thought about Lillian's smile as the van took him away from her.

Part Seven

Jallianwalla Bagh, Amritsar

13 April 1919, Morning

Rehill paid careful attention to Miles Irving, deputy commissioner of the Punjab, who was pouring himself another very large brandy. Irving was even redder in the face than usual and the hand he was using to hold the glass trembled. The man was losing it, thought the super-intendent; typical.

'Are there any orders, sir?' asked Rehill.

Irving shook his head. His eyes were red, the skin around them puffy. He looked very tired. 'Dyer and the rest of them have it under control,' he replied. 'I'm going home to try and get some sleep.'

Rehill held his tongue. There was no point in explaining the situation in the city to Irving – not when he had been out there all morning. The man had been complaining about sleepless nights for days now – he wasn't going to listen. It was as though he'd simply given up.

'Would you like an escort back to your bungalow?' added Rehill.

'No, no. My driver is armed and there are troops everywhere. I expect General Dyer will have orders for you.'

Rehill nodded as someone knocked on the door.

'Come!' bellowed Irving.

The door opened and Lieutenant-Colonel Smith, the civil surgeon, strode in. 'Ah, Miles,' he said. 'You look dreadful, old chap. Anything I can do?'

Irving sighed. 'I'm down four days' sleep. If you could get that back for me . . .'

Smith laughed. 'Afraid not,' he said breezily.

'I'm going home,' Irving informed him. 'Tell Dyer that I can be reached there if he needs me.' Not that he meant it. As far as he was concerned, Dyer was welcome to the city and its myriad problems. Irving was sick of Amritsar in particular and India as a whole; the sooner he could return to England, the better.

'Absolutely, old chap,' replied Smith. 'I'll hold the fort here.'

Irving thanked him, downed his brandy in one gulp and left. After the door had shut Smith turned to Rehill.

'Where is General Dyer at the moment?' he asked.

'Making plans to deal with any trouble, sir,' replied Rehill. 'There was a proclamation made across the city this morning. Commissioner Irving and I went out with General Dyer.'

'A proclamation concerning what?'

'Concerning protests and gatherings of more than four men. They're banned.'

Smith nodded. 'Good job too, after the other day,' he said.

'There may be a slight problem, sir,' ventured Rehill.

'And what's that?'

'It was read out in Urdu, sir.'

Smith raised his eyebrows in consternation. Urdu was just one of many languages spoken in the city.

'There were translators with the troops,' added Rehill.

'Ah, well, that'll help.' Smith smiled at the super-intendent – clearly a fine man who could be called upon in time of trouble, *unlike* Miles Irving. 'What is your assessment of the situation, Rehill?' he asked him.

Rehill shrugged. 'I've only just returned from Dharamsala.'

'Yes, yes – how are the two doctors? I take it they didn't give you any trouble?'

'None at all, sir,' said Rehill. 'But as far as the city is concerned, I've spoken to some of the men and had a quick scout around and I'm a little worried.'

'Really?'

'Yes, sir. Since the riots there have been a number of lesser incidents. There is talk of rebellion and I doubt if they'll stop this afternoon's gathering because of the proclamation. The deportation of the doctors has angered people, and news of Gandhi's exclusion is adding to the flames.'

347

Smith nodded. 'A city in turmoil . . . And our deputy commissioner has gone home for a nap.'

Once again Rehill held his tongue. It was one thing to agree with Smith about Irving; it was another thing entirely to air that agreement – not about a superior.

'And the gathering will happen – you're right about that,' added Smith.

'How do you know, sir, if you'll pardon the question?'

'No need to apologize, young man,' replied Smith. 'Let's just say that we have a man on the inside . . .'

'Yes, sir.' Rehill wondered why Smith would *need* such a man.

Smith sensed his puzzlement. 'There are many things that help keep our Empire together,' he told him. 'Sometimes we have to engineer certain . . . er . . . *situations* so that we continue to prosper.'

Rehill nodded but still didn't understand.

'It's nothing for you to worry about, young man,' added Smith. 'Just the machinations of the political beast. The Governor is well aware of the situation.'

He went and poured himself a brandy. 'Go and check on the situation as regards Dyer,' he ordered, 'and get back to me.'

'On my way, sir.'

As he left, Rehill wondered what the rest of the day would bring. His sources in the city had warned him that things were balanced on a knife edge; one slip and it would erupt. And the man in charge was not Michael O'Dwyer but General Dyer, not exactly a shrinking

342

violet when it came to the use of force. No attempt was being made to stop the meeting at Jallianwalla Bagh, neither by Irving nor by Dyer. No police or army patrol had been sent to prevent people from gathering. The only effort to try to avoid further trouble had been the proclamation. And then there was Smith's man on the inside, whatever that meant. It was as if those in charge *wanted* the gathering to happen. Much as he wished he was wrong, Rehill could foresee only one outcome: disaster.

Sohni held onto Gurdial's hand as if it was her life.

'I don't want you to go,' she told him. 'Stay here . . .'

Gurdial shook his head. Much as he would have liked to remain in the comfort of Sohni's house, he knew that he had to find Jeevan. 'I won't be long,' he replied. 'I'm just going to the orphanage to see if he's been back – or maybe I'll call in on Bissen Singh and ask him if he's seen Jeevan.'

'You heard what my . . . my mother said,' warned Sohni.

'I heard,' answered Gurdial, 'but I still have to go. Please understand.'

'Not to the gathering – *promise* me,' she insisted.

Gurdial shrugged. 'I *have* to find him. I won't be able to forgive myself if something happens to him. He is my brother and I can *feel* that something is wrong.'

'But she warned us not to go.'

'I'll be fine, I promise,' said Gurdial. 'You can't get

rid of me that easily. I'll be back before you know it.'

Sohni let out a sigh and then nodded. 'If you must, then go. But not yet . . .'

Neither of them had ventured out of the house since Heera had left the previous night. Sohni in particular was too full of shock and other emotions. Her eyes had seen everything but they were unwilling to communicate with her mind. Too much had happened; too much had been left unexplained. Her father and stepmother were gone, along with Mohni, and her mother had returned to her. She was no longer a virtual slave; she was now free to follow her own path – all in what seemed like the blink of an eye.

'I feel cold.'

Gurdial wrapped his arms around her and whispered into her ear. 'It *will* be all right,' he promised.

'I can't get it out of my head. Each time I close my eyes it's still there . . .'

Gurdial pulled her closer. 'Try to stay calm; we are together now, just as we wanted,' he said, his words acting as a soothing balm.

'I know,' Sohni whispered. 'I know.'

'Everything we have always wanted is right here,' he told her, 'right now. The rest is like a dream; it happened and we will never forget it, but *their* fate was not designed by us . . .'

Sohni nodded. 'They did it to themselves.'

'Yes, they did,' said Gurdial.

He stood and held Sohni for another few minutes

before leading her to her bed. He watched as she undressed and lay down. Once she was settled he leaned across and kissed her on the forehead. 'I will be back before you wake,' he told her.

'How do you know that I'll sleep?'

Gurdial smiled as he looked into her red and weary eyes. 'I know,' he said. 'Dream of beautiful things and forget about the events of last night.'

He stood and watched her as she sank into a deep, deep sleep, occasionally whispering words of love. Only when he was sure that she wouldn't wake up did he leave her side. He had promised her mother that he'd look after her and he wasn't about to break that promise. He walked around the rest of the house, making sure that the windows and doors were shuttered and bolted, then left the house by the kitchen door, locking it behind him.

From somewhere up ahead, out on the street, he could hear people talking. A few whistles sounded in the near distance alongside the *pap-pap* of a car horn. As he reached the street, he saw crowds of people walking towards the Golden Temple complex and, beyond it, Jallianwalla Bagh. It was Vaisakhi, and Sikhs from across the region had come to the city to enjoy the festivities. Only this year, with all the violence of the past days, there was something else in the air: a sense of unease and foreboding. Touching the concealed knife that he'd taken from Sohni's kitchen and tucked into his waistband, Gurdial turned and made his way towards Bissen Singh's.

★ ★ ★

On his return from another fruitless trip to the post office, Bissen felt a growing unease. Parts of the city were almost deserted, which was strange given that it was the Sikh holy festival of Vaisakhi, and there seemed to be no sign of the military presence he had seen over the previous three days. Here and there he passed people going about their business, and in the more crowded streets all seemed normal. But down the quieter back alleys, things had taken on a funereal feel. He remembered hearing the English talk about the calm before the storm, and the *pheme* that was still running around his system only added to his sense of dread. Something was wrong; he could *feel* it.

He went across the railway line and into the streets around Gole Bagh, hoping to catch the priest at the local *gurdwara*. Bissen had many things on his mind; thoughts that were weighing him down. And his dependence on opiates was drowning him. He knew that he had to get mind and body clean, summon up his courage. Deep inside, he knew that his destiny lay elsewhere. His return to Amritsar had always been a stopgap. Not so much a homecoming as a temporary retreat. There was only one place he wanted to be. Only one person he wanted to be with. Both were a long way away.

The priest sat cross-legged on a straw mat, his royal blue turban sitting high on his head. He asked Bissen if he needed some water.

'*Nay, gianni-ji,*' replied Bissen, taking in the aroma of rose incense.

'This woman – is she truly what you want?'

'Yes.'

Bissen was sitting opposite the priest, his eyes focused on a terracotta-coloured water gourd that sat beside him. Part of him felt foolish for bothering him with his own troubles, and this prevented the soldier from meeting his gaze. Instead he looked at the ripples in the rough clay finish of the gourd.

'And she is a *goreeh* – an English nurse?'

'The one who took care of me,' replied Bissen, hearing an insect buzz past his ear. 'She wrote to me for a while, but then the letters stopped and now I am in despair.'

'Perhaps her love was not as strong as yours?' suggested the priest.

Bissen shook his head vigorously. 'There are not many things of which I am sure, but Lillian's love for me is certain—'

'Is that her name?' asked the priest.

'Yes,' replied Bissen.

The priest stroked his salt-and-pepper beard. 'There will be many people coming into the city today,' he said, changing the subject. 'Vaisakhi will bring them streaming in.'

'The streets seemed oddly calm this morning.' Bissen didn't comment on the change of subject.

'Not for long,' replied the priest. 'And with all the

trouble of the past few weeks . . .' He shook his head sadly, his brow furrowed.

'There is more trouble coming,' added Bissen. 'The talk around Amritsar is of rebellion. This Rowlatt Act has upset many people.'

The priest nodded. 'The riot would not have happened if the two doctors hadn't been sent to Dharamsala.'

The two doctors, Kitchlew and Satyapal, had been deported without trial three days earlier – the spark that had ignited the powder keg.

'There will be a great deal more bloodshed,' Bissen told the priest.

'God willing they will show caution,' he replied, more in hope than anything else. The mood on the streets of Amritsar was ugly. Godless even.

'The weaver told me that Mahatma Gandhi was also barred from entering Punjab,' said Bissen.

'I heard that too – just when his presence is most required.'

'I'm not sure that I believe in his methods,' admitted Bissen.

The priest grinned, laughter lines etched deep into his seventy-year-old face. 'What else would I expect from a soldier?' He chuckled, showing yellowing teeth.

Bissen looked him in the eye for the first time. 'There is something else that has taken a grip of my mind,' he said.

'*Pheme.*'

'But how—?' asked Bissen.

'From the beads of sweat on your forehead to your sunken cheeks,' the priest told him. 'Sometimes you look like a ghost.'

'I don't know what to—' began Bissen.

The priest tried to comfort him. 'You need say nothing. With your injuries and the nightmares you suffer I am surprised you don't look worse. Like the real addicts who crawl around the seedier districts.'

'I must get free of it,' said Bissen. 'I have to go back . . .'

'To England?' asked the priest.

Bissen nodded, his grey eyes glazing over with longing. 'To *her* . . .'

Gurdial was sitting on the steps of Bissen's lodging house when he returned. Bissen hadn't seen the boy for a while, but the moment he saw his face he knew something was wrong.

'What is it this time?' he asked. 'Is it about Sohni again?'

'No!' insisted Gurdial, his young face twisted in angst. 'It's about Jeevan – I think he's going to get into trouble.'

Bissen sat down beside him and put an arm around his shoulder. 'What makes you think that?'

'I tried to get him to listen but it was no good,' continued Gurdial. 'He's in danger. I can feel it.'

'Do you know where he is?' asked Bissen.

Gurdial shrugged and calmed down a little. 'I have

not seen him for three days, *bhai-ji* – he took off with his new friends.'

'And you're still worried about them?'

The boy nodded. 'He is so distant. Always standing in little groups with Pritam Singh and those others.'

The 'others' were angry young men, recruited by agitators and used to carry out attacks on the British. Bissen had no doubt that Pritam in particular had been centre stage during the riots. There was something missing from inside him – a lack of humanity that showed itself in his cold, dead eyes. It reminded Bissen of some of his fellow soldiers, back in France; those who had grown to love the death they'd been ordered to inflict.

But Bissen had never seen it in one so young. At barely nineteen years of age, Pritam was far from being a war-weary soldier. Nor was he an orphan like Gurdial Raj and Jeevan Singh; motherless young men who yearned to belong, to find new families. Pritam came from a wealthy family – and had no more reason to hate the British than anyone else. In fact he had less: his merchant family had made fortunes out of the increased prices that recession and British taxes had brought. Yet, despite all this, hate seeped through his pores in the way that sweat did with other people. Bissen had smelled it on him.

'Was Jeevan involved in the riot?' he asked.

'I think so, but he only *watched*. My friend Bahadhur Khan told me what happened. Jeevan didn't hurt anyone.'

'Good. When you see Jeevan, tell him to come and see me – maybe I can talk to him.'

'If I can *find* him,' replied Gurdial. 'I'm going to try the orphanage but I'm not sure he'll be there.'

'Is there anywhere else he might be?' Bissen asked.

'I have a bad feeling,' admitted Gurdial. 'There is a gathering at Jallianwalla Bagh this afternoon. I think he will be there.'

'I thought all public gatherings had been declared illegal by General Dyer.'

'They have. But that won't stop people from going.'

'Dyer won't allow it,' said Bissen. 'Just this morning the British warned us not to gather. When was the announcement for the Vaisakhi celebrations made?'

'After the British warning,' Gurdial replied.

'They won't allow it,' repeated Bissen.

'It's Vaisakhi. People will gather like they do every year.'

Bissen shook his head. 'After the riots?' he said. 'There is too much tension in the city. There are too many agitators . . .'

'That's why I'm worried. What if something happens at the Bagh?' Gurdial looked away for a moment, wondering whether to tell Bissen of Heera's warning to steer clear of the gathering, but deciding against it. He had been told in good faith, and he didn't want to break that trust. Instead he remembered the task he'd been set.

'Oh, by the way,' he said, 'the shopkeeper from across the road told me to give you this. It was delivered to him by mistake.'

Gurdial pulled a battered and worn envelope from his pocket, attempting to straighten it out before he handed it to Bissen. The letter hadn't come from any shopkeeper but Gurdial had been forbidden from telling Bissen the truth. Instead he tried to keep a straight face as he told his white lie.

'It looks like it may be from overseas,' he said, fishing for information.

Bissen looked at the envelope in his hands. He tore into it, not worried about reading it all. He was only interested in one part: the words that would destroy his dreams or send him to heaven a happy man. It was handwritten, on expensive paper; four pages in all. Bissen scanned them all, quickly and quietly, until his eyes fell upon the words he had waited so long for. A single tear began to fall down his left cheek.

'*Bhai-ji* – are you feeling unwell?' asked a concerned and slightly embarrassed Gurdial.

Bissen turned to the boy and pulled him into a bear hug. '*YES!*' he shouted.

'*Bhai-ji* . . . ?' began Gurdial, confused. The woman who had given him the letter had told him that Bissen would understand its provenance but Gurdial understood nothing.

Bissen let him go before wiping his cheek. 'I have to go,' he said. 'My wounds are aching and I need to rest . . .'

He excused himself and made his way quickly to his room. Once there he found his pipe and smoked a small amount of *pheme*. When he was done, he lay back and read the letter over and over, until first tears and then sleep overcame him.

Gurdial knew he was in trouble the moment he saw Mata Devi on the steps of the orphanage. For a moment he considered turning back but there was no point. She had already seen him and, more importantly, he wanted to find out about Jeevan. He approached her, his head bowed.

'Where have you come from, you dog?' she shouted.

'I'm . . . I . . .' stuttered Gurdial.

'Are you such a man now that you do not need to return to your own bed?'

'Something happened,' he tried to explain.

'Really?' she asked sarcastically. 'Did someone kidnap you? Perhaps you fell down a well?'

Gurdial grinned. Mata Devi's sharp tongue hid her love and concern. She had been worried about him, that much was obvious. He decided that his best course of action was to tell a small, insignificant but entirely apt lie.

'I couldn't tell you,' he said. 'I was looking for Jeevan—'

Mata Devi's face changed immediately. 'Do you know where he is?' she asked with genuine concern.

Gurdial shook his head.

'He is in serious trouble,' she said. 'Someone recognized him during the riots and now the police want to talk to him.'

'But he wasn't there,' replied Gurdial. 'Bahadhur told me—'

Mata Devi shook her head. 'They were *all* there,' she explained, the sorrow heavy in her voice. 'They say that Jeevan killed two bank managers—'

'*No!*' shouted Gurdial. How could his friend have fallen so far? It just couldn't be true. No matter how much he had wanted to follow Pritam and his gang, to *belong*, Jeevan could not have killed anyone or anything. He simply didn't have it in him.

'It's true,' Mata Devi insisted, her eyes beginning to water. 'The assistant postmaster saw it with his own eyes.'

Gurdial's stomach churned. The assistant postmaster, Gurpal Singh, was a devout Sikh and would not have made it up. It had to be true.

'I need to find him,' he said. 'To help him.'

'He hasn't been here,' Mata Devi told him. 'The other boys haven't seen him either. He could be anywhere.'

'What should I do if I find him?'

'Bring him here,' she ordered. 'If he is in trouble then we can help him. Perhaps we can save him from the gallows.'

'And what if he won't come?'

Mata Devi held her hands up to the heavens. 'Then his fate is in the hands of a higher power.'

'I'll try the market first,' said Gurdial, only for Mata Devi to shake her head.

'Everyone is going to the Bagh,' she told him, 'to celebrate Vaisakhi and protest to the British.'

The thought pounded inside Gurdial's mind. He knew Jeevan's so-called revolutionary friends would want to be at Jallianwalla Bagh. Where else were they guaranteed to find yet another conflict with the *goreh*? There was no way the British would allow the protest, not after the violence that had started three days earlier, not when people had been murdered. He considered Heera's warning for a moment before putting it out of his mind.

Gurdial's heart began to pound as fast as his head and he said goodbye to Mata Devi, then turned and ran for the Bagh.

Afternoon

After three days of lying on a mat on the floor, trying to get images of dying men out of his head, Jeevan's whole body ached. He stretched himself out, pushing his arms up; as his muscles relaxed he heard little pops in his shoulders. The rest of the gang had left earlier, on another round of Pritam's 'revolution'. Jeevan had complained of feeling unwell and told them he'd join them later, at Jallianwalla Bagh. Pritam, perhaps out of pity or anger, had agreed that he should remain behind. But Jeevan had no intention of joining them. Instead he wondered what he could do to stop Pritam before he killed other innocents. Now, as he stood opposite the Golden Temple, he knew that he had to find the priest. There were so many thoughts flying around his head, so many emotions fighting for space in his chest. He *had* to tell someone and could think of no better person.

The complex was busy for mid-afternoon – people

had thronged here for Vaisakhi and the ensuing celebrations. Everywhere he looked, Jeevan could see rural families, lining up to pray inside the temple or simply strolling around. He pushed his way through the crowds, hoping he'd be able to find the priest before he got too busy. As he turned a corner he saw Udham Singh. Unwilling to stop, he tried not to make eye contact but a sudden surge in the crowds pushed him into Udham's path.

'Careful, *bhai*!' said Udham with a smile. 'What's the rush?'

'Nothing,' replied Jeevan. 'How are you, *bhai-ji*?'

'Very well.'

Udham's black eyes danced with light and his smile was warm. He clapped Jeevan on the shoulder with a strong hand.

'I have not seen you in a very long while, Jeevan,' he said. 'Are you keeping out of trouble?'

Jeevan nodded. 'It's always the same, *bhai-ji*. Mata Devi has us working our fingers to the bone.'

Udham laughed. 'Are you coming to the Bagh today?' he asked.

Jeevan shrugged. 'I have some things to do first. Perhaps when they are done . . .'

'It is important that you come along, *bhai*. We must protest at the British and their actions.'

'They won't allow it,' warned Jeevan. 'Not after the riots.'

Mentioning the events of three days earlier made him

357

gulp down air; his hands grew sweaty and his scalp prickled.

Udham didn't seem to notice. 'It will be peaceful, *bhai*,' he said. 'Even the British will be able to see that.'

An image of Pritam snarling, eyes filled with blood-lust, sprang into Jeevan's mind. If Pritam had his way, there would be no peace at all.

'I must go,' he said. 'I'll see you there perhaps.'

'I'll be near the well,' replied Udham, 'helping to serve water.'

The priest nodded sagely as he listened to Jeevan. The boy was lost and confused, it was clear. The words that fell from his mouth were unrehearsed and hurried, colliding with each other in random patterns that made very little sense. He let the boy exhaust those words before he spoke up.

'Calm down,' he said, 'and tell me, slowly, what it is that you are talking about, *beteh*. Try to think about what you want to say *before* you say it.'

Jeevan, flustered and red in the face, nodded. 'I was at the riots,' he repeated, watching the pace of his words this time. 'I *killed* people . . .'

Saying it out loud sent a shudder through his body. He put his hands to his face and wept. The priest sat and watched him as he stood in the doorway. When the boy had finished, he asked him why he had come to see him.

Jeevan shrugged. 'I wanted to talk to someone. I have

no parents and no family and I just wanted to try and explain that it was . . .'

The priest stood up and came over. He put a hand on Jeevan's shoulder. 'Why did you kill those people?' he asked softly.

'Because he told me that I had to,' whispered Jeevan. 'He told me that India was my mother.'

'Who?'

'Pritam – the one who leads the gang.'

The priest said nothing.

'I stood there, over those men,' continued Jeevan. 'I lit a match. I set them alight . . .'

'Which men were these?'

'The bank managers . . .'

As the boy began to sob again, the priest shook his head. The men he had killed had died as gruesome and frightful a death as it was possible to imagine. Nothing about them – not the colour of their skin or their position in society – warranted what they had endured. They had been innocents, caught in a vicious storm. And now here, in his presence, was one of their killers. The question of what to do with the information reared its head. Should he let the boy go or call for the police? Either decision, the priest knew, would weigh heavily upon his shoulders.

Half an hour later Jeevan stood outside Bissen Singh's door, knocking for all he was worth. The priest had told him to go, informing him that he himself had a duty, legal and moral, to summon the police and pass on everything that Jeevan had told him. 'But I will allow you to leave before I do so. God is willing to forgive all, but you *must* pay the price . . .'

Jeevan had nodded his understanding and promised to turn himself in. 'But there are some things I need to do first,' he'd said.

Now here he was, hoping to talk to a man he had cursed and been told was weak. A man who had killed out of duty and understood the toll that it took on a person. Jeevan did not understand why he sought out the soldier and had no idea what he wanted to say; all he knew was that he needed to talk to him. But Bissen wasn't answering his knocks and there was no sound from within. In despair, Jeevan slumped down on the step that he and Gurdial had sat on so many times in the past.

At the end of the lane he saw a woman walking towards him, her eyes fixed on his. He lowered his gaze and looked away, hoping that she would walk on by. Instead she stopped in front of him, removed her shawl and then took a seat at his side.

'Hello, Jeevan,' she said, her voice warm.

Jeevan looked up at her, wondering how she knew his name.

'There is very little I *don't* know,' the woman told him. 'I know your friend, Gurdial, for instance, and I know that you sit outside the residence of an ex-soldier, a man whom you once admired; a man who is enslaved by *pheme.*'

Jeevan's eyes widened, filled with shock and fear.

The woman laughed. 'You have nothing to fear from me,' she said, reading his mind. 'I have been sent here to help you. My name is Heera.'

'How can you know anything about me?' he asked. 'Are you a witch?'

Heera shook her head. 'No, not a witch – a ghost.'

'I do not believe in ghosts,' replied Jeevan.

'Your face is filled with sorrow, *beteh*,' continued Heera. 'There dwells within you anger and guilt.'

'No . . .' said Jeevan.

'You killed two men—'

'*NO!*' he screamed. 'You can't know! How can you know?'

Heera placed her hand on his and told him to remain calm. 'I *am* a ghost,' she repeated. 'And I am here to save you.'

Suddenly Jeevan felt a sense of calm descend over him. He looked into the woman's eyes and saw that she meant him no harm. Instead, deep in her amber eyes, he saw what Fate held in store for him. He looked away, feeling nothing. All he had ever wanted was to belong, to be part of a family. And now the ghost had shown him where he would find that family.

'Do you see?' Heera asked him.

Jeevan nodded.

'It is your only path to forgiveness,' she added. 'But no one can make you choose this path. You must want to take it.'

Again he nodded. 'I *want* to take the path,' he replied.

Heera smiled and placed a hand on his shoulder. 'Good boy,' she said.

'There is one thing I would like,' he told her.

'Name it.'

'I would like to tell Gurdial that I am sorry . . .'

'I'll see what I can do . . . Now, do you understand what is required of you?'

'Yes . . . No more innocent people will die.'

'Innocents will always die,' she told him. 'That is the way of the world. But not by your hand – not today.'

Jeevan shook his head. 'Not by his either . . .' he said defiantly.

At close to four in the afternoon Rehill learned that the meeting at Jallianwalla Bagh had started. Though apprehensive about what the general might do, he realized that he had no choice but to inform Dyer. He found him explaining his plans to two captains, Crampton and Briggs.

'What is it, man?' the general asked.

'The meeting at the Bagh has begun, sir.'

Dyer looked into Rehill's eyes for a moment and then turned away. 'Damn!' he muttered under his breath. He looked as weary as Irving had. His greying hair was greasy and clung to his head, and there were deep, dark circles under his eyes.

Rehill coughed. 'What would you like me to do, sir?' he asked. 'Shall I send a patrol?'

Dyer shook his head. 'It is too late for that,' he replied. 'There is too much danger. I'm briefing Crampton and Briggs regarding our response. Stay and listen.'

'Yes, sir,' he replied.

Dyer quickly went over his plans, detailing which troops would accompany him to the gathering. A plane had already been dispatched to fly over the Bagh to give an indication of crowd numbers. There were to be two separate responses. The first Dyer called his 'special force' – fifty men drawn equally from the Gurkhas and from Indian troops; although the Indians were Baluchis and Pathans, ethnically different from the people of the Punjab. Rehill immediately realized that Dyer was planning something drastic. Non-Punjabi Indian troops were being used for a reason. The pit of his stomach flooded with acid and a sense of dread filled his heart.

'All the men in this force will be armed with rifles, although the Gurkhas will obviously have their *khukuris* with them too,' explained Dyer.

The men in front of him, including Rehill, nodded.

'I'll also take forty Nepalis with me as an escort. These men will not require extra arms . . .'

Rehill felt himself sweating. He glanced at Crampton and Briggs but they showed no outward signs of concern. Briggs he hardly knew, but Rehill had stood alongside Crampton during the riots three days earlier, when both men had seen the anger and resentment on the faces in the crowd. Surely Crampton could see that they were heading for trouble.

'The second detachment needs to control the area outside the Bagh and at the gates of the city. To that end I'm ordering five troops of ten men each – is that clear?' asked Dyer.

'Yes, sir,' the three of them replied.

'We are going to *crush* this rebellion, this act of defiance. Stopping them in the alleyways and lanes would have been a problem, but out there in the open – well, out there we can *get* them.'

'It looks peaceful, sir,' said Rehill, worried now.

Dyer snorted at him. 'Those who have peaceful intentions will leave when we arrive, Superintendent. The ones who stay choose their own fate. We will send the rest of India a message today. Now, is everybody absolutely certain they know what their orders are?'

All three men nodded, Rehill with deep reluctance.

'Right then, men – no time like the present!' said Dyer.

Rehill couldn't work out exactly what it was that he heard in Dyer's voice. It was either anxiety or resolve, or perhaps both. Whatever the case, he could sense what was coming and it worried him deeply.

RA–TAT! RA-TAT-TAT! Suddenly Bissen found that he was alone, running straight at the German defences. Bullets whizzed past, etched with the names of others, not a single one meant for him. Mud and guts squelched beneath his feet as he approached the sand bags. He threw himself across them, rolled over and came up firing. *RAT! RA-TAT-TAT!* The earth shook as a shell

364

landed not fifteen feet from where he stood. Shrapnel – deadly red-hot slivers of metal – flew about in all directions like fireflies disturbed on a summer's night. But yet again they failed to touch him. He turned to his right and saw Gobar Singh Negi at his side, rifle raised, the back of his head missing. And then, to his left, the boy Jiwan, still smoking his cigarette as blood poured from the bullet hole in his forehead; blackened scorch marks puckering the skin around it like the underbelly of a mushroom. Another shell landed behind them—

RA-TAT-TAT-TAT! He found himself opening a door; the door to the room he had been given by Uncle Bertie. Lillian stood naked before him, her small upturned breasts flushed with colour. But within the blink of an eye the room disappeared, replaced by a snow-covered field. Bissen felt her hands wander down his back, across his buttocks, the left one settling on his wounds. He pushed against her, losing control as a film of perspiration covered her face and the scent of straw-berries clung to the porcelain skin of her neck. Bissen arched his back—

RA-TAT-RA-TAT! The doors to the van flew open and the Persian brothers ordered Bissen to step out. The stench, foul and rancid, of animals long dead had seeped through the pores of his skin. His clothes were ragged, covered in blood and excrement. He stepped out into a biting cold wind and was led to a gangplank. The ship in front of him stood tall and proud as it bobbed up and down at the quay.

'You get on!' he heard someone shout. 'Come quick!'

He looked down at his feet, saw that they were bare and wondered who had taken his shoes. He felt a crack on the back of his head and the world turned to darkness all around him—

RA-TAT! RA-TAT! RA-TAT-TAT-TAT!

Bissen awoke with a start, sitting up instantly. The room was baking hot and sweat fell freely from his armpits. His turban felt wet around the back, where it met his neck, his wounds ached and his loins still burned with desire. He swung his legs round and sat on the edge of the bed, shaking his head vigorously. Images from his dream, still fading, swam before his eyes. He rubbed them and looked down at his bony feet, then stood slowly and stretched out his arms as yet another knock sounded downstairs. Straightening his clothes and turban, he wiped his mouth free of drool and made his way down to answer the door.

The bright sunshine nearly blinded him when it opened, and there, standing with a huge grin on his face, was the weaver, Gurnam Lal.

'Did I wake you, *bhai*?' he asked.

Bissen blinked a few times before replying. 'Just taking a nap, *bhai-ji* . . . What can I do for you?'

Gurnam shook his head. 'No, no,' he replied. 'Think about what *I* can do for *you*!'

Bissen shook the final remnants of his dream from his head. 'I do not understand,' he said.

'I am here, under strict orders from my wife, to

make *sure* that you come to the celebration today.'

'I'm not sure I want to come,' replied Bissen. 'I have much to do—'

'No, no, *bhai*,' insisted Gurnam. 'It is not a request, it is an *order*! Will you let me return to my wife, accurate as she is with her rolling pin, and admit defeat? *Never!*'

Bissen asked Gurnam why he had been knocking so loudly.

'That wasn't me,' replied Gurnam. 'The last knock was mine, I'll admit, but the ones before that were those of a young man—'

'What young man?' Bissen asked.

'One of those orphans you seem to collect. He was standing on your step when I came round the corner, talking to an old woman. I asked him if he was looking for you and he said that he was but that he needed to go—'

'Did he give you his name?'

Gurnam nodded. 'Jeevan . . . And then he and the old woman left. I turned to knock at your door and when I looked back again, they had vanished.'

'Vanished?'

Gurnam grinned again. 'Perhaps they were ghosts,' he joked.

'I won't be able to get rid of you, will I?' said Bissen in a resigned tone.

'Just half an hour, *bhai*,' pleaded Gurnam. 'That's all I ask. And besides, my wife says there may be a pretty young woman for you to glance at.'

The letter! Bissen told Gurnam to give him five minutes. Without waiting for a reply he turned and ran back up the stairs. In his room, lying on the floor by the bed, was Lillian's letter. He looked at it and read it once more, thanking God that it said what it did. Fate had dealt him many blows over the years, agonies from which it had been difficult to recover. If they had been advance payment for this one blessing, this one glorious, glorious blessing, then without any doubt they had been worthwhile.

He tucked the letter into his pocket, then poured some water into a bowl and splashed it onto his face, savouring its cooling effect. He dried himself before changing his shirt and straightening his turban once again.

When he returned to the door, Gurnam was sitting impatiently on the step.

'You are worse than a woman, *bhai*!' the weaver scolded. 'Were you making yourself decent just in case there *is* a pretty woman to glance at?'

Bissen, who had experienced Gurnam's efforts at matchmaking in the past, nodded. It made no difference: within weeks he would have all that he had ever longed for, back in that far-off country for which he had fought so hard. He smiled to himself as he set off for the Bagh, with Gurnam chattering incessantly. Soon Lillian's smile would be real again and not some distant memory. The touch and feel of her skin would be with him every night and he would awaken to her scent each morning. And she would no longer have to hide her secret, as she had done for these past three years or so. He would make sure of that. His time in Amritsar was drawing to a close and he welcomed it with open arms. Each Punjabi sunset he witnessed from this day would bring him one step closer to her.

As he walked along, he had the feeling that he'd forgotten something but couldn't recall what it was. It niggled away at the back of his mind but he ignored it, patting the pocket that contained Lillian's letter.

'Are you all right, *bhai*?' asked Gurnam.

'I've never been better,' replied Bissen, smiling warmly. 'It is going to be a beautiful day.'

By the time Gurdial entered the maze of narrow lanes around Jallianwalla Bagh, the sun had begun to burn blood red, so low that it might have been sitting on the rooftops of Amritsar. The sky around seemed to darken as wisps of cloud were drawn together to form one mass. A sudden breeze dried the sweat on Gurdial's face, making him shiver. He turned into one of the narrow passages that led down to the Bagh, pushing through the crowds on their way to the gathering.

As he neared the entrance Gurdial lost his footing and fell to the ground. Before he had a chance to pick himself up, two strong, calloused hands lifted him out of the dirt. Gurdial looked up and saw the face of Mani Ram, a trader from the marketplace.

'What's the hurry, boy?' Mani asked with a smile.

'I'm trying to find my friend . . . Jeevan,' replied Gurdial, stepping to one side to let people past.

'Well, you won't find him with your face buried in the dust, will you?'

Gurdial shrugged.

'You look worried, *beteh*,' added Mani.

'My friend is in trouble. And I'm worried because of the riots—'

'No, no!' Mani replied, shaking his head. 'We are here to listen to our people. There is no need for any trouble today, not on Vaisakhi.'

Remembering Heera's warning, Gurdial nodded but knew not to believe Mani. Besides, as he passed through the city he'd sensed the tension in the air. The British would want revenge for the riots, which had left many dead and injured. They would not care that it had been an act of revenge and despair. And as a teacher had once told him, revenge was self-propagating; like a seed that, once planted, flowers each year, over and over. He said goodbye to Mani Ram and walked into the Bagh.

It was full of people; thousands of them. They were listening to someone reading out a poem. A wooden platform had been set up as a stage, with a microphone and speakers. The poet finished and the stage was taken by someone else. Gurdial waded into the crowd, eager to find Jeevan. His short, wiry frame allowed him to duck and weave through the dense forest of bodies. He turned his head to avoid a pair of broad shoulders but walked straight into a heavily perspiring breast and a clip around the ears.

'*You dog!*' he heard the woman shout as her scent invaded his nostrils.

'I'm sorry,' he said. 'I was just passing through the crowd and I didn't mean to—'

But the woman had already turned away. Gurdial looked up and saw the sun once more; it looked as though it might fall right on top of them. The clouds – dark purple and orange – fought for space in the sky. Gurdial shuddered. Something felt wrong but he couldn't work out what it was.

He continued fighting his way through the crowds, hoping to catch a glimpse of his friend, but there were too many bodies, too many faces. Eager women and smiling children got in his way, and at each turn he saw determined-looking men watching and listening. At one point he spotted the man the crowd were listening to: the newspaper editor Pandit Durga Dass, who was gesticulating wildly as he spoke passionately about the evils of the Rowlatt Act. The Pandit was a man well known to Gurdial – a kind, decent man who had often visited the orphanage bearing sweets.

And then suddenly he was clear of the crowd. He was by the large well, behind and to the right of the stage. Udham Singh was there with some other men. They were talking and passing cups of water to those in need. Udham saw Gurdial and held up his hand. Gurdial returned the greeting. He looked over to the stage and saw that the Pandit was still talking. Next to him stood a little girl and her mother. Her hair fell in honey-brown ringlets and she held a battered old doll. Gurdial smiled and the girl giggled at him.

A shout went up from Gurdial's left. He turned to see a disturbance taking place in the crowd. People seemed to be running but he couldn't make out what they were running from. The speaker urged them to be calm.

'*They won't shoot!*' he insisted.

Then Gurdial heard the sound of whistles. And after the whistles, as people began to scream, he heard the first of the gunshots.

Jeevan fought his way clear of the crowd and out into the open to the left of the stage. He was facing the western entrance to the Bagh and noticed that it seemed strangely deserted. The other four passageways were much narrower than the one he faced yet these were heaving with people trying to make their way in. He shivered, recalling what he had seen in the eyes of the ghost, before turning to the task at hand.

On his way to the Bagh he had played things back in his mind: the first time he'd spoken with Pritam; the warmth in Hans Raj's smile. He had felt part of something real and important. And then he'd seen the faces of the bank managers, the fear and desperation in their eyes as they lay amongst the piles of wood, doused in kerosene. He'd replayed the match falling, the kerosene exploding into life. The screams of the burning men had filled his ears and he'd wept openly, ignoring the strange looks passers-by were giving him. It was too late for Jeevan to worry about his own fate; he knew that now. All that remained was to find Pritam and stop him from turning some other young man into a carbon copy of himself: a vicious, cold-blooded murderer.

Up ahead of him, halfway to the stage, he saw a familiar face, the dark skin pitted with acne scars: Rana Lal. Jeevan felt a surge of energy flow through his body as both determination and fear took hold in his heart. He sprinted towards Rana, hoping he wouldn't lose him in the ever-increasing numbers of people.

'*Rana!*' he shouted out, straining to be heard above the public address system and the general noise.

For a moment it seemed that Rana hadn't heard, but then he turned round, saw Jeevan and gave a gap-toothed grin. '*Bhai!* We thought you had run away.'

As Jeevan heard him say 'we', he smiled. Pritam was close by. He reached Rana and clapped a hand on his shoulder. 'I would never run,' he insisted. 'Not when there are battles to be won!'

Rana grinned at him again. 'Come,' he said, 'the others are nearby.'

Jeevan nodded but didn't have to go far because the others suddenly appeared. Sucha and Bahadhur greeted him excitedly, but Pritam, dressed in his usual black turban and grey kurta, his dark eyes manic, held back. When the four younger men had finished exchanging pleasantries, Pritam took Jeevan to one side.

'I didn't think you'd be here,' he told him.

'And why is that, *bhai-ji*?'

Pritam gave Jeevan a sardonic smile. 'Let's just say I saw something in your eyes after you killed those men.'

Jeevan gulped down air and his scalp began to prickle once more. The very mention of the dead men . . . 'I needed time to adjust,' he replied quickly. 'To make sense of things.'

'And *now*? Are you ready to fight on?'

Jeevan nodded firmly. 'I'm more than ready. I am willing to lay down my life, *bhai-ji*.'

For a moment Pritam's eyes betrayed his shock but he quickly recovered and held Jeevan's gaze with his cold, dead stare. Jeevan realized that he was searching for something – a sign of weakness that would give the game away. At that moment he heard Heera's voice telling him to remain calm. In his head he answered, but on the outside his eyes gave nothing away.

It was Pritam who looked away first. 'They say this gathering will be peaceful,' he spat. 'I say we will make some more traitors pay.'

'Where is Hans Raj?' Jeevan asked.

Pritam gestured towards the stage. 'He's over there. I'm waiting for him to give us our orders.'

Jeevan looked across at the wooden platform but couldn't see Hans Raj. Instead he saw Pandit Durga Dass, raging against the Rowlatt Act. He held back a smile as he remembered the Pandit's visits to the orphanage. For a moment his thoughts turned to

Gurdial, but then he heard shouts coming from the crowd. He looked over to the source of the commotion: the *goreh* were coming through the western entrance, carrying guns.

Pritam, who had also seen what was happening, did the last thing Jeevan expected of him. His face changed colour and his eyes melted until they held only fear. They turned this way and that, as though looking for the nearest escape route.

Jeevan realized the time had come. 'What are you looking for, Pritam?' he asked.

'Nothing,' muttered Pritam. 'I think we should make our way over to the stage.'

'But the *goreh* are over *there*,' Jeevan pointed out.

'Let's attack them!' suggested Rana Lal.

Sucha and Bahadhur looked from Rana to Pritam and then Jeevan.

He grinned. 'Do you want to die today?' he asked them calmly.

They shook their heads.

'Well then, *run*!' he commanded. 'Run and don't turn back.'

'What are you—?' began Rana, but Jeevan ignored him. Rana looked to the others and then, his eyes beginning to water, he ran. Sucha and Bahadhur followed seconds later.

'*Well*, Pritam – what are we waiting for?' Jeevan asked.

Pritam's cold stare was once more in place, but Jeevan

had seen the fear in his eyes, could almost smell his desperation.

'Are you *scared*?' he asked, taunting the other boy.

Pritam squared his powerful shoulders and threw a punch. Jeevan ducked it and buried his own fist in Pritam's midriff. It caught a rib and made him gasp for air. All around them the crowd began to panic and run as Pritam threw more blows at Jeevan, smashing the bridge of his nose. As Jeevan wiped away blood, he saw again the contorted faces of the men he had killed, smelled their skin and fat as it sizzled and popped. He glared at Pritam, the loathing burning in his eyes. And then the Pandit's voice rang out from the speakers.

'*They won't shoot,*' he told the crowd. '*Stay calm . . .*'

Jeevan turned, knowing that the soldiers would be taking aim. He heard the whistles sound. Realizing that everything he had seen in Heera's eyes was about to come true, he uttered a prayer before grabbing Pritam and holding him tight.

'Come, *bhai,*' he spat. 'Help me to free my mother!'

Jeevan waited until the first gunshot cracked out before surging forward into the fray, taking Pritam with him . . .

Rehill was sitting in a car that was trundling along behind General Dyer's. Dyer, in his open-topped car, had Sergeants Pizzey and Anderson with him to serve as bodyguards, with two armoured vehicles at each side, and troops marching to the front and rear. Rehill had been given Plomer, much to his dismay. The man spent the entire journey parroting General Dyer – talking of teaching the Indians a lesson – Punjabis in particular. He didn't have a clue – he was more likely to chew off his own foot than engage a native in conversation. The man was a buffoon, and the most dangerous kind at that; a fool with a uniform and a gun.

The entourage turned into Jallianwalla Bazaar and came to a stop outside the Bagh. In front was the only proper entry point – the rest were merely narrow alleyways or sewage channels. Dyer stood up and commanded the armoured cars to stay outside and make sure that no one left. Then he turned to Rehill, who grimaced.

'Rehill, I want you to go ahead with Captain Briggs under the watch of Colonel Morgan!'

Rehill got out of the car and joined Briggs. Morgan, a tall, distinguished man, strode up to them.

'Come along, men,' he said as the troops fell in behind.

Morgan led them into the passageway, walking purposefully. Rehill took a deep breath and followed, wondering what they would see when they entered the Bagh proper. Dyer had designed his response with a purpose and Rehill felt uneasy about it.

The scene that greeted them sent Rehill's stomach into spasm. There were thousands of people – the vast majority of them men, but women and children too, many of them wearing brightly coloured clothes – pink, red, blue and orange. To Rehill's left, about eighty yards away, was a wooden platform that was being used as a stage. A man whom Rehill didn't recognize stood at the microphone, addressing the crowd. His hands moved in all directions and his face was contorted with emotion. He mentioned the Rowlatt Act, and sections of the crowd jeered.

'Good God!' exclaimed Colonel Morgan. 'These people are angry.'

Behind the troops, General Dyer appeared, his face set like stone. He looked at the crowd and then at the stage. Within seconds he gave the order: '*Troops ready!*'

The riflemen filed in, the Gurkhas going to Rehill's right, the others to his left, taking up positions with their backs to the western edge of the Bagh. Dyer stroked his moustache before asking Captain Briggs how many were in the crowd.

'It's hard to tell, sir,' Briggs replied. 'At least five thousand – maybe more.'

Most of the crowd were eighty to a hundred yards from where Rehill stood, directly in front of Dyer and the other officers. Rehill looked across at the troops as they prepared themselves, and said a small prayer. There was no way people would be able to escape if the men were ordered to fire. But surely Dyer would never do that. Rehill had heard many rumours about him and his 'special' way of dealing with unruly natives, but not even Dyer could contemplate such a drastic course of action, could he?

The answer soon came. Some of the people in the crowd saw the troops and began to panic. The speaker shouted for them to remain calm, insisting that the troops would not shoot. But no one listened, and people began to run in all directions. Dyer, with the cold, calculating calmness of a snake, pounced:

'*FIRE!*'

Whistles sounded, the troops took aim, the firing began . . .

Gurdial heard the screams getting louder as he stumbled through the smoke; unsure of where he was – or where he wanted to go. Beneath his feet were bodies; young and old, male and female. He clambered over them as the fog around him grew denser, and the stench of blood, guts and death made him want to retch. There was another smell – scorched metal and gunpowder – that stung his eyes and prevented him from seeing exactly what was going on. After two or three paces he fell to his knees, the sound of the gunshots still ringing in his ears. He slipped again and fell forwards into a soft wet mass. He reached down and felt something slippery. Looking closely, he realized that it was the stomach of a woman; or more precisely the area where her stomach had once been. Her insides were open and lying on the dusty ground all about him. Gurdial threw up – one, two, three times – before scrambling to his feet, away from the woman. But once again he slipped and hit the ground. Only this time he stayed where he was as someone ran across his legs.

He turned over and lay on his back, spluttering and choking, trying to think straight. Where had he been in relation to the stage and the perimeter of the Bagh when the shooting started? And how was he going to find Jeevan in the rapidly descending darkness? From somewhere behind him he heard men's voices; someone was uttering a prayer in short, broken sentences. The boot that crunched down onto his head was only visible for the split second before it connected . . .

When he came round, Gurdial sat up gingerly; he felt warm blood trickling down his chin. It was dark now and he was confused; momentarily lost until the smells and sounds of the massacre flooded into his consciousness. He stood up slowly, painfully, and turned a complete circle, wondering which way to go. Suddenly a child appeared out of the gloom, screaming at him. Her face was covered in blood and bits of flesh were woven into her hair. She clutched a ragged doll – Gurdial recognized her immediately as the girl he had smiled at just before the shooting began. He held out his arms and the girl, at first hesitant, ran into them. He picked her up and told her that everything would be fine. She moaned before turning her face and burying it in his chest. Gurdial sucked down air, steadied himself and walked on, hoping that he was heading for one of the passageways that led out to the street.

Moments later he realized that he had gone the

wrong way: he walked straight into Udham Singh.

'*Bhai!*' Udham cried in a strangled, hoarse voice.

'What happened?' asked Gurdial.

'The *goreh* started shooting . . . For nothing.'

Gurdial saw a combination of anger, fear and confusion in the man's eyes.

'There are many injured . . . Help me take water to them,' said Udham.

Gurdial shook his head. 'I have to get this little girl out of here. And I want to find Jeevan.'

Udham shrugged. 'Good luck,' he said. 'It's hard to see anything here – although I did see Jeevan earlier, near the stage.'

Gurdial prayed that his friend had escaped the carnage. 'Is the stage this way?' He nodded to his left.

'Yes, *bhai*.'

'Will you stay here?' asked Gurdial.

'Until I can do no more,' vowed Udham.

'Then let me take this girl to safety and I will return.'

'Thank you, Gurdial,' said Udham.

'Will you be all right?'

Udham shook his head. 'Not until the dogs that did this have gone to their graves,' he whispered.

By the time Gurdial reached the stage area there were many more people walking around. Some were helping the injured, but the majority were simply dazed and trying to find their way out. The little girl hadn't moved since he'd picked her up. He stroked her hair and she mumbled something. He whispered softly into her ear and then walked on, his eyes searching the ground all around. There were many, many dead, of all religions and castes. Tears began to fall from his eyes as he remembered Heera's warning. But, he asked himself, if she had known this was going to happen, why hadn't she done something to stop it?

'Because I couldn't,' her voice told him through the darkness. And then she was standing in front of him, her beautiful face full of sorrow.

'This is not right,' he told her.

'No, it isn't. But it *is* what Fate decreed, and even the ghosts of Amritsar cannot argue with what has already been written.'

Gurdial told her that he understood.

'The little girl in your arms has lost all her family,' Heera told him. 'She needs you to be strong.'

Gurdial frowned. 'I still haven't found Jeevan. That is why I came.'

'Come,' she said, 'let me take you to your friend . . .'

Before Gurdial could speak, she walked off into the darkness. He followed without question. After fifty yards Heera stopped and knelt down. Gurdial felt his heart trying to jump out of his mouth.

'He killed two men during the riots,' Heera explained. 'And then he saved himself . . .'

Jeevan lay on the ground, his eyes open and his mouth set in a smile. Two blackened holes burrowed into his face, one in his forehead, the other in his left cheek.

Next to him, peppered with bullet holes, was the body of Pritam. His face was contorted and the acrid smell of excrement rose up from his corpse. Tears, as bitter as vinegar, streamed down Gurdial's face.

'I'm sorry,' Heera told him. 'This is the way it had to be—'

Gurdial shook his head. 'No,' he whispered. 'I should have stopped him, *saved* him . . .'

She told him to look around. 'There are many dead here . . . Could you have saved them all?'

'No,' he said. 'But he was my friend, my *brother*.'

'He made his own choices, Gurdial,' Heera replied. 'Just like you, he wanted something from this world – a chance to belong, to be part of a real family.'

'I know,' whispered Gurdial.

'He made the wrong choice but he paid for it,' she continued. 'And now he has what he's always desired.'

'But he's dead,' replied Gurdial. 'How can he—?'

'I'm dead too,' Heera reminded him. 'Look . . .'

She pointed towards Jeevan. Gurdial blinked, then looked away. When he turned back again, Jeevan was gone.

'Where—?' began Gurdial.

'Amritsar has many ghosts,' she told him.

Gurdial held the little girl a little more tightly. She mumbled again and then nuzzled him. He looked into Heera's eyes. 'There is so much I don't understand,' he told her.

'But you will. Your life has been blessed, Gurdial. It

will be long and full of happiness. This is not because you are special, although you *are* a fine young man. It is simply the way it is . . .'

Gurdial nodded. 'Let me take this little girl to Sohni. I want to come back and help with the wounded . . .'

'Like Udham Singh,' said Heera.

'You know of him too?'

'Yes,' she replied. 'The spirits of those who lie dead here today, they will not rest for a very long time. They will wander the same alleyways, streets and fields that they did when they were alive. But one day Udham Singh will set them free.'

'How?'

'Exactly as it has been written by Fate,' she replied. 'I cannot tell you any more.'

'And what about you?' asked Gurdial. 'Where will you go?'

Heera smiled. 'Give me the child,' she said. 'I will take her to my daughter. You stay and help Udham Singh.'

She took the little girl from Gurdial, all the while whispering soothing words, and then, without looking back, walked off into the smoke. Gurdial stood for a moment and looked at the ground where Jeevan's body had been. He wiped his eyes and smiled a little. Life and Fate were confusing, he decided, but Heera was right. He was alive and he had been blessed.

'Why argue?' he said out loud.

He turned and walked back towards Udham Singh.

★   ★   ★

Heera stopped at the southern entrance to the Bagh and knelt down by a low stone wall; the child was now asleep on her shoulder.

He was sitting slumped against the wall, his legs stretched out in front and his arms dangling between them. In his chest was a single bullet wound, which had stained his white shirt a rich crimson. Heera reached out, closed his eyes and stroked his cheek, letting her long, slender fingers linger for a few seconds. Reaching into her clothes, she pulled out a single-stemmed rose that matched the colour of his blood exactly. She placed the rose by his hands and stood up.

'I warned you not to come,' she whispered softly. 'You should have taken your letter and gone, just like I told you . . .'

She looked down at his hands; hands that were still clutching his precious letter. Shaking her head, she turned and walked away . . .

Lillian Palmer's letter to Bissen Singh – excerpts:

. . . hiding it from you for so long. I had to wait, my love, until I was certain that we could be together. Uncle Bertie believes that we can – he has already spoken to some people he knows. There is no more danger for you here, now that the war is over. You will be employed by him as a butler, but only to make it look official. I hope with all my heart that you will still want to be with me and our son. I'm truly sorry for hiding his birth from you, but I was at my wits' end and did not know what to do. The year after you left was so difficult, so agonizing, and when you didn't reply for so long I grew afraid that you had forgotten me or perhaps been hurt.

Our son was born on 1 October 1916 – soon he will be three years old. I have called him Thomas after my own father, but if you do not wish it to be so, we can change it once you return to England. His eyes are like yours and his nose is proud and strong. I tell him about you every day and he cannot wait to meet his brave, handsome, courageous father. He even smiles as you do, and I am sure, when he has grown to be a man, he will be the image of you . . .

. . . the roses in the gardens. Each time I see them they remind me of our short time together. There is one bush, with flowers that are crimson, that I have even named after you. You will think me a fool when I tell you that I talk to that bush and pretend it is you. I long to feel your hands on my face once more and to watch you as you sleep. My life without you would have been empty. Had it not been for Thomas and Uncle Bertie I would have been driven insane. Now we have only a short time to wait until we can be a family – my heart beats faster just to think of it.

I remain, truly and deeply, your sweetheart, and send to you all the love in my heart,

Lillian

Author Note

'**An episode without precedent or parallel in the modern history of British Empire . . . an extraordinary event, a monstrous event, an event which stands in singular and sinister isolation.**'
Winston Churchill (8 July 1920)

A few years ago I discovered something about the First World War that sent my imagination into overdrive; one third of all the soldiers who fought for Britain during that war were non-white. Having studied the Great War, I was shocked. No mention of these non-white soldiers was made during my time at school. I'd never seen any representation of them in the media either. Perhaps it was my own ignorance, but for me these unknown soldiers seemed to have vanished from the pages of history.

Very many of these non-white troops were Indian, mostly Sikhs and Muslims. And all of them ended up fighting for the very country that had colonized them. How did they feel about fighting what one of my characters termed a 'white man's war'? And what was the reaction to them when they returned to their homeland; a place of simmering anti-colonial tensions?

My research led me to many places, all of which were interesting. But the most exciting of all was Amritsar; the holy city of the Sikhs and the scene, in April 1919, of the worst atrocity ever carried out by British troops against civilians. Coming from a Sikh background I knew of the Jallianwalla Bagh massacre; it's a part of Punjabi and sikh folklore. But how was I going to connect the massacre and the Great War? That was when Bissen Singh, who for me is the central character (you can choose your own favourite), appeared.

He was followed swiftly by many more characters, young and old, Indian and British. Eventually I had a huge cast list and a story that had spun itself into a web. Love, honour, brotherhood, loss, family, magic and myth became tangled together inside it. I did even more research, working out, over the course of a full year, where each of my characters' journeys would begin and end. The result is this novel.

But I must explain. *City of Ghosts* is *not* rooted entirely in fact, as some people will no doubt point out to me. Rather than worry about the details that I had painstakingly noted down, I decided to put them away and let my mind run wild. The central characters are both real *and* made-up; the city scenes are *entirely* imaginary. France in the First World War, Brighton in 1915 and Amritsar in 1919 are the landscapes I dreamt up in my imagination, not the real places. The result is a multilayered novel with elements of history, fantasy and magic working in tandem.

And because of this, *City of Ghosts* is very different to anything I have previously written. I'm very excited about it and I hope that you enjoyed it. And I also hope that you can forgive the liberties I have taken with the facts.

Warmest wishes,
Bali Rai

Some notes:

How was I going to present factual events and real historical figures in a work of fiction? What were the events that I researched and who were the key characters? To answer those questions I have compiled a quick guide for you below:

Udham Singh (aka Ram Mohammed Singh Azad)
'I have nothing against the English people at all. I have more English friends living in England than I have in India. I have great sympathy with the workers of England. I am against the Imperialist Government.
Udham Singh (15 July 1940)

Udham Singh became a hero to millions of Indians when he avenged the 1919 Amritsar Massacre by assassinating Michael O'Dwyer in London. His act was seen as a strike against the inhumanity shown by the British, not just in Amritsar but across India during the Raj.

Udham Singh was an orphan and spent part of his life at the Khalsa Orphanage in Amritsar. He went to Iraq when the war started, as a sixteen year old, and served the Raj. But he soon returned to Amritsar and witnessed first hand the massacre at Jallianwalla Bagh. He swore revenge and became a radical, influenced by the growing independence movement, and particularly by the armed struggle led by a rebel called Bhagat Singh.

He spent much of the next decade attempting to procure weapons from the US, and other places, and was captured and imprisoned. Upon his release he left India and went abroad. He travelled widely and was known to have visited the USSR and other countries. By the mid 1930s he was in England, planning his revenge, having renamed himself Ram Mohammed Singh Azad. The name is Hindu, Muslim and Sikh, and signified the united India for which Udham Singh stood.

Very little is known about his time in England. Friends' testimonials, police documents and studies by experts reveal that he frequented the Shepherds Bush gurdwara (the first in the UK) and also spent some time in Devon, close to Michael O'Dwyer's home, perhaps working as a bus driver. In 1940 he surfaced at Caxton Hall and carried out his revenge. He was hanged in Pentonville prison the same year.

Britain, Colonialism and Independence in India

The East India Company arrived in India during the 1600s and, using its own army, took effective control of the subcontinent by the 1790s. In 1858 British Crown Rule was established and became known as 'The Raj'. India was Britain's largest and most-favoured colony and was often called 'The Jewel in the Crown'. British companies and individuals made huge fortunes trading in India's natural wealth and resources.

But for the ordinary Indian population, British rule wasn't welcome. The British gave India many things, including the railways and democratic systems, but in reality they ruled with an iron fist. Over the years there were many uprisings against British rule but all of them failed.

By the time of the Amritsar massacre, opposition to the British was widespread. No longer secure in their colony and hounded by peaceful and violent opposition, the British did all they could to prevent the inevitable – Indian independence. But, in trying to hold on to their prized jewel, the British lost the support of the people.

The Jallianwalla Bagh atrocity was one of the pivotal moments in the move towards independence. For most of the Punjab, an area that was a key to British control, the massacre was the last straw. Although it took another three decades for the last of the British to leave, Amritsar certainly helped to make it happen by radicalizing an entire generation of young people against the British.

India gained its independence from Britain in 1947.

Reginald Dyer

'It is only to an enlightened people that free speech and a free press can be extended. The Indian people want no such enlightenment.'
Reginald Dyer (21 Jan 1921)

Reginald Dyer was the officer in charge at Jallianwalla Bagh and became known as the 'Butcher of Amritsar'.

Cast as both hero and villain, Dyer was much more complex in reality.

He was born in India during 1864 and saw himself as more Indian than English. After being sent to school in the UK, an unhappy Dyer couldn't wait to return and moved back to India as soon as he was able. Soon after the massacre, he was forced to return to England once more, and this seems to have broken his spirit – he died in 1927. He fought many campaigns alongside Indian troops of all religions throughout his time in India and was a well-respected soldier and officer. Dyer believed that he knew what the Indian people wanted because he was so close to his troops.

His role in the massacre is well documented. Dyer wanted to teach the whole of India a lesson with his actions. And he is rightly remembered as the instigator of an atrocity. But Dyer was also baptised as a sikh *after* the massacre, something which shows how complex both he and the events of the time were. On his return to England, many people saw him as a hero and 'The saviour of India'.

Dyer never apologized for his crime, and to this day there is a dispute over how many people were actually killed in Amritsar. But for Indians and their descendants, Dyer will always remain a villain. The Amritsar Massacre remains the largest atrocity ever carried out on civilians by British troops.

Hans Raj

Hans Raj has been described as a shady character and very little is known about him. His only link to Amritsar was that he was present in the city during 1919 and was one of the organizers of the Jallianwalla Bagh gathering. But after the massacre he disappeared and nothing more was heard from him.

One of the more controversial theories surrounding Hans Raj's role is that he was working on behalf of the British to create unrest. This allowed the British to take stricter control of India at a time when there was growing resentment to their presence. Revolutionary actions were spreading across India and in the Punjab the Ghadar party and others were advocating armed struggle. The theory is that Hans Raj acted as a double agent, helping to spread unrest, to give the British an excuse to rein in militants.

It is *just* a theory but a very fascinating one. The simple fact that Hans Raj disappeared after the massacre is mysterious enough and led me to write my own version of events. Many people will argue that he wasn't a double agent and that may well be true. But *City of Ghosts* is only rooted in real events. It isn't a blow-by-blow account of what actually happened and was never meant to be. For me Hans Raj's role remains very mysterious and became essential for Jeevan's story.

The 'Brotherhood' of which Hans Raj and Pritam speak in the novel is also entirely fictional.